Kate froze. She could scarcely believe Deverill was about to kiss her—or even less, that she would permit him. When he bent toward her, she braced herself, knowing his breath-stealing kisses would make her light-headed and weak.

He seemed in no hurry, however. Intent on drawing out the moment, he raised his hand to touch the side of her jaw, a light brush of his fingers. A rush of sensation shot through Kate at the unexpected caress. When he spread his hand and stroked his thumb over her lower lip, tendrils of heat shimmered inside her, sending small shivers along her skin. She was vividly aware of everything about him: his strength, his hardness, his barely restrained power.

An unwanted surge of excitement only added to the tautness in her body. And when finally, slowly, he lowered his head, the delicate pressure of his mouth almost stopped her heart. Even forewarned, she was unprepared for the flash of pleasure that staggered her senses. Despite the softness, his kiss was just as explosive as six years ago. It gave her chills, set her body on fire, filled her with delicious feelings. . . .

BY NICOLE JORDAN

Legendary Lovers
Princess Charming
Lover Be Mine
Secrets of Seduction
The Art of Taming a Rake
My Fair Lover

The Courtship Wars
To Pleasure a Lady
To Bed a Beauty
To Seduce a Bride
To Romance a Charming Rogue
To Tame a Dangerous Lord
To Desire a Wicked Duke

Paradise Series
Master of Temptation
Lord of Seduction
Wicked Fantasy
Fever Dreams

Notorious Series
The Seduction
The Passion
Desire
Ecstasy
The Prince of Pleasure

Other Novels
The Lover
The Warrior
Touch Me with Fire

My Fair Lover

A Legendary Lovers Novel

BALLANTINE BOOKS • NEW YORK

A Ballantine Books Mass Market Original

Published in the United States by Ballantine Books, an imprint of Random House, a division of Penguin Random House LLC, New York.

BALLANTINE and the HOUSE colophon are registered trademarks of Penguin Random House LLC.

ISBN 978-0-553-39257-9
Ebook ISBN 978-0-553-39258-6

Cover design: Lynn Andreozzi
Cover illustration: Alan Ayers

Printed in the United States of America

randomhousebooks.com

9 8 7 6 5 4 3 2 1

Ballantine Books mass market edition: September 2017

To my wonderful readers,
for faithfully sticking with me over
the years. You make the long hours
at the computer worthwhile.

A special shout-out to Charlene and Jennara.
Your two cents on Kate and Deverill's story
was worth many, many times more!

And finally, my heartfelt appreciation for
my superb editor, Junessa Viloria.
You always make my stories and
characters better, and I thank you.

My
FAIR LOVER

Chapter One

London, May 1817

The last time she visited Brandon Deverill in his hotel rooms, she had climbed into his bed naked—a foolhardy scheme that ended in utter disaster.

Wincing at the scalding memory, Lady Katharine Wilde raised her hand to knock on the door to Number 7, then promptly lowered it again as the swarm of butterflies resumed dancing in her stomach. Gaining access to the second floor of Fenton's Hotel this afternoon was the easiest phase of her clandestine mission. Disguised as a nobleman's liveried male servant, she didn't fear recognition. No, her anxiety stemmed from having to face Deverill again after six long years.

She fervently hoped that history wouldn't repeat itself today. Before, when she'd brazenly thrown herself at his head, he had rebuffed her offer, gently but firmly.

"That is far enough, Kate."

She froze in confusion, wishing she could express all the yearning she was feeling. All the chaotic mix of uncertainty, desire, and hope. "But I thought . . ."

His jaw flexed with determination or regret, she wasn't sure. "You were mistaken."

Remembering her abject humiliation that night, Kate bit her lower lip and stepped back from his door. How she had longed to crawl into a hole and die! Maddeningly, her wounded pride still stung all these years later, as did her foolish heart.

Turning, she paced the corridor in an effort to drum up her courage. Unmarried young ladies simply did not visit gentlemen's hotel rooms unaccompanied—although at four-and-twenty, she was hardly *young*. And Brandon Deverill—a rich American merchant and former privateer whose fleet of ships had battled the British Navy—was barely considered a gentleman, even if he *had* recently inherited the title to an ancient English barony.

Yet she had numerous reasons for risking scandal today: To prove she had recovered from her hurt and show him she was not still nursing a broken heart. To test her fortitude and confirm that she could handle meeting him alone. To deal with her certain embarrassment out of the public eye. And to make her unusual proposition in private.

She'd vowed to have nothing more to do with Deverill, but her aunt by marriage, Lady Isabella Wilde, had asked for her help in turning him into a proper English lord. Since Aunt Bella was her dear confidante and the prime mother figure in her life, Kate felt she could not possibly refuse. Not at least without good reason.

Which would mean confessing the mortifying details of the most lowering experience of her life, when she'd pursued Deverill like the lovesick, starry-eyed, half-witted females she deplored.

Scolding herself for her cravenness, Kate returned to his door and managed to subdue the violent flutters raging in her stomach long enough to rap lightly. Last time, Deverill had unequivocally rejected her amorous advances. This time, however, she had something he wanted.

When eventually the door swung open, the first thing that struck her was his bold, dark eyes. They were much as she remembered—deep, penetrating, black-fringed. His arresting eyes had always matched his daring demeanor and actions, she thought in bemusement.

In their dark depths she saw his instant recognition of her, even though she was garbed in her noble family's livery, complete with silvery powdered wig covering her auburn hair.

She had clearly taken him by surprise. Kate herself was startled by the sight of Deverill wearing only breeches. He was bare-chested and barefoot, while his overly long raven hair was damp and curling. Apparently he had just bathed and was about to shave, for he held a razor in one hand.

A stubble of beard shadowed his strong jaw, a raffish look that only accentuated his appeal, much to her vexation. A ruffian—a pirate, at that—should not look so blasted appealing. He smelled delicious as well, deuce take him.

Confounded by his unwanted impact on her senses, Kate stood staring back at him speechlessly.

When his gaze drifted down over her attire, one eyebrow lifted and she could see amusement spark in his eyes.

"I should have expected you to act unconventionally," he remarked in that rough-velvet voice that never failed to rake her feminine nerve endings.

She could say the same of him. He didn't seem at all nonplussed to be caught in a state of near undress. But then Brandon Deverill was the most infamous man of her acquaintance, which was saying a great deal, considering that she hailed from the scandalous Wilde family, who could boast centuries of notorious ancestors.

There were lines on Deverill's face now that made his striking features more mature. But shirtless, with his sun-bronzed, muscular torso exposed, he was even more devastatingly handsome than she recalled. His masculine beauty put classical statues to shame—

Oh, merciful heavens, gain hold of yourself, you moonling.

She was badly mistaken about having conquered her vulnerability, though. She most certainly was *not* over him. Deverill still had the power to make her knees weak. And she was still swamped by the undeniable, unquenchable attraction that had hit her the first moment she met him so long ago.

Kate gave herself a violent mental shake. She would be in deep, deep trouble if she couldn't contain her captivation.

Thankfully Deverill interrupted her muddled ruminations. "How did you find me?" he asked with a note of curiosity.

"At my request, the harbormaster was on the lookout for your ship and alerted me when you docked. I sent a servant to question him about where you were lodging."

"I admire your resourcefulness, if not your prudence. What the devil are you doing here?"

"May I come in?" Kate pressed. "I wish to speak to you, and I would rather not hold our conversation out here in the corridor."

After a moment's hesitation, he stepped back to allow her entrance and closed the door behind her, although he didn't appear elated by her presence. "Could you not have waited until I called on you tomorrow?"

"I felt sure there would be awkwardness between us, and thought it best to deal with it in private."

"Will you be seated?"

Glancing around the small chamber, she saw a table and two chairs, a washstand, and a bed that reminded her uncomfortably of their last ignominious encounter. Kate smiled amiably to cover her discomfort. "I will stand, thank you. This should not take long."

"Good. It would be best if you weren't seen visiting my bedchamber. Does your brother know of your whereabouts?"

"No, and I don't intend for him to find out."

"Beaufort would have my head if he knew you were in my rooms."

"You needn't worry. Ash is in the country and is not expected to arrive in London until tomorrow."

Deverill scrutinized her costume. "You aren't concerned that someone might recognize the beautiful Lady Katharine Wilde?"

"No one looks twice at a footman."

"Thus the disguise. You make a fetching lad."

His compliment flustered her, but he followed it with a censorious remark. "Evidently you haven't changed. You make a habit of frequenting gentlemen's hotel rooms."

"Not all gentlemen," she returned archly. "Only yours."

"Should I be flattered?"

She sent him her most charming smile. "Indeed, you should," she quipped before catching herself. She had no business engaging in spirited repartee with Deverill as they'd enjoyed in the past.

Fortunately, he changed the subject by rubbing the stubble on his jaw. "Would you object if I continue shaving while we talk? My cousin Trey should arrive shortly to convey me about town. I have business with my solicitor regarding issues of the inheritance, and then plan to dine with Trey and his wife, Antonia, this evening."

Kate had met Brandon's distant English cousin Trey Deverill years ago, although she had not seen him recently and had not met his new wife. "No, I wouldn't object."

Deverill went to the washstand and picked up a cake of soap. "It has been a while since I last saw you," he mused aloud as he began making a lather.

Six years, two months, and nine days. With another mental shake, Kate focused her thoughts on the future, not the past. "Aunt Bella has generally kept me abreast of your situation. I was sorry to hear of your uncle's passing."

Deverill nodded solemnly. "Reportedly Valmere was in a great deal of pain, so perhaps it was a blessing. I plan to travel to Kent this week to pay my respects to his remaining kin and make arrangements to provide for them."

Kate was aware of Deverill's lineage. His late grandfather, a younger son of a British baron, had immigrated to Virginia in America decades ago and married into a prominent merchant family that owned a fleet of sailing ships. This past January the current Baron Valmere—Augustus Deverill—had succumbed to a lingering illness, leaving behind a widowed daughter and two young granddaughters. The title and entailed properties had devolved to Brandon as the closest male relation.

For a moment, silence reigned as he lathered his

face with soap. Watching, Kate found herself distracted by the sheer allure of his bare torso. Without volition her gaze skimmed over his wide shoulders and followed his tapered back to his lean waist, then lower to his tight buttocks and powerful thighs encased in buff knit breeches—

She looked away quickly so Deverill wouldn't catch her admiring his lamentably impressive body. "Would you mind donning a dressing gown?"

"Regrettably, I don't have one with me."

"A shirt, then?"

He hesitated. "I will when I finish shaving." Deverill glanced over his shoulder at her. "Have you turned missish all of a sudden?"

That tender, amused light that she'd loved so well had returned to fill his eyes. Seeing it, Kate remembered another provoking quality of his: No other man could make her blush as he could. She always felt as if he knew what she was thinking. And sometimes he seemed to be laughing at her—or at himself—inviting her to share a private jest.

It had been that way from the very first. He'd always taken vast liberties with her and never stood on formality. On the contrary, he'd teased her intimately, the way her brothers and cousins did. She could also count on Deverill to be candid, even brutally honest.

She had never minded his casual familiarity before, for it felt amiable, comfortable. Indeed, she had prized his frankness after all the sycophants who had toadied to her all her life as a wealthy, noble heiress.

They had met seven years ago when Deverill was visiting his uncle in Kent, the introduction made by Lady Isabella, who knew him from the days when he worked for the British Foreign Office. It was an unusual occupation for an American—a career that had originated because of his cousin Trey Deverill, and was cut short when war broke out between their countries.

"I have not been completely sheltered," Kate answered lightly. "I grew up with male relatives, so I've seen partially unclothed men. But you and I are not at all related. Just because I dared call at your rooms twice does not mean I am unaware of the impropriety."

"You forget I've seen your charms as well," he murmured.

With her face flaming, she ducked her head. "You needn't remind me," she said in a low voice. "I once felt a foolish infatuation for you, but that is long over."

Realizing how fainthearted she sounded, Kate raised her chin and met his gaze bravely. It was best to confront her embarrassment head-on.

Deverill was regarding her with that penetrating look, as if he knew all her secrets. Defensively, she flashed him her most winsome smile. "Never fear, Mr. Deverill. I am not here to throw myself at you again. I promise I won't accost you or try to sneak into your bed."

He looked as if he might reply, for his mouth curved

for a moment, but he only shook his head and commenced shaving.

When he turned his back to her again, she noticed a wicked-looking scar beneath his right shoulder blade, perhaps three inches long, as if a knife or bayonet had speared his flesh. It must have hurt dreadfully, Kate thought, biting her lip in sympathy. She started to ask how he had come by the scar but stopped herself. The condition of his body was far too personal a matter for her to contemplate.

She changed her mind about taking a seat, however. Pointedly ignoring the bed, Kate crossed the small chamber to one of the chairs and sat down so she wouldn't have to gawk at him directly. Deverill was pure physical temptation. More than that, he possessed the type of raw, vital presence that was supremely dangerous to any woman's virtue. *Any woman's but mine,* she amended. *Her* virtue had been perfectly safe in his hands, to her immense regret.

Kate cleared her throat. "Aunt Bella wishes she could be here to greet you, but she recently travelled to Cornwall to attend the lying-in of a friend's daughter and needs to remain there a while longer. Meanwhile, she solicited my aid in her absence. I don't know all the particulars of your correspondence with her, but I understand you intend to fully assume your role as Baron Valmere?"

"Yes."

"I would like to hear from you what your aim is."

He complied as he scraped off his whiskers. "You know that when the conflict between our countries escalated, my father requested I come home to Virginia? When he died a year later, I assumed the reins of our shipping company. I've spent the past several years rebuilding, since commerce suffered significantly during your British blockades of our harbors, and a portion of our fleet was destroyed. Now we are finally on solid enough footing that I can turn the enterprise over to my younger brother and fulfill my duties here."

Kate eyed him inquiringly. "You actually mean to settle here in England?"

"In all likelihood, although my mother is not happy about it," Deverill said dryly.

"I find it surprising that you would even consider it, given where your loyalties lie."

"My loyalties?"

"To America. It is no secret that you were devotedly engaged in privateering."

When his gaze sharpened at her disapproving tone, Kate pressed her lips together. There was no point in arguing the past with Deverill. The fact remained that he was the bold American seafarer who had stolen her heart and left her pining, which was his greatest offense.

She'd thought he could be her perfect mate, but he'd spurned her and then gone off to fight a war against her countrymen, and thus had become her enemy. Now, not only was he back in England but she had promised to consider helping him.

"What do you wish of me?" she finally said.

"To start, I need an introduction to society. The enchanting Lady Katharine is the toast of the polite world. Who better than you to help pave my way? From what I hear, you rule the ton with your charm and wit."

Kate laughed. "Hardly. But with Ash being a marquess and my cousin Quinn an earl, I do have noble family connections that might benefit you." Her expression sobered. "Aunt Bella also mentioned that you are looking to wed."

Deverill nodded. "I am three-and-thirty. It's time I settled down and took a wife."

Hearing him confirm what she already knew—that he wanted to marry—affected her oddly. But she had vowed to repress any rebellious pangs of jealousy and turn his need to her advantage. "Are you interested in making a marriage of convenience? Or something deeper?"

He cast her a swift glance, although his expression was inscrutable. "Nothing deeper. Isabella claims that you can find me a suitable bride. She says you are a matchmaker at heart, and that your past endeavors have been highly successful."

"I have developed something of an expertise at matchmaking, true," Kate admitted. "Not to boast, but I aided most of my family in finding their ideal mates. I am willing to advise you as a favor to Aunt Bella, but I would like to make a bargain with you in exchange."

"What sort of bargain?"

She took a deep breath. "If I find you a bride, you must escort me to France at the end of the Season."

Deverill rinsed his face with water from the washbasin and began drying it with a towel. "Why do you wish to go to France?"

"I believe you know how my parents were killed?"

"They perished at sea when their ship sank in a storm."

"So we thought." Kate frowned. "It is rather a long story, but to be brief . . . You may remember that my aunt Angelique was French—the daughter of the Duc and Duchesse de Chagny, who were guillotined during the Revolution."

"Your cousins Quinn and Skye's mother?"

"Yes. Angelique wed my uncle, Lionel Wilde, Earl of Traherne. Their branch of the Wilde family is somewhat distant from ours. . . . In any event, the priceless de Chagny jewels were hidden while Britain was at war with Napoleon's armies. Then during the Peace of Amiens, my parents travelled with Angelique and Lionel to southern France to recover the treasure, and on their return shortly before Christmas, their ship sank just off the coast. For years we believed everyone on board perished, but recently we learned that their ship was actually sabotaged and that my mother made it to shore and survived a short time before succumbing to her injuries."

Falling silent, Kate stared down at her hands as she recalled the shock and pain of discovering the truth about the shipwreck two months ago. She'd been ten when she lost her mother and father to the tragedy, and with the new revelations, she had relived her grief all over again.

Moreover, imagining the suffering her mother had endured and picturing her father's watery grave beneath the sea had only added to the persistent nightmares she'd had since childhood.

Kate twisted her fingers together as her voice dropped to a murmur. "Mama had a pauper's burial, and Papa and my aunt and uncle had no burial at all. I would like to visit Mama's resting place to put a headstone on her grave, and search for the shipwreck while I am there." She gave a faint, apologetic smile. "I confess, it has become an obsession of mine. Perhaps I am foolish, but I want her to have a decent burial."

"I would not call you foolish."

She lifted her gaze to find Deverill watching her, a gentle look in his eyes, as if he understood her need. She was grateful that he wasn't teasing her about an uncertain—perhaps perilous—undertaking that was so close to her heart.

"Anyway," she went on, "the saboteur was brought to justice and most of the treasure recovered, although some of the jewels sank with the *Zephyr.*"

"And you wish to salvage the rest?"

Kate hesitated. "I doubt that is possible. It has been over a dozen years. But I hope at least to locate the ship's remains. We can guess at the general site based on reports from that night and where pieces of wreckage washed ashore. The *Zephyr* was rocked by an explosion and caught fire. Although attempting to limp back to port, it only came close to shore but may have sunk in shallow water. Quinn has done actual calculations and drawn maps for a salvage effort. The problem is, there are pirates inhabiting the nearest villages along the coast."

"You seem to know a great deal about the circumstances. How did you obtain your information?"

"I believe you know Beau Macklin? He was a colleague of yours in the Foreign Office, along with Skye's new husband, the Earl of Hawkhurst."

"I know Macky."

"Well, some months ago, he went to France to investigate for my family."

"So why do you need my escort? Why can't you call on Macky?"

"He has done enough already. But mainly, I need an experienced sailor. Someone I can trust."

Deverill's mouth curved. "And you trust me?"

She suspected he was trying to lighten the moment by provoking her, so she answered in the same vein. "Amazingly enough, yes. You know more about the sea than anyone of my acquaintance. In fact, you own an entire fleet of ships, and now you have your own right here in London."

"I had planned for my ship to return to America in a week or two."

Kate felt her heart sink. "Oh. Well, perhaps I could

make it worth your while. I can afford to pay a great deal."

"You have your own extensive fortune, I know."

She ignored his amused drawl. "I could hire a ship and captain, perhaps, but I would rather not depend on strangers in this endeavor. You see . . . I am not very fond of sailing."

A vast understatement, Kate reflected. In fact she had a base fear of ships—not unreasonable considering how her parents had perished. "I can swim quite well," she explained. "You will recall the lake at Beauvoir where I grew up? But I have a morbid fear of drowning at sea."

"And you need someone to cosset your sensibilities."

Certain now that he was ragging her, Kate smiled. "Alas, yes. I concede that I am craven. But there are other reasons you would be a better choice. Even if I could employ men to search for the wreck, I might have to deal with the pirates. I am English. After decades of war, the French are not exactly our bosom friends. I suspect pirates are much fonder of you Americans, since many of them aided you during the war."

Deverill frowned as he pulled on a linen shirt and began tucking the hem into his breeches. A pity to cover all that bare flesh, Kate thought before scolding herself and concentrating on what he was saying.

". . . it could be dangerous."

"Perhaps, but pirates are unlikely to threaten *you*."

He cast her a wry glance. "I am not concerned about my own skin, but yours. A young lady travelling along the coast needs protection."

"Which is why I am asking you."

"What about your family? Will they be accompanying you?"

"Although they would all very much like a resolution, they are not as adamant as I am. And they are all busy starting their own families."

Kate watched as Deverill wrapped a length of cambric around his neck and began tying a cravat in a plain knot. The white fabric contrasted appealingly with his tanned skin. Indeed, clean-shaven, he was even more attractive— *Stop that, you ninny.*

She drew a steadying breath. "So you see, I want to lay to rest the memories of my loved ones with a proper burial of some sort. That is my one condition. I will help you find a bride if you will help me by taking me to France afterward."

Deverill hesitated while he donned a coat of serviceable brown kerseymere. "Very well. I agree."

Her eyebrow rose skeptically. "You do?"

"Why do you seem so surprised?"

"I thought it would require more effort to convince you."

"But you are Princess Katharine. You have always been able to wrap men around your finger and persuade them to do your bidding."

She gave him an arch look. "Some men, perhaps, but not *you*. And you oughtn't call me princess since

I am not of royal blood. Clearly you have more to learn about British customs in addition to your new responsibilities as a lord." She paused as the urgency occurred to her. "We have very little time to secure you a bride—merely a month till the end of the Season. We should begin working on a plan at once."

Fetching his stockings and boots, Deverill crossed the room and sat down in the adjacent chair to put them on.

Kate disliked his proximity but forced herself to remain seated as she studied his attire. With his superb physique—all broad-shouldered, rugged—he put her more effeminate, aristocratic beaux to shame. But his black mane made him look rather uncivilized, and although his coat fit well enough, the style screamed "provincial."

"Our first order of business," she said, "should be to find you a good tailor. You don't want to look like a backwoods colonial, Mr. Deverill—Lord Valmere, I mean. I suppose I should address you by your new title."

"Pray, don't. I prefer you call me Deverill—or Brandon as you once did."

"You must grow accustomed to it, my lord."

He grimaced. "I will have a difficult time."

"It will become easier with practice. I, however, will have my work cut out for me if I hope to turn a brash American merchant into an acceptable English nobleman."

An amused gleam reentered his eyes. "I am part

English. My paternal bloodline should count in my favor."

"But you are a scandalous privateer," she said sweetly.

"Says the lady shockingly dressed as a lad. You've never objected much to scandal before, if I recall. None of your family has. With you advising me, I should fit into the ton well."

His retort was reminiscent of the sparring they'd done when they were both younger, but as pleasant as it was, Kate knew she would be unwise to encourage him. "I have had to curtail my scandalous inclinations of late, and I trust you will do the same if you wish to attract a genteel bride. We should begin as soon as possible. Are you free tomorrow morning?"

"As far as I know. I won't be leaving for Kent for another day or two to see the Valmere estate and my relatives."

"Could you call at my house at eleven tomorrow?"

"Why so late?"

"Usually I ride in the park in the mornings."

"I could accompany you. I haven't stretched my legs on a horse since leaving Virginia several weeks ago."

Consorting with Deverill in their old haunts would *definitely* be unwise, Kate realized. At least until she had more control of her feelings. She would do better to face him on her own ground with her companion present to preclude any chance of intimacy. "No, you cannot be seen in public looking like a ruffian. And it will be more appropriate if we have a proper chaperone."

Her comment made his brow rise. "You can't be serious."

"Indeed I am. When my brother married last year, I hired a companion . . . a middle-aged widow . . . although she will be marrying soon, so I must seek another. I recently found an ideal match for her also, by the way."

"Do you truly need a chaperone at your advanced age?"

Deverill was roasting her again, but his teasing stung a bit, since *he* was chiefly the reason she was still unattached, drat him.

She forced herself to answer lightly. "Sadly, it is one of the frustrations of being a single lady living alone in London. Ash and his new wife, Maura, prefer the country, especially since they recently had a son. So, while I am old enough to wear caps, if I hoped to remain here to enjoy the Season, I was required to bow to propriety. I will ask Mrs. Cuthbert to join us tomorrow when you call."

Deverill studied her thoughtfully. "If you are such an expert at matchmaking, why have you never made a match for yourself?"

Because no one lived up to my memories of you. "I never found the right match. I have no intention of marrying without true love."

His dark gaze moved over her with more intensity. "By all reports you've rejected countless suitors. And

I know for a fact you've always had a bevy of swains at your beck and call."

It was true. As a wellborn heiress, she'd been sought by numerous men, from awkward lads to hardened rakes. Her appearance, too, tended to attract male attention. With her dark red hair, she stood out among the fair young ladies making their debuts.

At eighteen, however, she had been brought up short by Deverill. For the first time in her life, she'd felt vulnerable to a man and uncertain of her powers. She had learned a valuable lesson in humility then. As a result she'd resolved to be kinder to her lovelorn suitors and let them down gently, settling into an amiable friendship with most.

But this conversation was growing far too personal for her comfort. Striving for casualness, Kate rose to her feet. "If your cousin Trey is arriving shortly, I had best go. Tomorrow morning we can discuss our plan and review exactly what sort of bride you are seeking. Meanwhile, I will begin thinking of possible candidates. I have enlisted Ash's aid as well—to advise you on government and legal matters and the like. In truth, that is primarily why he is coming to town tomorrow."

Deverill's eyes narrowed, but she could see amusement there. "You were certain of my agreement, weren't you? But then you usually manage to get your way."

She smiled ruefully. "I could never count on getting my way where you were concerned." When Deverill stood as well, she gazed up at him. "I trust you won't mention my visit here to your cousin Trey?"

"Your secret is safe with me."

"It is your secret as well. I could be ruined, but if you are complicit in my downfall, your plans to take a genteel bride would surely suffer."

His teeth flashed white in his tanned face. "I seem to recall you instigated both trysts."

"This time is not a tryst. And neither was the last time, actually—or at least, not entirely. True, I was enamored of you. I have always been overly romantic. It is my worst failing—or among my worst. But my original purpose that night was not to seduce you. I had convinced myself that I could persuade you to stay in England."

"I explained to you at the ball why I could not."

"So you did." Kate managed a careless laugh. "Forgive me, but I had some thought of trying to save your life."

"My worthless hide, you mean?"

She dimpled. "I did not say that. I did not even think it."

"I imagine you were angry with me."

She had been furious and heartbroken and afraid for him. Deverill had hurt her, although it was not wholly his fault. Apparently he had never harbored the same feelings for her that she had felt for him.

"I have forgotten all about that unfortunate incident," she lied. "A true gentleman would endeavor to do the same."

His smile was wry. "That is one event I could *never* forget."

"Well, *I* distinctly recall my mortification."

The laughter left his eyes. "I admit, I was greatly to blame. I led you on by kissing you the previous night. But refusing you was my only honorable course."

She lowered her gaze to a button on Deverill's coat. "You clearly didn't want me."

"Untrue. I simply had to discourage you from making an irreversible mistake."

Even as a sop to her pride, his admission was not particularly heartening. "Your discouragement was highly effective," she said softly.

"Kate—" He stopped and reconsidered whatever he had meant to say. "What kind of man would I be if I'd taken your innocence? My duty was to my country. I had to leave, and I didn't know when or if I would ever return."

She met his eyes again. "If you would be killed in battle, you mean."

"Yes. If I had taken you, I would have been obliged to stay."

That had been her goal, persuading him to stay instead of sailing off to fight a war against her own countrymen.

In her defense, she had thought she stood a chance. The night before at a ball, Deverill had given her a stunning farewell kiss, meant as goodbye. That thrilling, stolen embrace had shaken her down to her satin slippers and set her world askew. Worse, it had started her dreaming.

She'd wanted to tell him how she felt as well as beg him not to leave England. So she went to his hotel rooms and waited for him to return. Her scheme to seduce him truly was not premeditated, however. The longer she waited, the greater the temptation to use her budding feminine wiles, which had served her well in the past. Impulsively she'd undressed and climbed into his bed.

Memory descended in vivid detail: the flaming embarrassment flooding her body, the hurt stabbing her heart at his unceremonious rebuff. She had never behaved so wantonly—and had ardently vowed never to risk such painful rejection again.

Willing the memory away, Kate smiled brightly. "You will be pleased to know I have conquered my obsession with you. I will not make a fool of myself a second time."

When he didn't answer, she searched his face. "Surely you are relieved, my lord. You won't have to send me packing as you did the last time. You needn't fear my unwanted advances."

"A pity," he murmured.

His comment confused her. "What did you say?"

"Nothing of consequence." Oddly, his gaze softened. "If it is any consolation, I was extremely flattered by your offer. I was wildly attracted to you. I simply couldn't act on my desire."

His concession captured her full attention. "You desired me?"

His faint chuckle was self-deprecating. "Of course I desired you, as did countless other hapless males."

It was gratifying to think her own wild attraction then had not been wholly one-sided. As foolish as it was, beneath her surface confidence, self-doubt had been eating away at her all these years since.

Kate gave a slight shrug of her shoulders. "It doesn't matter now. It happened a long time ago. I was a mere girl then. Girls are inclined to do idiotic things."

"And now you are a beautiful woman."

"Your flattery is unnecessary."

"It is not mere flattery." To her surprise, Deverill reached up to finger a stray tendril that had escaped her wig and brushed it back from her face. "I hope you have not taken to wearing caps. It would be a shame to cover your lovely hair."

That brief gesture sparked a fiery awareness in Kate and caused her to take an involuntary step backward. If he was attempting to keep her off balance, he was succeeding. And strangely, his scrutiny only grew more intense.

"What if I wanted to claim another kiss?" he murmured.

His unexpected suggestion made her inhale sharply. "That would be entirely inappropriate."

"Aren't you curious?"

"Curious?" she repeated breathlessly.

"Wouldn't you care to see if there is still any attraction between us?"

The notion was absurd. Of course there was still an attraction between them. A potent one. At least on her part.

"No, I don't want to know. I mean . . . there is nothing on my side. I don't need to kiss you to know how I feel."

"Perhaps I do."

When he stepped closer, Kate felt her heart leap, whether in alarm or anticipation, she wasn't certain.

"What are you about, Deverill?"

"Answering a question."

His gaze captured hers, making her heart pound. His mouth was close, his body closer. . . .

Chapter Two

Kate froze. She could scarcely believe Deverill was about to kiss her—or even less, that she would permit him. When he bent toward her, she braced herself. She was not the type of woman to swoon, yet she knew his breath-stealing kisses would make her light-headed and weak.

He seemed in no hurry, however. Rather, he appeared intent on drawing out the moment. Surprisingly, he raised his hand to touch the side of her jaw, a light brush of his fingers. A rush of sensation shot through her at the unexpected caress, making Kate tense even further. In response, he spread his hand and stroked his thumb over her lower lip. Tendrils of heat shimmered inside her at the contact, sending small shivers along her skin. She was vividly aware of everything about him: his strength, his hardness, his barely restrained power.

An unwanted surge of excitement only added to the

tautness in her body. And when finally, slowly, he lowered his head, the delicate pressure of his mouth almost stopped her heart. Even forewarned, she was unprepared for the flash of pleasure that staggered her senses. Despite the softness, his kiss was just as explosive as six years ago. It gave her chills, set her body on fire, filled her with delicious feelings. . . .

Her hands rose reflexively to press against Deverill's chest, yet she didn't truly want to make him stop. Especially not when he changed the slant of his head, insistently coaxing her surrender as he drew her against him.

She had dreamed of this moment, Kate realized in a haze of need. Of Deverill kissing her again. Of his tender, passionate embrace. Even knowing her imaginings were pure fantasy, she had never entirely given up hope.

His lips moved over hers with exquisite pressure, his kiss slow and erotic and extremely thorough . . . cajoling, seducing. Then his tongue parted her lips, penetrating her mouth. Stunned, she arched toward him, wanting.

When he delved farther inside, exploring, she gave a helpless moan. He was assailing her with tender languor . . . molding, tasting, teasing.

Her body melted instinctively against his. All her senses felt assaulted as his tongue stroked provocatively against hers, tangling in a sensual dance. The effect was spellbinding. The heady sensation he roused made her light-headed and giddy.

With a sound between a sigh and a whimper, Kate gave in completely and wrapped her arms around his neck. Deverill made a more guttural sound and drew her closer, a reaction that thrilled her. She clung to him, wishing the moment would last forever.

To her awe and delight, his kiss went on for an endless, enchanting moment. Kate was achingly aware when he shifted against her, for one of his knees separated hers. Through her breeches she felt the pressure of his sinewed thigh against her femininity. She stifled a gasp as another shaft of desire struck her.

Her startled movement must have jolted Deverill, however, for his embrace loosened. When he pulled away, she swayed in his arms, her eyes still closed. He had left her dazed and flustered and hungry for more of what she'd tasted.

It was a long moment before he spoke. "I thought so," he said with husky satisfaction.

There was a note of triumph in his tone as well. His confidence—his certainty that she would fall into his arms again like a half-wit—rubbed Kate the wrong way. It made her feel helpless, impotent—and she didn't deal well with either.

She pushed her hands against his chest, holding him away as she stared up at him. Her breath was coming in rapid bursts while her pulse raced wildly. It was so unfair that she should find herself unable to speak, unable to think of anything but Deverill and his marvelous mouth, his beautiful eyes.

His eyes held a dark fire that called to some primitive instinct deep inside her. While she stood mesmerized, he lifted a forefinger to her throat and lightly stroked. "You felt it also."

She most certainly had. She was profoundly shaken. She still felt a strange quivering between her thighs, a restless ache low in her feminine center.

She took a deep, unsettled breath. "It is no matter."

When she struggled to extricate herself from his arms, Deverill released her, but when she turned for the door, his query brought her up short. "Have you considered resuming where we left off?"

She glanced over her shoulder, her gaze narrowing. "You are making game of me."

"No."

A tangible desire shimmered between them, filling the air. It took Kate all of her willpower to shake her head. She would *not* make a fool of herself again. At least she earnestly hoped not.

"There is no chance of resuming where we left off," she finally replied.

"None?"

"No, *none*. Whatever feelings I had for you are all in the past."

"All of them?"

Kate swallowed hard, not wanting to answer. "Enough of them. In any case, there will be no more kissing, my lord. You will behave like a civilized gentleman, not a pirate, or I cannot continue. Our agreement will be strictly a business arrangement."

"You drive a hard bargain, sweetheart."

"Yes, I do. I will expect you at eleven tomorrow."

She turned then and fled across the room. Scrambling out the door, she shut it quickly behind her and stood there breathing heavily. Heat flushed her body, while her lips still tingled with sensation.

For a moment, Kate closed her eyes, chastising herself for giving in to Deverill so readily. Then she realized she would be seen if someone happened upon her.

Fortunately the corridor was deserted. Reaching up to make sure her wig was not askew, she hurried down the hallway, toward the servants' narrow back staircase in search of her trusted coachman who awaited her on the street.

Just as her endeavor six years ago, this encounter with Deverill had been an abject failure also. She had hoped to prove her indifference, but she'd only confirmed that her witless captivation still existed.

Willing her racing pulse to slow down, Kate muttered a vivid oath. She simply *must* forget this regrettable incident and pretend it had never happened.

The trouble was, Brandon Deverill was the most compelling, most unforgettable man she had ever met. And his devastating kiss just now had refreshed her memory in spades.

Pirates. As he stared at the closed door, Brandon shook his head in bemusement. Leave it to Kate to surprise him. She was the most unpredictable woman of his acquaintance, but even so, he hadn't expected her proposition just now—trading her matchmaking skills for his potential protection from French pirates.

His reaction to kissing her was no surprise, however. Voicing an oath, Brandon adjusted his breeches in an attempt to tamp down the lustful ache in his body and turned away from the door. *Get hold of your urges, man.*

At least two questions were now settled in his mind. He'd wanted to see if Kate was as special as he remembered, and the answer was an emphatic "yes." And the attraction blazing between them was as combustible as ever—he'd proven it to them both. All his male instincts told him Kate wasn't as indifferent as she pretended, either, which spawned numerous other intriguing reflections.

In an effort to distract himself, Brandon fetched a leather satchel from his valise and pulled out a sheaf of documents. He glanced briefly through the lot, mostly correspondence with his late uncle's solicitor regarding his inheritance.

He wasn't particularly eager to assume the barony, knowing it would require a vast change of lifestyle. He'd left England with grave reluctance six years ago, to honor his duty to family and country, but now he finally was free to follow his own inclinations for his future. He hadn't yet settled on a specific course, beyond determining if he wanted Kate for his wife. Which had meant taking advantage of the moment to kiss her. He'd purposely caught her off guard, knowing she would refuse his advances otherwise, given how they had parted.

He'd needed all his willpower to release her. No doubt his keen response was even stronger because he knew what charms lay beneath her male-servant's attire. He knew what her bare breasts looked like, how perfect her lithe, naked body was. Even garbed as a lad, with her masses of glorious hair hidden beneath a powdered wig, she was just as bewitching as ever. She had flame-dark hair and warm green eyes and a mouth made for sinning.

Brandon blew out a breath and raked a hand through his own hair. He thought he'd overblown Kate's impact in his mind. That war, blood, pain, and guilt had warped his memories. But she was the same bold beauty he recalled, intensely vibrant and so full of life, she made *him* come alive.

He wanted her in his bed, that was for certain.

He'd felt desire for Kate from the very first. Isabella had spoken about her for years—and warned him that few men were able to handle Lady Katharine Wilde. He'd expected a willful, independent belle, but upon finally meeting her when she was seventeen, she had unexpectedly entranced him. Admittedly, her adventurous, lively nature had attracted him even more than her physical attributes. Kate was fresh, direct, honest, spirited. . . . The very opposite of the dull debutantes he usually encountered.

By that time she had countless suitors at her feet, clamoring for scraps of her attention. Men flocked to her, and Brandon was determined not to become a lovelorn lackey who vied to do her bidding. Yet her effervescent personality had won him over.

It was the only time he'd ever been tempted to consider matrimony. Upon severing ties with Kate, he couldn't help feeling he'd lost something vital. He'd acted for her own good, though. Succumbing to a reckless night of passion would have been disastrous for them both.

He regretted having to leave her, regretted more hurting her. Indeed, the following years had been filled with regrets. He'd seen death, caused it. Killed people who might have been friends and neighbors under other circumstances.

Memories, heavy and relentless, descended upon him. When he strove to push them away, sweat broke out on his brow.

With another curse, Brandon restored the legal documents to the satchel, then strode over to the window and opened it, letting in the sounds and odors of the bustling London street below. He was supremely glad those grim years were over. He might have returned to England sooner, but he'd had multiple obligations to fulfill. First to his father and the war, then his widowed mother, his younger brother, and his shipping business. Now he had duties to his new title.

Yet it was Kate herself who was the strongest draw. She was like a beacon of warm light—

A knock on his hotel room door thankfully interrupted his brooding thoughts. When he opened it, his cousin Trey stood there. They were of similar build and appearance, except that his cousin had lighter brown hair.

As soon as his ship arrived at the London docks, Brandon had sent Trey a message, but he wasn't certain what his reception would be after all these years, since they had fought on opposite sides.

He needn't have worried. Trey flashed a broad grin, stepped forward, and seized him in a powerful bear hug.

"It is about time you showed your sorry hide, Brand," Trey said, clapping him on the back heartily before releasing him. "You waited far too long to return."

"I finally had good reason."

"Ah, yes . . . Lord Valmere," Trey replied, sketching a mock bow. "I suppose congratulations are in order."

Brandon grimaced. "You are better equipped to assume an English title."

"But you always knew that your fate was tied to England."

Trey was by far his favorite relative. They'd once been as close as brothers, less from blood ties than from being comrades in arms. As members of a covert branch of the British Foreign Office, the Guardians of the Sword, they had carried out missions and faced danger together numerous times.

"Are you ready?" Trey asked. "Your uncle's solicitor is expecting you, so we ought to be on our way."

"Yes." Brandon fetched the satchel and accompanied Trey from the room. "My thanks for conveying me. I will need to hire my own carriage, but I welcome your advice on inheritance matters."

"I am at your service. Very glad to have you back, old man."

"What the devil have you been about?" Brandon responded. "What of the Guardians?"

As they made their way downstairs to the street where his curricle awaited, Trey discussed their mutual friends and their league's leader, Sir Gawain Olwen, who had recently retired. The secret society, headquartered on an island paradise near Spain, had been formed in medieval times and charged with protecting the weak and vulnerable across Europe and Britain. But defeating the French at Waterloo nearly two years ago had ushered in a new era of peace.

"With Boney vanquished, there is less need for foiling tyrants and battling warmongers, but we still have a good deal of work to do," Trey said. "We have all missed you."

"I missed you all greatly also. One of my chief regrets was having to leave the Guardians."

"I can imagine."

He'd been torn between two countries, with loyalties to both. The war had forced him to choose sides and put his American blood kin above his English ancestry and friendships. And given his family's various shipping enterprises, he was in the thick of things during the war.

"Most of us are happily wed now," Trey added as they climbed into his curricle. "Some with families." Taking the reins, he guided his pair of grays into the busy street. "Hawk was the most recent."

"So I heard." The Earl of Hawkhurst had married Kate's cousin, Lady Skye Wilde.

"Which leaves you, Brand. It staggered me when you wrote that you would be seeking a bride. You never were one for marriage."

Brandon's mouth curved. "No." He'd never been eager to relinquish his freedom or be tied down to one woman. But if he had to wed, Kate was his only choice. Yet he needed the time and opportunity to verify his instinct that they would suit in married life.

"You surprised Lady Isabella as well," Trey remarked. "But she thinks you could be happy with the right woman, just as I am. My wife, Antonia, is eager to meet you this evening, by the way."

"And I her."

He'd been invited to lodge at Trey's house but had declined. For his pursuit of Kate, he wanted more privacy.

Trey fell silent as he negotiated the curricle through heavy traffic. After directing the grays across a crowded intersection, he continued the conversation.

"Bella told me something of your plan—that you intend to ask Lady Katharine Wilde to find a match for you. I'm acquainted with her brother, Beaufort, but I don't know her well. Isn't she the one who rescued the child injured in the ruins at Beauvoir?"

"Yes, the young son of a tenant farmer. He might well have died had she not discovered him after his accident and risked her life to save him."

A wagon lumbered into the middle of the street, claiming Trey's full attention, leaving Brandon time to recall the incident at Beauvoir—the lavish Beaufort country estate—a few months after he had met Kate.

That afternoon had given him a new appreciation for her courage. A superb horsewoman, she never missed a chance to ride. Although it was a chilly, stormy afternoon, they'd been galloping hell-for-leather across the Kentish countryside. If he lived a hundred years, he would never forget the enchanting picture she made, laughing with exhilaration, her face flushed from the wind, her vivid hair streaming out behind her.

When eventually they came upon the ruins of an ancient church, they slowed their horses to a walk. Just then the wind died down long enough for her to notice a misplaced sound.

"Listen . . . Did you hear that?"

Kate insisted she heard a moan coming from inside the ruins, and when they rode closer, the faint weeping sound grew stronger. She dismounted and scrambled over the rubble, calling out, "Hello?" Brandon hastily joined her and warned her to take care.

"I will. It looks as if several walls have collapsed."

"More than that," he replied, pointing across an open space.

Evidently the floor had partially given way, bringing down much of the adjacent room into what must have been the cellar. Through a gap in the rotten boards, they could make out a pile of stones and debris strewn with wooden beams.

When the weeping stopped, followed by a pitiful cry for help, they ascertained what had happened: While exploring the ruins, a ten-year-old boy named Billy had fallen through the opening and broken his ankle, so that he couldn't climb out.

Brandon intended to hazard a descent, but Kate objected. "No, I am smaller. You cannot squeeze into the crevice where he is trapped like I can. And you are much stronger, so you can pull us out. We can fashion a rope from my petticoats. . . ."

They had argued briefly, since Brandon disliked the risk she would be taking with the structure so unstable. The remaining stone walls could crumble and crush her at any moment or bury her alive. Yet he knew her plan stood the best chance of rescuing the boy.

While they tied strips of her linen undergarment together, Kate kept up a steady stream of soothing words for Billy, focusing his attention away from his agonizing pain by asking about his family.

When they were done, she took a deep breath and carefully inched her way down the stone incline as Brandon fed the makeshift rope to her. All the while, he felt his gut clenching. But after an endless time, she reappeared, gritting her teeth but smiling grimly in triumph.

She had crawled back up the pile of rubble, with Billy gamely clinging to her back, despite his pain. Her lovely face was smudged with dirt and sweat, her hands and knees lacerated and scraped by sharp fragments of rock and mortar, but she was grateful to have helped the lad. They splinted his ankle as best they could and conveyed him to her own family physician, who managed to heal the injury well enough that months later, Billy could walk with only a slight limp.

She'd become a local heroine that day. Few noble ladies would have risked their lives to save a commoner child. Kate had also earned Brandon's admiration that day. Her fearlessness was one of the things he liked most about her. That and her selflessness. In the intervening years, he had never met any other woman like her.

He could never forget her or her passion. Thus, it was no wonder that she'd stayed on his mind the entire time during the war. In the initial months, visions of a fiery redhead had haunted his sleep. He'd tried to ignore them but finally gave in. Thoughts of Kate had gotten him through the long, lonely nights at sea. In his worst hours, after a raging battle, he would call up memories of her.

Those memories had led him back to her after six long years. He'd orchestrated a reason to share her company, and used Bella to hook her into finding him a bride.

Naturally he couldn't tell Kate what he was contemplating, not after rejecting her once already. But he couldn't shake the suspicion that this could be his second chance. That he needed her freshness, her warmth. That he needed her to wash him clean with her inner fire, her strength of mind and spirit.

Her vitality was contagious, Brandon reflected. A mere quarter hour in her presence this afternoon had made him feel more alive than he had in a long while.

And yes, he wanted to explore this remarkable heat between them. To find out if her lovemaking was as sensual and wild and uninhibited as he imagined it would be.

He was under no illusions, however. If he decided to pursue Kate, she wouldn't be easy to win. Overcoming her hurt and wariness would prove a definite challenge, although in truth he had expected her to be angrier with him.

And then there was another, greater obstacle. She wanted love, she'd made that very clear. He wasn't certain he was even capable of love. Perhaps it wasn't in his character. Or perhaps his experiences had deadened him to any deeper feelings.

His return to England had opened new possibilities, though. It was tempting to think he could forget the blood and battles, that he could live a normal life, perhaps with a wife, a family. As for marriage, he'd been profoundly unsatisfied with any of the conceivable candidates he'd met over the years, especially after knowing Kate.

Today had shown him that she was still an enchantress, accustomed to getting her way through charm and sheer persistence. She threw herself into every endeavor—and her search to formally mourn her parents would likely be no different.

Her bargaining had presented him with a dilemma. Unquestionably, he much preferred to put the violent elements of his past behind him. The prospect of clashing with hostile buccaneers held no appeal whatsoever. Yet he had no choice but to aid Kate in her quest to properly lay the memory of her parents to rest. He couldn't let her go haring off to the Continent, intent on tackling a horde of French pirates on her own.

Moreover, despite his reluctance on several fronts, he was glad to be back in England. And for the first time in a very long while, Brandon acknowledged, he felt eager and hopeful about the future.

When Kate arrived home moments ahead of an impending rainstorm, she discovered her companion in the library as usual, curled up on a window seat, scribbling in a notebook.

Smiling fondly, Kate went to the hearth to stir the fire. She considered herself quite lucky to have found Nell Cuthbert, a middle-aged widow of good breeding who was respectable but not puritanical. Normally a bit scatterbrained, Nell seemed even more dreamy-eyed and unfocused of late. With her nuptials approaching in a few weeks, there was also a hopeful feeling of romance in the air.

When Kate fetched Nell's shawl and wrapped it around her plump shoulders, the widow looked up from her writing. "Thank you, my dear. I was growing chilled."

"It is no wonder. You are wearing a summer gown on a blustery spring day. Do come away from the window, Nell. Have you had your tea yet?"

She looked around her blankly. "I believe they brought a tray in some time ago. The tea must have grown cold, though."

"I will ring for a fresh pot, but there are sandwiches and scones here."

While Kate went to the bellpull, Nell stood stiffly and stretched, then carried her notebook, pen, and inkwell to the desk. "My, how I let the time get away from me. I wished to jot down one more page of notes."

That was regularly the case, since she was trying her hand at writing a novel, a brooding gothic romance set in a haunted castle.

When a footman entered, Kate gave orders for more tea and settled on the sofa. Realizing the servant had eyed her oddly, she pulled off her powdered wig and combed her fingers through her hair.

Rather than disapprove of her male attire, however, Nell clapped her hands together in delight. "What fun your unconventionality is. You have given me a capital idea for a new plot." She frowned. "Where are my spectacles?"

"Atop your head. Will you join me on the sofa?"

"Yes, indeed."

Complying, Nell reached for the plate of sandwiches and began to nibble. "How fared your meeting with the pirate, dear?"

"Well enough, I suppose. Deverill agreed to help me locate the shipwreck in exchange for my finding him a suitable bride."

"How comforting to know he will aid you. But will you truly be able to secure a genteel match for him as you did for me? At best he is a sailor and merchant, at worst a pirate."

"To be precise, he was a privateer. There is a difference."

"What difference?"

Kate had posed the same question several years ago. "Pirates are typically rebel citizens with allegiance to no country. Privateers are sanctioned by governments by letters of marque. In Deverill's case, the American government granted him legal authority to conduct hostilities against declared enemies, meaning us British."

"The distinction will be lost on the ton," Nell predicted.

"I expect so," Kate agreed. "But he is quite wealthy, not to mention outlandishly handsome. And now that he possesses a distinguished title, I suspect there are any number of ladies who would leap to become his wife."

"You said you quarreled with him before he left for America. I imagine it was awkward for you today, meeting him again after all this time," Nell said sympathetically, reaching out to pat Kate's hand.

Kate squeezed her companion's fingers in return. Sometimes Nell surprised her with her compassion and insight. In the past year, Kate had come to love Nell, for dotty-headed or not, she was a real dear and a jewel of a friend. She would be sorely missed when she married and left her position in the Beaufort household to begin a fresh stage of her life with her new husband.

"Our meeting was indeed awkward," Kate said simply, preferring not to expound on the details. "But we came to a satisfactory business arrangement."

"Merely business? I thought your past acquaintance with Mr. Deverill was romantic in nature."

"Once it was, but no longer."

"A pity. I want you to be as happy as you have made me."

Managing a smile, Kate attempted to change the subject. "I hope I may find such happiness also, Nell. May I count on your presence when Deverill calls here tomorrow at eleven?"

"Of course. With a man like that, it is only prudent for me to attend you."

Nell apparently was not ready to give up her line of questioning, however. "Wasn't he supposed to be your ideal mate? Skye told me something of your history with Mr. Deverill and your conjectures about legendary lovers."

Avoiding an answer, Kate reached for a biscuit. Last season, she had speculated that the five Wilde cousins would find their mates based on myths and classic tales of legendary lovers throughout history—and had successfully predicted four of them.

"What was your tale to be?" Nell persisted. "Pygmalion?"

Kate made a face. "Yes." She'd originally presumed her cousin Quinn's courtship would follow the Greek myth of Pygmalion—a sculptor whose artistic creation had been brought to life by the gods. But after Quinn had married pursuing a different tale, she'd thought Pygmalion might do for her instead, only in reverse.

In this instance she would have to mold a bold American privateer into a proper English nobleman.

Her heart had sunk when she realized that Deverill might be her legendary lover. And now she was determined to prove otherwise.

"I am ready to abandon my theories about legendary lovers, Nell."

Nell suddenly looked dismayed. "But you are the last unmarried Wilde cousin. You cannot give up now."

"I am not giving up entirely. Merely on this particular legend."

"Good. Your premise thus far has been extremely fruitful. Your siblings and cousins would agree."

Kate couldn't repress a droll smile. "Yes, they *finally* appreciate my prodding." She chewed thoughtfully as she recalled the battles she'd had with Ash and Quinn and her adopted brother and first cousin, Lord Jack Wilde.

Her desire to matchmake had begun when she was just a young girl—the craving to make something out of tragedy, to turn grief and loss into happy endings. In truth, after their parents' deaths, all the Wilde cousins had felt a need to take fate into their own hands, to shape their own destinies.

"Well," Nell said, "*I* certainly appreciate your prodding. You thrust me into society against my will, against my very character, and now I am preparing for an entirely new life with Horatio. I am still pinching myself for my good fortune."

Kate nodded. She had dragged bashful Nell out of her shell and found her a genteel widower who properly treasured her.

"You deserve all the happiness in the world, Nell."

"As do you, dearest Kate. I worry about you, you know."

Sensing her companion's desire to press further, Kate again tried to change the subject. "You won't mind if I focus my efforts on Deverill's bride search now? I don't want my project to interfere with your nuptials."

"It won't. We have the wedding arrangements well in hand. But you should not forget about yourself, my dear. I know you have always longed for love."

"I want love, yes, but it will *not* be with Deverill."

"Why not?"

She gave her friend a patient look. "I was mistaken about him, Nell. I no longer believe he is my destiny."

"No?" Nell frowned in disappointment.

"No," Kate repeated emphatically. "And if I can find a bride for him, it will confirm that he was never meant for me."

"But perhaps you can rekindle your romance with him."

"There is no chance of that happening."

"Why not?"

Because she refused to risk rejection again, to expose her vulnerability in so painful a fashion.

"May we *please* speak of something else?" Kate said, unable to hide her exasperation any longer.

"Yes, if you wish. But I only want to help."

Nell's hurt tone was a pretense, Kate knew, which made her smile. "We agreed long ago that I am the matchmaker in the family. Truly, I am capable of seeing to my own future."

Nell returned a knowing smile of her own. Fortunately, just then the footman returned with a fresh pot of tea and claimed her attention.

While Nell busied herself pouring two cups, Kate couldn't help reflecting on how she had come to be so obsessed with romance. Loneliness had played an enormous role, of course. She had been orphaned at a young age and sent off to boarding school with only Skye for company. Perhaps that was why she'd developed such a great affection for Nell; because in those latter years of her childhood she'd been motherless. She had missed that mother-daughter bond, ached for it.

Her ardent desire for a soul mate also stemmed from the loneliness driving her. One of her biggest fears was that she would never find love with a man who loved her in return. The kind of all-consuming devotion her parents had known in their marriage. She had wonderful memories of her parents—their joy, their loyalty, their adoration for each other.

She wanted that same soul-deep commitment for herself. She yearned for love with a devoted husband, for friendship, for completion.

Over time, though, she'd refined her aspirations for the ideal mate. She had wanted someone adventurous and exciting to claim her heart. She was searching for lightning, for fiery passion, for heart-searing intensity.

With Deverill she'd thought she had gotten her wish. He was infuriating, delightful, provocative, deliciously risqué. He made her think; he made her want to box his ears. In short, he enthralled her. Her fervent attraction had swiftly become far more than adolescent lust. She had fancied herself falling in love.

And his rejection had not merely wounded her pride. The hurt had felt much deeper than merely a young woman scorned.

Deverill's divided loyalties, too, had only complicated her conflicted feelings about him—a man who had fought against her country, who had killed her countrymen. Kate pressed her lips together with renewed resolve. She refused to believe that he was her destiny. And if she could marry him off, then he obviously was not her legendary lover.

No, she had one main goal now: to travel to France and resolve her family's tragic ending.

But to achieve that, she had to take Deverill under her wing, so to speak. She would groom him for his new role as a nobleman and find him a bride befitting his new title.

Admittedly, her heart would not be in her work. She had no wish to dedicate the next month or more to making a match for Deverill. But for good or ill, she was committed. She would force herself to discharge her pledge with good grace.

Of course, when he called on the morrow, she needed to be better prepared than she'd been this afternoon. In the flesh, Deverill was far more potent than in any dream or fantasy.

Images of his big, hard body kept sliding into her mind at the most inappropriate moments. The tanned skin, the broad shoulders, the lean, muscled torso. And his mouth . . . his marvelous kisses—

"Here you are, my dear."

"Thank you," Kate said, gratefully accepting her teacup from Nell.

With effort she shrugged off her vexing memories. No doubt she would have to fight temptation every step of the way. At least she had laid down rules for their future relationship. Whether Deverill would abide by them, however, was highly questionable.

But she would manage to control him and her own deluded yearnings somehow. She would find him a bride, and she would prove that he wasn't the match for her. And then she could move on with her life and set about locating the shipwreck and properly laying her late loved ones to rest.

Promptly at eleven, Brandon arrived at the elegant Beaufort mansion in Grosvenor Square, his anticipation of seeing Kate heightened by his vivid dreams of the previous night. In his nocturnal fantasies, they had finished what she'd started in his hotel room six years ago. He'd spent the hours until dawn making love to her, glorying in her delectable body, her passion.

When he was shown into the drawing room by a footman, Kate immediately drew his focus. Politely rising from a sofa, she pasted a faint smile on her lips and came forward to welcome him, clearly bracing herself for the jolt of eye contact.

Brandon felt the powerful jolt as well. Without volition, he found his gaze raking over her lithe figure. She wore a fashionable gown of pale green kerseymere with a demure neckline and long sleeves.

Her modest attire did nothing to curb his natural

lust. His instinctive desire to claim her, however, was tempered by the presence of a small, plump woman with graying hair who was seated on the sofa.

"Lord Valmere, may I make known my companion, Mrs. Cuthbert?" Kate said.

When the introduction was made, he judged Mrs. Cuthbert to be a pleasant, well-bred matron there to guard the virtue of her charge.

Brandon much preferred having Kate alone without a chaperone, but he repressed his feelings of possessiveness and took a seat in a chair opposite the ladies. Fortunately, Mrs. Cuthbert occupied herself with her needlepoint and made no further comment.

Even so, the conversation was somewhat stilted at first, not the least because Kate maintained a determined air of formality. Only when they began discussing potential candidates for his future wife did she warm to her subject and thus to him.

"Before I begin my search, I need to know what kind of bride you are seeking. What sort of character appeals to you—and any other parameters you have in mind . . . appearance, interests?"

"I have no one particular in mind. I am not overly fastidious."

Her brows drew together. "Seriously, I will have difficulty helping you if you don't give me some kind of hint as to your preferences."

"Very well, then. Someone meek and mild who will do my bidding."

She wrinkled her nose. "A biddable female. How

revolting." The glimmer of laughter that entered her eyes was reminiscent of the old Kate. "I confess disappointment, Lord Valmere. I would have expected you to favor a lady with a little spirit, but if a doormat is what you want, I will do my best to oblige."

He leaned back in his chair, enjoying her rejoinders. "There are advantages to having an obedient wife rather than one who seeks to rule me."

"In other words, you want someone quite unlike myself."

"I suspect there is no one else like you," Brandon said truthfully.

Kate gave a light shrug of her shoulders. "You would not be content with a wife like me. We are both too strong-willed ever to suit. We would forever be at loggerheads."

"You are right. You and I would be in constant conflict."

Her slight frown suggested she was not happy with his reply, but then her brow cleared. "You are saying that to provoke me."

He smiled. "Only a little."

Chuckling, Kate seemed to relax, appearing once more in control. "Take my advice, my lord, and learn to behave yourself. If you want to win a genteel bride, you cannot treat gently bred young ladies as you do me, or you will frighten them off. You cannot be overbearing, and you certainly cannot act like a heathen."

With emphasis on the word "heathen," she pointedly scrutinized his coat. "I will endeavor to find the perfect bride for you, but our first task should be to repair your appearance. After weeks at sea, you are in desperate need of a haircut. I intend to send you to my brother's barber—and tailor and bootmaker as well."

Kate rummaged through the papers on the tea table in front of her and handed him a list. "Here are their names and directions. I have alerted these particular tradesmen so they will be expecting you. If your measurements are taken before you leave to visit your new dependents in Kent, work can begin on your new wardrobe while you are away."

Brandon studied the list, recognizing Weston, London's premier tailor, and Toby, a superb bootmaker. "Is such haste necessary?"

"Yes. You want to make the best possible impression. Indeed, I suggest you postpone any public appearances until you have a proper wardrobe. You should probably hire a valet also, unless the late baron had one in his employ who can continue to serve you. If not, I can recommend a reputable employment agency on Bond Street."

"You have planned thoroughly, haven't you?"

"Not *thoroughly*. I haven't had the time. But rest assured, I will. Making your formal debut in society requires a careful strategy."

"You sound like a general conducting a campaign."

A wry smile curved her mouth. "It is rather similar. I mean to transform you into London's most eligible bachelor." Her gaze again settled on his coat. "A new wardrobe will be the least of our challenges, I fear. You will have to conform to polite social strictures and cultivate a sense of decorum and disport yourself as a gentleman and develop more formal manners. . . ."

Judging by her amusement, she was purposely exaggerating the ordeals ahead of him because she knew he disliked such trappings.

"You never objected to my manners in the past," he pointed out.

"I made allowances and put up with you because you are American and a friend of my family, but now I mean to make you over with a new image. It will be impossible to turn you into an ideal husband otherwise."

"You intend to emasculate me," Brandon murmured, "by converting me into a stuffed shirt."

"Not at all. But I cannot stress enough that you must strive to be *gentle,* not so forward and threatening. I have several candidates in mind, and they all have more delicate sensibilities than I."

"I imagine so," he said dryly. Leaning back in his chair, he crossed his arms over his chest. "I am intrigued to see how far you will go to change me into a namby-pamby."

Kate laughed. "There is little danger of *that.*"

"But you are set on highlighting my shortcomings and overlooking my sterling qualities and manifold charms."

Her green eyes sparkled. "Your charms, hmmm? Modesty is not your strong suit, I see."

"You are enjoying having me at a disadvantage, aren't you?"

"Quite. I believe it best to speak plainly."

"Your plain speaking is one of the things I always liked about you."

For a moment, she looked reluctant to accept his praise. Then she cleared her throat and returned to the matter of his reformation. "We must emphasize your fortune and title and estates and remain vague about your former occupation . . . downplay your actual career as a merchant, even a wealthy shipowner, and embrace your new nobility instead."

"I warn you, I have no intention of becoming an idle fop."

Kate shook her head. "If you care for your dependents and tenants, you will not be idle in the least. Done well, estate management is hard work. You can hire a bailiff, but an absentee lord benefits no one. Ash will be happy to advise you. He can also help you to better understand the peerage and our royal government and the workings of Parliament—although none of that is a priority at the moment."

Her expression turned thoughtful. "It might even be wise for Ash to accompany you to Kent. That would help to expedite your education and make good use of what little time we have. When he arrives in London this afternoon, I can ask him if he is willing. As for our plan . . . while you are away, I will work on refining a list of candidates. I will also start planning various engagements for you to attend—balls and routs and assemblies and such."

"How delightful for me." He offered her a cynical smile. "Behold me in raptures."

In response, Kate gave him an exasperated look. "I am not inviting debate, Deverill."

"Now who is being overbearing? I shall start calling you 'Little Dictator.'"

"If I am dictatorial, it is for your own good. You should be grateful I am willing to expend so much time and energy on your behalf."

Brandon gave her a mock salute. "As you wish, princess."

"You may deride me all you like, but you will have to make a sincere effort if we are to succeed. You cannot scare the ladies with talk of weapons and battle. You ought not speak about the conflict with America, either, and especially not your former privateering."

"Why not?"

Her expression sobered. "I should think it obvious. For most of the Beau Monde, 'privateer' is merely a polite term for marauding pirate. I heard that you even captained a schooner against the British Navy."

Brandon shrugged. "An exaggeration. I was merely aboard as owner, although in my youth I did spend two years apprenticing as a sailor aboard our ships at my father's behest."

"But you went to war against England, which made us enemies."

At her accusation, he sharpened his gaze on her, while his tone held an edge when he replied, "If your navy hadn't illegally impressed thousands of American seamen for over a decade, there would have been no need for war."

Kate's own tone was clipped when she retorted, "So you spent years harrying our fleet and sinking our ships and killing our sailors."

"How would you feel if you were torn from your home and family and forced to serve on a foreign warship, perhaps to die in captivity?"

She pressed her lips together, clearly trying to hold back a rebuttal. "We will always disagree on this subject, so there is no point in quarreling about it."

Perceiving her genuine ire, Brandon softened his approach. "I can see I have ruffled your feathers."

"I do *not* have feathers, my lord," she said tartly.

"Don't get your back up, love."

Visibly striving for composure, she gave him a cool look. "I don't know how they do things in America, but here the appropriate interval for a gentleman's social call is fifteen minutes. You have overstayed your welcome, my lord."

Brandon shifted his glance to Kate's companion. Mrs. Cuthbert was concentrating on her needlepoint, a vague air about her, but he suspected she was listening intently to their clashing.

He disliked leaving Kate on such contentious terms, but rather than dispute the point, he rose to his feet.

With a polite bow, he took his leave of Mrs. Cuthbert, then her charge.

To his surprise, Kate accompanied him to the entrance hall—to finalize their plans, he presumed.

Instead, she sounded contrite when she spoke. "I am sorry for losing my temper."

"I will contrive to forgive you."

"I mean it, Deverill. I ought not have scolded you for a past that cannot be changed. We should let bygones be bygones."

"You needn't apologize, princess. We have too much of a history to stand on formality."

She searched his face intently. "Indeed, we do. And in all seriousness, I well know the people you hope to influence. Many will turn on you and cut you dead if they perceive the slightest social advantage, and all your high marital aspirations will be for naught."

Brandon held up her list of merchants. "I appreciate your efforts and will upgrade my wardrobe as you instruct. In fact, I shall display admirable forbearance in all your dictates. When I return from Kent, I intend to impress you with my sartorial splendor."

Kate seemed relieved by his genial response and glad to return to their former easy friendship, for her tone lightened. "And I shall gamely carry on while you are away. Meanwhile, if you fix your interest on any specific lady, you should inform me at once so that I can revise my strategy."

"I doubt *that* will happen. I am unlikely to find a

suitable bride on my own. I told you, I will need your expertise."

"And I told you, I will do my best."

"I am all gratitude." Bowing over her hand, Brandon brought her fingers to his lips for a lingering kiss, apparently startling her. She was flustered by his gesture and keenly aware of the intimate physical contact, if the fresh bloom in her cheeks was any indication.

"See, I can feign gentlemanly behavior if pressed," he pointed out, flashing a slow smile.

With a visible effort at composure, she smiled back and allowed her amusement to show. "I only pray you can continue your sham for several weeks, Deverill."

Chuckling, Brandon turned toward the door. He could feel Kate's gaze following him as a footman let him out the front entrance.

As he descended the steps to the drive, Brandon felt satisfied overall with this second meeting. Obviously Kate was still angry at him for leaving England, perhaps even for spurning her all those years ago, but her ire was mellowing.

As for his own feelings toward her . . . Kate was just as captivating as ever, with her endearing charm and ability to laugh at herself. Indeed, she seemed even more special now because she had matured. She was no longer a girl, but a fully grown, infinitely desirable woman.

After directing his newly hired coachman to Bond

Street and climbing into his rented carriage, Brandon sat back against the leather squabs and contemplated his dilemma: what to do about Kate.

Not only was she more mature and seasoned, she was far more controlled now. More guarded. Less trusting. She'd once looked at him as if he were the most fascinating, desirable man alive—and he badly wanted that look back.

Moreover, he wanted *her.* He relished her spirit and how she challenged him. Admittedly, he would rather fight with Lady Katharine Wilde than make love to any other woman.

Which settled the question for him. He wanted a future with Kate. The prospect of taking her to wive felt . . . right. Even more profound, he knew he would be the best husband for her.

Love or no love, they would make a fine match.

Yet he couldn't just waltz back into her life and claim her after rejecting her and being absent for years. No, he would first have to make up for hurting her, for wounding her pride and her heart.

He could start by showing her how utterly desirable he found her. Kate was rightly gun-shy with him now. And clearly, she intended to use her chaperone as a piece of her defensive armor.

Brandon's brow furrowed as a strategy began to take shape in his mind. He would have to woo Kate without being overt about it. Which meant he needed to maintain the pretense of relying on her matchmaking skills to seek some other genteel lady to wed.

And of course, he couldn't conduct a seduction under the watchful eye of her companion.

A bemused smile curved Brandon's mouth. He looked forward to finally getting Kate alone upon his return to London. In the interim, he would plot ways to separate her from her chaperone.

With luck, the next time he saw Kate, he would put his plan into action.

Woefully flustered, Kate made her way back to the drawing room, her hand tingling, her body hot, her thoughts bordering on dismay. Deverill had only to kiss her fingers and she felt sparks deep in her core.

And that sensual smile of his . . . The impact had left her reeling, as did his easy mastery over her physical responses. He was fully in control, effortlessly using his masculine powers to beguile her. When she was younger, she had often employed her feminine wiles to her own end, and now he was employing similar methods on her, blast him. He knew how deeply his mere touch affected her.

"I must say," Nell observed in an admiring voice, "Lord Valmere is . . . an *overwhelming* sort of man." She fanned her face in mock heat. "A handsome pirate figure whom a heroine in my novel might wish to ravish her."

I would like to be ravished by him also.

Although Kate lamented the unbidden thought, such a risqué observation coming from her companion surprised a smile out of her. And silently, she heartily concurred with the sentiment. She had dreamed of Deverill last night, reliving her most cherished, long-held fantasies of becoming his lover. Her imagination had grown more powerful after seeing him wearing only breeches yesterday, baring his strong, sinewed body.

A few moments ago, when a lock of raven hair stubbornly fell into his eyes, she had fiercely resisted the urge to push it back. That disheveled look became him, as if he'd just risen from his bed after a long, lustful night of passion.

"I could almost envy you," Nell said in a dreamy voice. "Although Valmere will undoubtedly prove very difficult to handle."

"A vast understatement," Kate replied dryly. She gave a disgusted snort. "I cannot believe he truly wishes a meek mouse for his bride. I will have to show him what a mistake he would be making."

Nell looked at her curiously. "What do you intend to do, dear?"

"Why, find candidates who match his requirements. I predict he will grow weary of them in short order."

Kate spent the next two hours drawing up plans and making lists of possible candidates. She decided on two who fit Deverill's definition of mousy, with three more who better matched her own specifications, and a few less appealing prospects thrown in for good measure. By the time her brother and his wife arrived, Kate was far enough along in her planning to lay it aside for the time being and go outside to meet them.

Since Maura had fair hair and Ash had dark, they made a striking couple as they descended from their carriage. Maura, one of her dearest friends, embraced Kate warmly. Ash likely would have done the same, if not for his infant son sleeping soundly in his arms.

Named Stephen after Ash and Kate's late father, the baby was not yet two months old, and his parents doted on him.

Kate properly—and quietly—admired her young nephew, and after settling her guests comfortably in the drawing room and arranging for tea, brought them up to date about her intentions to find Brandon Deverill a bride in exchange for his escort to France.

Ash showed his amusement with an appealing grin. "Deverill *willingly* means to subject himself to your machinations?"

"What machinations?" Kate asked innocently.

"You know precisely, minx. We endured your meddling for years."

"And *you* know that I had the best of intentions. I would do it all again without question. Need I remind you that my meddling turned out extremely well for *you,* dear brother?"

Maura intervened. "I for one am very glad you persevered, Kate." She gave a fond glance at her husband. "Ash is also, even if he is averse to giving you credit."

"Loath as I am to admit it," Ash said with fabricated reluctance, "I am profoundly grateful."

Kate was beyond thrilled to see her beloved brother and dearest friend so much in love, but she was willing to concede her methods might not have been the easiest to abide.

Just then their son woke and started fretting, so Ash turned the infant over to Maura, but he continued addressing Kate. "I see Bella arranged to be out of town at a crucial time. You do realize she is setting you up with her own machinations?"

"Would Lady Isabella do that?" Maura asked.

"Oh, yes," Ash replied emphatically. "She has advocated for love matches among our clan for far longer than Kate. In this case, she wants Deverill for Kate."

"I am not entirely naïve," Kate said with a grimace. "I know Aunt Bella is trying to throw us together."

"How does it feel to be the victim for a change?"

"You have a point." It was easier to press for a love match when the target was someone else, especially since her own situation was far more complicated than she had ever anticipated.

When her brother smiled, Kate settled for changing the subject. "I told Deverill that he could rely on you to instruct him about a nobleman's duties and obligations. You will aid him, won't you, Ash?"

"Yes, for Bella's sake, and for yours as well. I know how much this trip to France means to you."

"Thank you. Deverill is headed to Kent tomorrow,

and it would help greatly if you would consider accompanying him."

"You don't ask for much, do you?"

"It is hardly anything at all. A few days of your time, no more. And you will agree because you are the best of brothers."

Ash chuckled, and Kate beamed back at him in return, secure in the knowledge that their good-natured ribbing was done out of love.

She deeply cherished her family. As orphans raised together, with ties of blood and loss, the Wilde cousins had come to love each other dearly and were fiercely loyal to one another. In truth, their family tragedy had brought them closer together. Moreover, they had learned to live as though every moment counted—because it did.

Their closeness was also why she was so adamant in her matchmaking efforts. She wanted her loved ones to find happiness.

It had taken Ash many years to finally come around to her viewpoint. She could take comfort in his happiness, even if her own quest for love might prove hopeless.

Now, however, Kate told herself, she had to deal with finding a match for Deverill before she could return to her own search.

Strange how the prospect of being quit of him once and for all was not so very pleasing.

Chapter Four

Three afternoons later found Kate staring out her drawing room window at a drizzling rain, feeling restless and dissatisfied.

"What troubles you?" Maura asked while rocking young Stephen in her arms.

The trouble was Deverill, Kate thought in consternation. Or rather, her idiotic preoccupation with Deverill. He had gone to visit his new barony and meet his dependents, and absurdly, she *missed* him.

Not caring to admit how eager she was for his return to London, Kate settled for a half-truth. "You know how little I relish waiting. The sooner I can find a bride for Deverill, the sooner I can journey to France."

"You have found some good marital candidates for him?"

"Yes. They are not ideal, but adequate enough, I suppose."

"Are you reluctant to seek a bride for him when you once loved him?"

Kate couldn't resent the intimate question from her dearest friend. Maura was the only one who knew the full history of her romantic debacle with Deverill. She had never even told Skye about climbing into his bed nude. "I confess, I am reluctant."

"Because you are not yet entirely over him," Maura said sympathetically.

Ducking her head, Kate repressed a sigh. "I will have to be over him. He couldn't—or wouldn't—love me in return. Even so, I am concerned about him. I can't help thinking he deserves better than a mere convenient marriage. I don't want him to become the victim of fortune hunters and title seekers."

"Which may be the case."

"Yes. It began last night."

"At the soiree I missed because Stephen was fretful?"

"Yes. Do you remember Julia, Lady Dalton? The gossip rags refer to her as Lady X."

"Isn't she the wicked widow of a baronet? The one who was Quinn's paramour for a short time and caused a public scandal?"

"The very same." Kate tightened her jaw at the memory of the raven-haired beauty. "Lady Dalton approached me last night to quiz me about Deverill. Not only does she claim a long acquaintance with him, she practically boasted about her intention to pursue him now that he is a lord."

Maura frowned. "I thought she currently has a protector."

"She does, but he is a 'mere' commoner. Her brazenness galls me. She tried to come between Quinn and Venetia two months ago, and now she has her roving eye pinned on Deverill."

"Was he intimate with her in the past, do you think?"

"I don't know. And truly, his former liaisons are not my business." Kate shrugged in frustration. How was it possible that she felt so protective of Deverill—and worse, so jealous? It would be far easier if she didn't like him so blasted much. If she didn't still have irrepressible feelings for him.

Kate scoffed silently at herself. She had seen nothing of him in six years, and suddenly she couldn't stop dwelling on him? How pitiful.

During his absence this week, she had kept busy with prosaic activities—riding and social functions in particular—remaining out late in the evening and falling into bed exhausted so she wouldn't have to think about Deverill. All her efforts were for naught, which vexed her to no end.

She had done everything in her power to forget him, but she couldn't keep him from stealing her dreams . . . or overwhelming the quiet moments of her waking hours.

Muttering an oath, Kate squared her shoulders and turned away from the window. She was self-sufficient and independent-minded, perfectly capable of arranging her affairs without relying on anyone else for her happiness. She did *not* need Deverill to enliven her life or satisfy her longing for adventure and passion. And she most certainly refused to pine after any man, even him, or worry about his past relationships with wanton beauties like Lady X.

Still, she was glad when her brother returned the next day and reported on the happenings in Kent.

"I am impressed with Deverill's willingness to accept responsibility and do right by his dependents," Ash told her. "He is plainly serious about learning his role as Baron Valmere. Furthermore, he's a quick study, so I've had an easy time advising him. He'll return to London by midday tomorrow, by the way."

Although also impressed by Deverill's efforts, Kate deplored how her heart leapt at his impending return. When, the next afternoon, she received his note saying he hoped to ride with her in the park early the following morning and break in his new boots, she quickly wrote back agreeing, conditioned on his suitable attire.

She found herself waiting with breathless anticipation for his arrival at eight o'clock, and when Deverill strode into the drawing room, the impact of seeing him was as intense as ever—as if she'd been struck in her core by a bolt of lightning. His bold, dark eyes locked with hers, and suddenly all she could think of was him.

Then her own eyes widened at his appearance. Most men did what she wished of them, but surprisingly, he had followed her every dictate, and his sartorial elegance surpassed all her expectations.

His curling black mane had been marginally tamed by a shorter cut. His exquisitely tailored green coat, buff breeches, and shiny Hessian boots molded his tall, athletic form to perfection. And a pristine white cravat set off his bronzed features.

The combined effect turned Deverill into a rugged Adonis who made her pulse race.

"Do I pass muster?" he asked, seeing her scrutiny.

Though silently admiring his splendor, Kate flashed a vague smile and answered dispassionately, "You do look more civilized. Doubtless you will make the society mamas swoon."

Amusement tugged at his mouth. "I am more interested in making their daughters swoon."

An easy task if my response is any indication.

Kate banished the wayward thought. It vexed her that Deverill could still make her want him without even trying, especially when she'd vowed to remain immune to his irresistible allure.

He, however, was scrutinizing her in return. She had bound her tresses into a chignon and donned a jaunty, plumed, military-style hat. His approving gaze swept over her forest-green riding habit, then returned to her face. "That color complements your eyes."

Ignoring the feminine thrill of his masculine praise, Kate murmured a polite thank-you, then gathered her gloves and put them on as she led the way outside, where their mounts awaited.

"Your chaperone won't be joining us?" Deverill asked.

"Nell doesn't enjoy riding. I have a dependable groom who regularly accompanies me on my morning rides."

"Are you permitted to be alone with me?"

Her mouth curved at his taunt. "We will hardly be *alone* in a public park with my groom following behind. Besides, it is a shrewd tactic for me to take you riding and show you off. We want to incite curiosity and interest and tantalize prospective candidates. This morning I will present you to only a few people, but I've already put out word with the busiest gossips that you are looking for a bride. That by itself will garner you immediate attention wherever you go."

Her groom stood in the drive, holding the reins of her flashy chestnut mare and his own sturdy cob, while a footman held a strapping gray for Deverill. Deverill helped Kate mount her sidesaddle, and when he had swung up on his own horse, she led the way from Grosvenor Square, through the elegant streets of Mayfair to Hyde Park, with her servant trailing respectfully behind, far enough for their conversation to remain private.

"This is more satisfying than convening in your drawing room," Deverill observed. "I hoped to see you without your watchdog hounding my every action."

"Nell would make a poor watchdog since she has no teeth," Kate said, smiling, before steering the topic to a safer one. "How did you find the Valmere estate?"

Deverill looked thoughtful. "It was in better shape than I expected."

"I must commend you. Ash spoke highly of how you are meeting the obligations that come with noble privilege."

"I am happy for his guidance."

"I shall have him attend your formal debut. His friendship and patronage can only help you become accepted."

"It already has," Deverill said. "I was welcomed more graciously than I anticipated. Lady Melford and her daughters didn't seem overly distressed that the title and lands have changed hands and left them financially at my mercy."

"Because they were raised to believe that the laws of primogeniture are the natural order of things—and because, according to Ash, you provided them with an extremely generous settlement. I know Barbara Melford but have yet to meet her two daughters. Harriet and Mary are too young to be out in society yet."

"Lady Melford agrees that it is fitting for a man of my age and circumstances to settle down." Deverill glanced over at Kate, as if judging her response. "Now that I've dealt with my first priorities, I can turn to providing a mistress for the estate."

Kate was not happy to be reminded of Deverill's

desire to marry someone else, or that her emotions were such a confusing mess of contradiction. She ought to be pleased by this proof that he was serious about conquering the British upper class.

She shook off her ridiculous pang of jealousy. "I have identified seven possible candidates. Two I would categorize as 'obedient' in nature. Two more are fairly 'docile.' But you should beware of getting what you wish for. I doubt you truly want a meek wife. You would be bored witless."

"Perhaps."

"I think compatibility is vitally important when making a match," she began, then caught herself. "But, of course, the decision will be yours."

"You are all consideration, allowing me to choose my own bride," Deverill said dryly.

Kate continued as if he hadn't mocked her. "I plan for you to meet all the contenders over the next week. To that end, I've accepted invitations for a musical evening, two balls, a tea, and an afternoon garden party."

Deverill looked pained. "A tea? Must I?"

"Yes, indeed. I intend for you to take the ton by storm. Your formal debut is set for tomorrow night, but if you now have an adequate wardrobe, you could accompany me to a ridotto tonight. I am also trying to secure vouchers to Almack's—which are London's premiere assembly rooms, if you didn't know."

"Isn't that where you are required to dress properly and toady to the hostesses?"

"Yes. Jack was once refused entrance for not wearing proper evening attire. And two seasons ago I was banned altogether."

"Whatever for?"

"I antagonized one of the patronesses by waltzing without permission."

"How shocking," Deverill drawled in mock dismay. "What were you thinking? You said you were determined to remain circumspect."

"I am now, but not two years ago when the waltz was coming into vogue. It was considered highly scandalous then."

"And you Wildes have always courted scandal."

"Not intentionally. We just don't allow the threat of scandal to dictate our every action."

Deverill's gaze sought hers. "Is that what you are doing now? You don't seem to be living life on your own terms. Instead you are letting yourself be stifled by strictures."

Before she could respond, they reached the entrance to the park. Personal conversation became impossible when a number of other riders stopped Kate to speak to her. After making introductions, she turned onto Rotten Row and urged her mount into a canter. Deverill easily matched her gait, and when she pulled up, there were more greetings and introductions.

To Kate's mind, only one sour note occurred during their excursion: They came across Lady X driving her phaeton with one of her female friends—a rare, early-hour appearance that was likely no mere coincidence.

Kate wouldn't put it past Julia Dalton to be lying in wait for Deverill.

When the widow expressed delight at his return to England and invited him to call on her "to renew our acquaintance," her suggestive tone grated on Kate's nerves. But Kate held her tongue when they parted ways and refrained from asking Deverill about his relationship with the witch.

Otherwise, she was relatively satisfied with the progress of her plan. By the time they left the park a half hour later, Kate pronounced herself pleased. "I knew you would be a curiosity," she told Deverill.

"I was not the chief attraction. Your many beaux were eager to win your attention."

And the ladies were eager to win yours.

Unexpectedly, Deverill returned to their former conversation. "Are you satisfied with your life?"

Not entirely was her first thought. She wanted to feel as if she was truly living, not simply letting life pass her by, as it seemed now. "For the most part."

"You used to run barefoot and wear your hair down."

"That was in the country, when I was much younger and carefree."

"And independent."

"No doubt my independence came from being raised by my bachelor uncle and having three older brothers and cousins."

"If I recall, you can swim and ride as well as your brothers, and play cricket, too."

"Because they were always short of players. I confess, I am also a fair hand at archery, swordsmanship, shooting a pistol, and even a little fisticuffs." When his eyebrow rose, Kate smiled. "Ash thought it important for me to be able to defend myself."

"Remind me never to challenge you."

She doubted Deverill meant it literally. With his teasing provocations, he had always challenged her and encouraged her rebellious tendencies.

"I would think you fret under your current restrictions," he remarked.

"Sometimes," Kate agreed. After her humiliation with Deverill, she'd learned to curtail her rasher inclinations and act with more prudence. "But I am resigned now to being practical. Society imposes vastly greater limits on ladies, but there is little to be gained by fighting it."

"American women are freer to disregard the rules. In fact, America is a more equal society in general, without such vast differences between classes."

She glanced over at Deverill, wondering at his sudden philosophical mood. "True. To our discredit, we English overly esteem rank and status. But you can use our class prejudices to your advantage in your search for a bride. Your title is a prime matrimonial inducement. It is only natural that women will pursue you for the chance to join the nobility."

"Is that the only reason?"

"Of course, there is your wealth."

"And my dashing appearance also," he prodded good-humoredly.

"Well, you are a handsome, virile man."

"You find me virile?"

Disregarding his laughing eyes that made a jest of humility, Kate gave him a brief perusal. Deverill possessed an air of breathtaking virility that commanded attention, while his melting masculine charm was potent enough to capture the iciest of female hearts. "I am only pointing out your attributes as others see them."

"What other attributes do *you* see?"

She gave a snort of exasperation. "You well know your attractions, Lord Valmere. You don't need me to puff up your vanity. You would do better to worry about concealing your many flaws."

A chuckle shook his chest. "Pray, don't spare my feelings."

"What feelings are those? Yours seem impermeable." Kate met his warm eyes and laughed in return. "You can be supremely aggravating, you know."

"As can you. You are still set on turning me into a milquetoast."

"Only for your own benefit."

Deverill made a *tsk*ing sound. "Your brother warned me that when it comes to matchmaking, you are the embodiment of a meddlesome female."

"I merely want to make a valuable difference in people's lives."

"And you never do anything by half measures."

"What is the saying? If it is worth doing, it is worth doing well. . . . Which reminds me of an issue we need to discuss. I wish you would find someone to marry you for yourself rather than for your fortune or title. No doubt countless ladies will fall all over you, but for superficial reasons."

His look turned considering. "You aren't fixed on wedding a nobleman yourself, are you?"

"No, but I put less store in lineage than most of my acquaintances. We Wildes can trace our bloodlines back to the Normans, but while roots and blood kinship are important, ties of friendship and love are much more vital to me."

Deverill shook his head. "I told you, love isn't a requisite for my marriage."

"I remember. But you *should* want love. If you put your mind to it, you could even have the special kind of love that most of my family have found."

A muscle flexed in his jaw. "My parents had a strict marriage of convenience. Love played no part in their arrangement."

She frowned. "My experience was vastly different from yours, thank heaven. My parents were madly in love."

At the memory, Kate felt the old ache again. She knew what it was like to lose loved ones, to feel alone, to yearn for love to fill the hole in your heart. "Loss can change your perspective. So can growing up without a mother."

His gaze grew thoughtful. "That I cannot relate to.

But my own mother was rather cold and indifferent."

Kate frowned at his revelation, even before Deverill added, "My father was just as cold in his own way, strict and autocratic. I confess I always envied your family's closeness."

His tone was surprisingly sober, which roused a powerful surge of sympathy in Kate. "I am sorry your family was not so warm and loving as mine."

When Deverill caught her watching him, his somberness abruptly disappeared. "I know—you are a hopeless romantic."

She flashed a smile. "I willingly admit it. It offends my sensibilities for you to marry for mere convenience. I have seen it over and over again. Love makes an enormous difference to the chance for a happy marriage."

"I doubt I can summon the tender emotions you consider so crucial."

He thought himself incapable of love? Kate wondered. "Even if you cannot form a strong affection for your wife, you could attempt to elicit hers. For a union to be successful, a meeting of hearts and minds is invaluable."

"What are you suggesting?"

"If you want your wife to care more for you than for your fortune and title, you will have to win her heart."

"And just how do I manage that?"

"Well . . . you could start by wooing her."

He was silent for a moment before responding unexpectedly, "I think you should teach me."

Kate gave him a questioning glance, and Deverill explained, "You are the expert in romance. You know how an Englishwoman wants to be courted, and what she wants from a suitor."

It puzzled her, why Deverill would ask her to tutor him when thus far he had resisted her efforts to change him more than superficially.

When she didn't reply, he pressed her. "Who else can I call on for help? No one else would dare to take me on." Seeing her continued hesitation, he added, "How difficult can it be?"

"To convert a vexing American privateer into the ideal suitor who can win an English lady's heart?" she said lightly. "Exceedingly difficult, I would imagine."

"Taking you to France will require a great deal of time and effort. You could make a small effort in return."

"I already am making an *enormous* effort," she pointed out indignantly, before spying the warm laughter in his eyes. "You are hoping to make me feel guilty, aren't you?"

"I am appealing to your sense of fair play."

A chortle escaped Kate, even as she questioned her own common sense. She couldn't believe she was actually considering teaching Deverill how to woo his potential bride.

"I suppose I could show you a thing or two," she said cautiously.

"Good. We can begin this morning, once I escort you home."

Her exasperation returned. At her first hint of yielding, he had taken charge. "Nell has a fitting for her wedding dress this morning and won't be free until this afternoon."

"You don't need to hide behind your chaperone's skirts. Moreover, I am meeting your brother at Brooks's club this afternoon."

"I will need a chance to think on it."

"Well, think quickly. As you said, we have very little time before the Season ends."

At the reminder, Kate relented. Maura would likely be home this morning, even if Nell wasn't. And the introduction of Lady X into the equation added urgency to her task of finding Deverill a suitable bride who would value him for himself.

"True. And we could review my list of candidates. You should be prepared to encounter any of them at the ridotto this evening. Very well. We can begin when we conclude our ride."

The smile Deverill gave her was potent enough to curl her toes. At his intimate look, she couldn't deny the jolt of excited anticipation that shot through her—

Kate brought herself up short as all her defenses shouted "Beware!" Teaching him to romance her peers? Whatever had possessed her to agree? Clearly she needed to have her wits examined.

Dragging her gaze from his, she directed her eyes

straight ahead. Even more than her fierce attraction for Deverill, her tangled emotions made her far too vulnerable.

No, Kate thought, steeling herself for the engagement to come. She would have to take great care if she hoped to remain unscathed. Otherwise, she could be in real danger of resuming her former idiotic romantic infatuation.

Chapter Five

Maura and Ash were out, Kate learned upon arriving home, yet she led Deverill to the drawing room anyway. Surely she could handle him for a short while.

When he was seated on the sofa, she gave him a copy of Debrett's Peerage. "You should study this to familiarize yourself with the ranks of nobles and knights."

Then she pulled out her list of potential candidates and settled beside him in order to review the names. "Here are the ladies I have identified so far."

"You put great store in lists," he said, visibly amused as he skimmed over her notes.

"Because they help me to organize my thoughts."

He looked up at her. "Have you made a list for our excursion to France?"

"Only in general terms."

"We should discuss our plans soon. I want to hold up my end of our bargain."

Kate was gratified that Deverill hadn't forgotten their agreement. "Where should we start?"

"For instance, will anyone be accompanying us? Your brother expressed little desire to make the voyage since he has a wife and newborn son to consider."

"Yes. And Jack is in a similar situation. His wife Sophie is great with child and is expecting any day now, so he won't risk a voyage."

"What of your cousin Traherne?"

"Quinn was only married two months ago, and since he brought our parents' murderer to justice, he doesn't crave a more decisive resolution as I do. As for Skye, she would rather Hawkhurst remain in England for now. He has finally found happiness after so many years of sacrifice abroad in service to the Foreign Office. However, my uncle Cornelius is willing to accompany us."

"I thought your uncle was a scholar. Searching for sunken treasure and thwarting pirates would seem contrary to his usual pursuits."

"Indeed." Her uncle Lord Cornelius Wilde was far happier with his nose buried in a Latin or Greek tome and had already sacrificed a great deal for their family—a bachelor raising his five orphaned, unruly relations as their legal guardian. "But he still feels responsible for me. Also, his new wife, Rachel, wishes to help me because I am scouting a match for her"—Kate paused to search for the appropriate description—"younger friend, Miss Daphne Farnwell. They know I will need someone along to observe propriety. I can't very well go alone with you to France."

Deverill's mouth curved, but he didn't rag her as she expected. Instead, he said, "I should arrange a meeting with Macky to learn what he discovered from his investigation of the shipwreck."

"I would like to be part of the planning."

"As you wish. It will be good to see Macky again," Deverill said absently. "And Hawk as well. I have missed them both."

"Has it been six years since you last saw them?"

"Yes." He turned to look directly at her. "Did you miss me while I was away in America?"

Kate hesitated, not wanting to confess that her dotage had continued long after Deverill left her. "I couldn't help but think of you now and then," she hedged. "Especially whenever I saw the casualty reports in the newspapers. I didn't want you to be killed."

"I am flattered."

"I was thinking of Aunt Bella also. I know how fond she is of you. I would not have wanted her to grieve."

"Would you have grieved for me?"

"Well, yes." She would have been *devastated* if Deverill had died, although confessing that would reveal how much he meant to her. "I did not pine inconsolably after you, if that is what you are implying."

"But you did miss me a small measure."

His insistence disconcerted her less than the intimate light in his eyes did. "Why ever would I? You made your feelings very clear that night. You didn't want me."

"You are being deliberately obtuse, princess. I told you I was trying to be honorable in not taking your innocence before I sailed away."

"I suppose it *was* honorable of you."

He smiled slightly. "Finally you admit it."

Shrugging, Kate attempted to regain the upper hand in their conversation. "May we please change the subject? Remembering my abject humiliation all those years ago is not particularly delightful."

"If it's any consolation, you are not the first woman to come to my bed uninvited."

Whether Deverill meant to tease her or reassure her, the thought stung. "Oh, I am certain there are *legions* of females flinging themselves into your bed," she said tartly.

"Not one I wanted there a fraction as much as I wanted you." His gaze dropped to her mouth. "I still want you, you know."

And instantly, just like that, the tension between them changed from contentious to something far more intimate and potent.

Kate froze. The light in Deverill's eyes was a curious mixture of intensity, desire, and challenge—with a hint of tenderness.

Leaning toward her, he raised a finger to her cheek, lightly stroking. Something warm and heavy settled in the pit of her stomach. When his attentive gaze wandered over her face, Kate's breath tangled in her throat. He was so disturbingly male. All her senses were alert to him, to the hypnotic intensity of his eyes.

Then he moved his thumb in a rotating caress that lingered at the corner of her lip, flooding her raw nerves in a warm bath of sensation.

"Does this trouble you . . . my touching you?"

"Yes . . . no." "Trouble" was not at all the right word. Exhilarate, thrill, inflame—

"Then why is your heartbeat so wild?"

How did he know? Her heart had started racing as heat flared between them.

When Deverill cupped her chin in his hand, as if intending to kiss her, Kate could only stare at his mouth and remember how wonderful it had felt on hers. Her tension increased, as did her longing.

He leaned even closer, his breath warming her lips, igniting sensual sparks in every nerve. Kate fought the urge to melt. It was deeply disconcerting, her instantaneous, wanton response to his touch. Profoundly unsettling, waiting for him to bring his mouth into contact with hers—

Before he could complete the action, she drew back abruptly, breaking the spell with a sharp inhalation. She desperately needed to maintain control, both over Deverill and herself.

"That is close enough, my lord. Now, if you don't mind, I should like to review these possible candidates for your hand."

When she took the list from him, Deverill relaxed against the back of the sofa. "I am all ears."

Since he pressed her no further, Kate expected her tension to subside, yet she still felt unsettled and highly annoyed at herself. She was suffering a mental derangement, to be disappointed that Deverill hadn't kissed her.

They spent the next several minutes discussing names, descriptions, and characteristics of each lady on her list. Kate began with the two who were on opposite ends of the scales, from the most forward—Miss Phoebe Armitage—to the shyest, Miss Kitty Smythe.

"Miss Armitage is likely to pursue you ruthlessly."

"Then why did you include her?"

"Because she is related to the Duchess of Devonshire, and if you were to wed her, your acceptance in society would practically be assured. On the other hand, you will need to treat Miss Smythe with extreme gentleness. Lady Grace Middleton falls somewhere in between. Her father is an impoverished viscount, so she is looking to marry a fortune, but she has a kind heart."

"And you will advise me on how to court them?" Deverill asked.

"Yes, but I told you, I would like time to consider the most effective ways. For now you need only become acquainted with each lady so you will be prepared for tonight."

"I would rather hear your plan to turn me into an ideal suitor."

Kate refused to be sidetracked. "Miss Emma Dodd is somewhat plain but has excellent breeding and a sharp wit that might appeal to you. Miss Eliza Rowe has impeccable manners and is welcomed everywhere, although I find her rather cold. Additionally, she is rumored to be on the verge of an engagement. Miss Ruth Osborne is soft-spoken and fits your requirements for 'obedient' and 'biddable.' "

"This list names six candidates. This morning you said you had identified seven."

"Yes, but I am saving the best for last. She meets all *my* requirements, although not yours. If you tire of wooing the others, I will introduce you."

"So tell me how *you* want to be wooed."

Kate sent him a chastising look. "There is no reason to talk about me, Deverill. You know my goals for marriage are different from most young ladies. I want true love."

"How do you define true love? I am curious."

Her gaze narrowed on him. "You only want to roast me."

"No, I am entirely serious. I should like to understand what you mean."

"It is simple, really. True love is a passion of the heart, shared equally by two people."

"Equally, hmmm?"

Kate hesitated, puzzled by his reply. His expression

was dispassionate, enigmatic. "Well, yes. The attachment cannot be one-sided."

When Deverill was silent, she expounded. "Love is kind and generous and unselfish and self-sacrificing, powerful and wholly consuming. It makes you feel complete and fulfilled. . . . Put another way, you can't imagine living your life without the other."

His grimace was slight but unmistakable. "You are speaking of ideal love, not reality."

She studied him thoughtfully. "Is it that you don't believe ideal love exists," she asked, "or that you can't see the possibility for yourself?"

"I suppose it exists. But it is extremely rare."

"Well, I have learned that life is too short and precious to live without it. In fact, it makes life worth living."

Deverill did not look convinced. "You have never known true love yourself."

"Not yet. But I have faith that someday I will. The proof is not only in my immediate family. A number of our Wilde ancestors were famous lovers. One of our enduring traits is that when we fall in love, we love passionately and for life."

His expression remained dubious. "I think you are creating a fantasy. A figment of your imagination. And you are bound for disappointment."

"Perhaps. But love is worth waiting for, fighting for, perhaps even dying for," she returned emphatically.

Deverill's response was a hint of a smile. Evidently her intensity amused him.

Kate firmed her jaw, unwilling to concede the argument. "I see your problem. You are a cynic like my cousin Quinn. He felt the same way before he met Venetia and discovered he couldn't live without her."

"And *your* problem is that you are too choosy when it comes to suitors."

"I am merely discriminating."

"I wonder that any man could live up to your high standards. I can see you checking off your list of requisite attributes."

Kate compressed her lips to hold back a retort. "It is not a matter of conforming to attributes or meeting standards. I intend to follow my heart, not my head. Love often has nothing to do with logic or intellect."

"So you follow your heart and wind up disillusioned when your ardor isn't reciprocated."

Her exasperation returned. "Even if a romance ends badly, it can be worth the risk. Even painful emotions make you feel alive."

"I would prefer to avoid the pain."

"So would we all."

She spoke from personal experience. Deverill's rejection had been extremely painful, and yet he always made her feel keenly alive. Since his return to England, her senses, her very spirit, had come back to life, as if they'd been dormant all this time. Furthermore, all the ardent emotions and deep longings she'd carefully kept tucked away had come flooding back.

But Deverill did not seem eager to discuss emotions. Shifting to face her, he stretched one arm over the back of the sofa behind her. "Perhaps your beliefs are not to blame. Perhaps the fault lies with your suitors and how they regard you. You should be treated as a woman, not a princess."

"What do you mean?"

"Your suitors worship at your feet. I doubt if any have dared seduce you or even kiss you as you were meant to be kissed."

Suddenly on guard again, Kate sat up straighter in her seat. "Trust me, I have been courted by expert seducers."

"But you prefer to remain a virginal spinster."

His gibe about her spinsterhood rankled. "You assume I am a virginal spinster."

Judging from Deverill's raised eyebrow, her retort was unexpected. "Why would you think I haven't taken any lovers?"

"Have you?"

"It is hardly your concern. But I have known passion." *At least in my dreams,* Kate clarified to herself.

When his gaze fixed intently on her, she stared back at him with a trace of defiance. She was shading the truth, yet it wasn't a complete falsehood. In her dreams, Deverill had always been her only lover. Neither was she completely ignorant when it came to men and physical relations. She had her aunt Bella to thank for educating her. Bella had wanted her nieces to be armed against the rakes who might try to tempt them.

When the charged moment drew out, Kate tried to

will away the blush rising in her cheeks while silently justifying her prevarication. After Deverill, she'd felt vulnerable and unsure. Secretly she'd even wanted to make him regret spurning her. An unworthy ambition, she knew; she hoped she was not that petty.

But she wouldn't apologize for the entirely rational feminine need to make him believe she was not a shriveled-up old maid, or feel much remorse if she pretended to have had a torrid affair. Showing him she was desirable, that other men wanted her, would be a salve to her wounded pride. . . . Although she wouldn't lie to him outright.

"I have had more than one suitor who is considered a marvelous lover," she declared. Which was completely true. She knew several rakish noblemen who were rumored to be remarkable lovers.

She could tell Deverill wasn't particularly pleased with her reply, which somehow made her feel better.

"However," Kate added, deciding it wiser to extricate herself from the web of deceit she was spinning for herself, "I value emotional gratification much more than physical."

"You say that because you don't know any better. If your physical experience had been at all pleasurable, you would rate it more highly." Deverill leaned closer while his voice dropped to a murmur. "Lovely Princess Katharine . . . I could show you pleasure."

Reaching up, he wrapped his fingers lightly around the column of her throat. This time, however, Kate was better prepared for the scalding impact. Suspecting that Deverill was testing her, she forced herself to remain still. If she had truly taken any lovers before, she would not be shy about his physical advances—and heaven help her, she wanted his physical advances.

As if reading her thoughts, he drew even nearer. She watched, spellbound, as his ebony lashes lowered to shadow his eyes. She knew she ought to pull away, but he took the decision from her. Raising both his hands, he slid his fingers along either side of her jaw and bent his head to kiss her.

Determined to pretend more experience than she really had, Kate made no protest, yet when his mouth settled on hers, claiming with a forceful tenderness, she found herself being swept up in the enchantment. The taste of him was gloriously arresting. When Deverill made her open farther for him, his tongue penetrating in an erotic invasion, an intoxicating rush of feeling assaulted her.

She ignored the warning voice of reason when he pressed her back against the sofa cushions. She couldn't summon the desire to fight him. Instead, her body softened instinctively against his, and she clutched weakly at his shoulders. She could feel the hardness of his corded muscles beneath her fingers, the heat of his powerful torso, could smell the arousing scent of him.

Caught up in the moment, she raised her hands to his black, curling hair, which was thick and silky. In response, his kiss only deepened; with one hand behind her nape, he held her head still so he could drink more fully of her.

He kissed like a possessive lover—or what she imagined a possessive lover to be, arousing with languorous strokes of his tongue, slowly driving, deliciously plundering. A whisper of a sigh escaped Kate. Compared to Deverill, she was an utter novice at passion, and she had no defenses against him. The sinful thrill of being captured against his hard, male body sent another hot ripple of weakness surging through her. The beguiling friction of his chest against her breasts only made her want more.

The kiss turned endless. Emotions whirled and clashed within Kate, leaving her giddy. Her head swam with drugged pleasure, her body trembled.

She was only vaguely aware of his hand molding her breast beneath the jacket of her riding habit. Shivering with aroused excitement, she gave a helpless moan and strained against his palm as he caressed the swelling mound above the confines of her corset. She could feel her nipples peak to a tingling ache—a result he seemed determined to encourage.

Still holding her entranced with his mouth, Deverill opened the front buttons of her jacket, then moved his lips lower, following the path his hand had taken. When he tongued her breast through her shirtfront and chemise, the sweet shock of it stopped her breath. Kate inhaled sharply as a tremor shook her. And when he suckled her nipple through the fabric, she whimpered and arched against his mouth.

It was the most incredible sensation. Wicked, marvelous, irresistible. Fire streaked through her body, flooding her veins with shuddering heat. Deverill was taking full advantage of her weakness for him, leaving her dazed and swooning.

It was only when his hand moved lower, down over her skirts, between her thighs, that Kate came to her senses and realized she was sprawled inelegantly on the sofa beneath him while he pleasured her breasts.

"Deverill . . ." she rasped. "You must . . . stop."

"Why?"

"Someone could enter . . . and see us."

"So?"

"So, this is madness."

"Yes, sweet madness. . . ."

Sliding her arms between them, she pressed her hands hard against his chest. "I won't be your plaything!"

Her ragged declaration made Deverill pause and lift his head. "Making you my plaything is furthest from my intentions."

Swallowing against the dryness in her throat, Kate found her voice, albeit a weak one. "Your intentions are beside the point. I don't need you to show me pleasure or prove your mastery over me."

Summoning all her willpower, she pushed at him in an effort to extricate herself from his embrace.

To her vast relief, Deverill eased his body off hers and sat up. Fighting the urge to scramble off the sofa, safely out of reach, she also sat up, though more unsteadily, and turned her back to him in order to adjust her bodice.

It was impossible to act as if she hadn't just felt a double lightning bolt annihilating her senses, or to disguise her shamefully husky voice. Yet she was proud that she managed to feign a tiny measure of aplomb when she said in a disgusted tone, "For a man who claims to be an expert lover, you have a decided lack of control."

"Perhaps I have been at sea too long," he murmured in a similarly husky voice.

"So you use your long voyage to excuse your randiness?"

"I could blame my randiness on your delectable charms."

Taking a calming breath, Kate turned to face him. "When I agreed to tutor you, I did *not* expect to be assaulted."

For a moment Deverill simply studied her. Then he gave a soft chuckle, amusement warring with irony in his eyes.

His nonchalance raised her hackles. "You are not taking this bride search seriously, Deverill!"

"I assure you, I am serious."

"Then if you wish me to continue, you must make more of an effort."

"I will try to do better."

She didn't trust his mild reply. "'Better' is not good enough. You will promise to behave as a gentleman, not a heathen pirate."

"If you insist."

"I do insist."

Bending, Kate gathered her list, which had fallen unheeded to the floor. "What lunacy seized you?" she muttered before adding in warning, "It will never do for you to be this forward with a prospective bride. You could find yourself in a compromising position, and then you would be forced to marry her."

"Have no fear, princess. I would never be so forward with anyone else."

"I should hope not." Not knowing whether to be pleased or disturbed by his reply, Kate tore her gaze from his and returned her focus to her list of marital candidates.

This had to stop! she reprimanded herself. Somehow, some way, she needed to conquer the sensual power Deverill wielded over her, but thus far she had been entirely unsuccessful.

She was very glad they would be among a large crowd tonight. And the next time she was required to meet alone with Deverill, she would insist that it not be here in her drawing room, but some other, less private setting where she wouldn't be so damned tempted to surrender to him.

Watching Kate at the ridotto that evening, Brandon found it hard to focus on the task of interviewing bridal candidates, since he kept remembering the pleasure he'd experienced that morning. Having Kate beneath him—kissing her, fondling her—had left him hard and aching and ready to burst.

Blowing out a breath, he forcibly turned his attention to the gala. He had to admire how she'd orchestrated his debut down to the smallest detail. The Wildes had picked him up in their carriage so that he could be seen arriving with Lord and Lady Beaufort. And once there, Kate made certain he was the center of attention while watching over him protectively.

It was a gay affair, where some fifty nobles and gentry had gathered for music and dancing, a lavish entertainment that mimicked the opulent balls in Venice during the last century. Many of the guests were masked, but Kate had only permitted him a demi-mask—to give him a mysterious air without entirely concealing his features, she said, the better to tempt prospective brides.

In her own demi-mask and gold-threaded, emerald satin ball gown, Kate was pure temptation herself. If her clan navigated the glittering world of high society with ease, she was the brightest star. Her vivid coloring—fiery hair, wide expressive eyes, creamy flawless skin—set her apart from her peers. Yet those peers seemed to flock around her as if to gain some of her lively essence by sheer proximity.

An hour into the evening, they were alone long enough for Brandon to compliment her on her triumph. "It is a pleasure observing the dashing Lady Katharine in action, with all of London at her feet."

She looked at him with slightly amused green eyes. "The ladies think you are dashing yourself. As I predicted, my acquaintances are clamoring for an introduction."

As for her matchmaking strategy, he met the two most extreme candidates on her list, one meek, one covetous and calculating. The poor meek girl—Miss Smythe—was so tongue-tied, she couldn't form a coherent reply to his simple greeting. Her face turned bright red, and when Kate tried to put her at ease, she finally stammered an apology, flashed a grateful look at Lady Katharine for her kindness, then fled the scene in mortification.

In another incident with a middle-aged matron who apparently was his chief detractor, Kate, rather than showing kindness, put the woman in her place with a sweetly cutting reprimand.

When later she found another private moment with him to discuss his progress, she justified her response in a tart tone. "That biddy is a terrible gossip, and I won't have her denigrating you."

"No, only you are permitted to denigrate me," Brandon remarked.

She gave a rueful smile. "Yes, but never in public in front of witnesses."

"I was touched that you came to my defense like a fierce mother tigress."

"I feel responsible for your success," she said. "So what is your opinion of Miss Smythe and Miss Armitage?"

"I didn't care for either one."

Her smile turned victorious. "I regret saying I told you so."

"No, you don't."

Kate laughed, a sound rich in pleasure. "Miss Armitage is more your style. She has already set her cap for you. It should be amusing to watch you elude her clutches."

Still later, after supper, he found himself watching Kate from a distance as she stood on the sidelines of the dance floor, apparently bantering with a tall, dark-haired gentleman. Brandon barely stopped himself from scowling. It was clear the man admired her—a sparkling-eyed beauty who radiated charm. What red-blooded male wouldn't?

And when her mouth twitched with a devastating smile, a flash of memory from six years ago hit Brandon—a vision of her lithe, beautiful, nude body—and he felt the impact straight in his loins.

When he next spoke to her, he asked the gentleman's identity.

"That was Lord Gallier."

"You seem on good terms."

"Yes. He is a longtime friend of Quinn's."

"Is he the one?"

"The one?"

"Your former lover."

For a moment, her eyes widened at the blunt question. Then her expression lightened. "Take care, Lord Valmere. One would almost think you jealous."

He was indeed jealous, Brandon reflected, although he wasn't ready to admit it aloud to Kate. "I am curious about how he appeals to you."

"I am comfortable with him, and I admire his sharp wit."

"I'll wager he treats you like a woman."

"Come to think of it . . . he does."

When another gentleman came to solicit her hand for a dance, she left Brandon standing there, acknowledging his powerful, almost irrational feeling of possessiveness.

If he'd had any doubts about wedding Kate, his fierce reaction just then would have dispelled them. He wanted her for himself. Clearly it was time to escalate his pursuit of her.

His plan was momentarily sidetracked, however, when Lady Dalton entered the ballroom to great fanfare and made a beeline straight for him. With a seductive smile, she maneuvered him into conversing with her for nearly a quarter of an hour—an event that, curiously, Kate did not seem happy to see, Brandon noted.

He had not the least interest in Lady Dalton. Kate must have had a contentious relationship with the widow, though, judging from her flashing eyes when shortly he spied them conversing together, or perhaps even arguing.

When Kate suddenly turned and strode from the room, Brandon stared after her thoughtfully, debating his best course.

Although seething, Kate forced herself to take a breath and calmly exit the ballroom. Her barbed exchange with Julia Dalton still echoed in her ears. Not only had the widow thrown down the gauntlet, declaring her intention of competing for Deverill's hand, but she had attacked Kate directly.

"You are fooling no one with your pretense at matchmaking," she purred. "You want to capture Lord Valmere for yourself."

Kate pasted on an icy smile. "You are mistaken, dearest Lady X. Unlike you, I needn't rely on deceitful tricks to land a suitor."

Her retort brought out Lady Dalton's own lethal

smile. "The larger deceit is your self-delusion, Lady Katharine. Clearly Valmere finds me far more appealing than he does you. You are too prudish and controlling to ever attract a strong, vigorous man like him."

It was all Kate could do to step back from their confrontation without pulling out the widow's hair. But while Julia Dalton had always rubbed her the wrong way, the cutting words stung keenly. Worse, the thought of Deverill consorting with that harlot made her stomach knot.

Needing time to cool her temper, Kate made her way to the supper room, where buffet tables were laden with domestic and imported delicacies. She gratefully accepted a glass of wine from a footman but had barely taken a sip when Deverill unexpectedly appeared beside her.

"There you are. I came to solicit your hand for a dance."

"You should be dancing with your potential brides," Kate pointed out.

"True, but I prefer your company to any of those tedious young misses." He glanced down at the buffet table, where a selection of fruits and cheeses had been artfully laid out. "Are strawberries in season?"

"These were likely grown in a hothouse."

"I haven't had one in ages." He picked up a plump red berry, then bit into it and made a small sound of approval. "As ripe as summer fruit. You should try it."

"I am not particularly hungry—" Kate began, before he brought the uneaten half to her lips.

When she opened her mouth reflexively, he slipped the strawberry inside. The tart sweetness was a burst of flavor on her tongue.

His gaze fixed intently on her mouth, Deverill watched her savor the taste. Then after she'd swallowed, he brought his thumb up to stroke the corner of her bottom lip.

Caught off guard, Kate felt the contact like a lover's caress, the pleasurable shock of it setting her pulse racing. Perhaps he was only wiping a drop of juice away, but he imbued the simple gesture with a sensuality that was unmistakable. And his eyes . . . How could a mere glance be so potent?

Kate shook herself. What was she doing, allowing him to feed her strawberries in public with the intimacy of a kiss? It would be safer to dance with him, she realized.

"We should return to the ballroom," she announced, setting down her wineglass.

Deverill's half smile suggested he had accomplished his goal. "My thought precisely."

He accompanied her back to the ballroom and led her onto the floor just as the orchestra struck up a waltz. No sooner had they settled into the steps, though, when she saw Lady X eyeing him from across the room. Reminded of her earlier contretemps, Kate felt her lips tighten.

Deverill must have noticed, for he bent his head so

that he could be heard over the music. "Was that an altercation I witnessed between you and Lady Dalton earlier?"

"Of a sort." Peering up at him, Kate debated whether to report on the beauty's sordid history. She was no tattletale and despised backbiting females, but Deverill deserved to be warned of the danger. "How well do you know her?"

"Thus far? Not well. Why do you ask?"

"Let us just say that she is up to her favorite sport—husband-hunting, with you as her target."

Deverill quirked an eyebrow at her acrid tone. "Now who is jealous?"

Although coloring at being caught out, Kate resorted to denial. "It is hardly jealousy. I merely would hate to see you tangled in her web. Julia Dalton is avaricious enough to make Miss Armitage look like a perfect angel in comparison. Her aim has always been to marry a wealthy nobleman."

"Why is that a mark against her when you've said that most of the unattached ladies in London have the same aim?"

A fair point, Kate silently conceded with reluctance. "Are you aware that her sobriquet is 'Lady X'? Dallying with her will reflect poorly on the respectable image you hope to cultivate."

"I expect my image can withstand the association," Deverill replied mildly.

Kate bit back a retort at his nonchalance. "Very well, if you must know . . . She is wellborn but practically a lady of the evening. Moreover, my dislike of her is personal because she attempted to ensnare Quinn two years ago. Actually, she was his mistress for a time and caused him a great deal of grief, embroiling him in a public scandal that was the talk of the town for weeks."

"I see" was all Deverill said.

"What do you see?" Kate asked suspiciously.

"Thank you for the warning, sweetheart. Your concern is duly noted." When she started earnestly to explain further, however, Deverill interrupted. "Enough about Lady Dalton. What do you say we simply enjoy the dance?"

As he swept her into the lilting rhythm, Kate found herself locking eyes with him again. And just like that, she became keenly aware of the tingling warmth Deverill aroused in her with his one large hand cradling hers, his other pressing lightly at her waist.

He steadily held her gaze, and when she fell silent, his faint smile of approval did strange things to her insides, reminding her vividly of his seductive kisses in her drawing room that morning.

Suddenly feeling flushed and overheated, Kate was glad to blame the exertion of the dance for her riotous physical state.

When he expertly whirled her around, she gave herself up to the music and the pleasure of having Deverill hold her. It was foolish to let that witch ruin her evening. No doubt she was the envy of every woman there, including Julia Dalton. Deverill was a swoon-worthy partner. Like everything else he attempted, he waltzed superbly.

And so Kate determinedly tamped down her jealousy and tried very, very hard to ignore the thrill of being in his arms again.

By the time Brandon returned to his hotel, the hour was well after midnight, but with sleep eluding him, he lay in his bed, recalling his recent encounters with Kate. Kissing her ripe lips this morning, touching her breasts, suckling her nipples, even through layers of fabric, had sent his erotic fantasies soaring. He was fortunate that he hadn't exploded then and there.

After being so long without female companionship, he wasn't surprised that his lust had gotten the better of him. Yet lust alone didn't explain his physical hunger for her.

No, it was Kate herself.

Dispassionately, Brandon reached beneath his nightshirt and took his cock in his hand, determined to see to his needs so that the next time he was with her, he would be able to maintain some semblance of restraint. However, a cold, perfunctory sexual release failed to quiet his persistent thoughts of her or prevent him from reflecting on his evolution.

He relished the fiery version of Kate from this evening. The passionate free-spirited woman who was ready to challenge the world. The same lovely, vibrant girl who had captured his attention so decisively seven years ago.

But his desire for her now went deeper than he had ever admitted. In Kent, he'd counted the days till he could complete his duty visit and return to her. A remarkable change in his long-held perspective, Brandon realized. He was accustomed to being alone and, until lately, content to stay that way. Yet now he was willingly, even eagerly, contemplating ending his bachelorhood.

The simple truth was, he wanted Kate for his wife. No other woman would do. Certainly not the two tiresome society misses he'd met this evening, or any of the other young ladies on her list, either.

The trouble was, however, Kate was too fixated on the elusive notion of ideal love. He'd always known he wouldn't readily fall victim to love. In fact, he doubted that any woman could have such an effect on him, even Kate.

Unlike her, he'd witnessed few examples of loving relationships, seen precious little joy. His own parents had been callous and unfeeling, their marriage a cold business arrangement, their procreation of children a mere duty. As for himself, the closest he'd come to experiencing any sort of emotional intensity was getting lost in a pair of vivid green eyes and a warm, sensual smile.

But that was before the war. Since then, he felt as if something inside him was missing. He'd hated killing and maiming, and the experience had left him a little scarred inside, Brandon suspected. Perhaps that was why the idea of marrying Kate had an irrefutable appeal. She could fill up the empty corners of his life.

For years, he'd had nothing but obligations and duty to look forward to. No one to make him smile, to warm him at night. No one to come home to, or even to care if he came home at all.

Kate could be that someone.

There was a strong bond between them already, even if it would never blossom into anything more ardent than friendship and affection. His challenge would be to make her recognize that bond and accept his limitations. If she wanted him badly enough, she wouldn't insist on love.

He had already succeeded to some degree; she wanted him but didn't like it. But he needed to press his advantage.

Kate was a handful under any circumstances, and although he preferred forthrightness and honesty, he couldn't reveal his ulterior motive or she would bolt. At minimum, he had to pretend to go through the motions of searching for a bride—which was why he'd proposed that she tutor him. So he could learn what she wanted in a suitor, how she wanted to be wooed. He would use her own counsel against her and compel her to let down her guard.

In short, he intended to pursue Kate with every means at his disposal, conventional or not. Even if he pushed the boundaries of fairness, or violated the accepted mating and marriage rituals, he would win her.

With his decision, Brandon was finally able to close his eyes and relax enough to let sleep overtake him. And just before he dozed off, he smiled faintly in satisfaction.

He had chosen Kate. Now he just had to convince her of the inevitable.

Chapter Seven

When Kate reached home late that evening, her temper was still simmering from her clash with Lady Dalton. She spent the night tossing and turning and woke with fresh determination to find Deverill a worthy bride. Obviously, she had been too desultory in her search thus far and needed to reconsider her strategy. No more tame, mousy girls for him. He needed someone much better.

Therefore, she would move up her plan to introduce him to her first choice, Daphne Farnwell. Daphne could be an excellent match for him. She was intelligent, beautiful, talented, a good conversationalist, and as the daughter of a baron, she held a respected position in society.

Indeed, Kate decided as she dressed for the day, she should be glad for her nemesis's warning shot since it had brought out her fighting instincts. Yes, jealousy played a role in her renewed resolve, but mostly she was thinking of Deverill. She would do everything in her power to keep him safe from the clutches of that witch.

This was no longer merely a favor for her aunt, or a means to persuade him to escort her to France. This was a battle for his future.

Before parting last evening, they had agreed to convene this morning at her home. Since both Nell and Maura would be away, Kate chose the folly in the rear gardens for her meeting with Deverill—a pretty, domed structure partially hidden in a copse of woods.

Surrounded on all sides by white trellises, which in turn were covered by thick ivy and climbing rose vines, the folly should provide privacy, yet because of the dreary, gray day, the setting was not romantic in the least. With a misty rain falling, the air was even a bit chilly, requiring outer garments. Kate rationalized that since she would be more heavily clothed Deverill would have less opportunity to fondle her bosom.

When he arrived at ten o'clock, she met him in the entrance hall. After donning a hooded cloak, she led him outside to the rear terrace and down the sweeping stone steps.

There was no sign of any gardeners as they traversed the graveled path. Deverill, however, seemed to divine her purpose, if his knowing gaze was any indication. He paused just inside the doorway of the folly, surveying the interior and the opposing wooden benches. "Shall I guess the reason you chose here?"

"I will happily tell you. I wanted a less intimate setting than my drawing room."

"The setting wouldn't stop me if I was determined to be intimate."

Kate found herself flushing, then scolded herself for her reflexive response. She was acting very much like the prude Lady X had accused her of being.

"We have a good deal of ground to cover so we should begin at once." Pushing back the hood of her cloak, she sat on one of the benches and indicated that Deverill should take the other. Instead of complying, however, he leaned one broad shoulder against the wooden door frame, waiting.

Kate took a breath. She should stop worrying so much about being alone with Deverill and get on with tutoring him. The trouble was, that intense stare of his—so tender and sensual—was unsettling.

"We must focus on increasing your appeal to your chosen candidate," she said. "Since I don't care to endure your roasting, I won't bore you with my myriad lists—"

"Praise the saints."

She cast him a narrow glance. "—but I will share some attributes of an ideal suitor. I believe most women will appreciate these same qualities in a husband."

Deverill folded his arms over his chest. "Pray, proceed."

"First, the negative. I have already mentioned that

sheltered young ladies may be put off by your provoking nature and warned that you cannot be intimidating or arrogant or dictatorial. At the same time, you should never belittle her or act as if you are better than she is."

"Do I act as if I am better than you are?"

"No, but you could take my advice a step further. It can be disarming if you can laugh at yourself. A self-deprecating manner can put a shy girl at ease. And you could strive to be a good conversationalist. At least some ladies want that."

"Such as yourself. I will practice developing my witty ripostes after tea."

Kate couldn't help but smile. "You should be quick with a compliment, but not in the obvious way. . . . Not necessarily with appearance or beauty, I mean. A plain woman will know you are feeding her falsehoods if you call her beautiful, but you could admire her best feature or praise an attractive character trait—something she takes pride in. Everyone has some attribute that is worthy of praise and admiration. But flattery must always be truthful, even if exaggerated a little."

"You have amazing eyes."

Heat bloomed in her cheeks. "That is overdoing it, my lord, but you are on the right track. It also helps to be forgiving of her flaws and accepting of her limitations."

"Such as you and your lists."

Kate flashed a bright smile. "Exactly. And at the top

of my list: Attentiveness is perhaps the most effective quality in a suitor, to my mind."

"What do you mean?"

"Listen to her, talk with her. And most important, you ought not close off your feelings."

"I thought you advised disarming her."

"There are many ways to accomplish that. Show a genuine interest in her. Care about *her* interests. Ask about her hopes and dreams. Be considerate of her needs. But one of the best ways is opening your own heart to her."

"Why?"

She leveled him a look tinged with exasperation. "The whole point is to try to make her fall in love with you, Deverill. I know you put little value on love, but if you want to earn her regard and perhaps even win her heart, you cannot come across as calculating or cold. She will warm to you if you sometimes share what you are feeling."

"You have created quite a lengthy list."

"You needn't do *all* these things, but some measure would go a long way toward earning her gratitude and affection."

"If I were to court *you* as you're advising, you would be bored out of your senses."

"We are not talking about me," Kate replied, voicing the same argument she had made several times before. "Stop being so provoking, Lord Valmere. You could also strive to be a little romantic."

"Command and I will obey."

She gave a dubious laugh. "You, obey my commands? That will never happen. Besides, this is supposed to be a courtship, not a naval battle."

"What else am I to do?"

"Well, try to observe the proprieties whenever possible. For example, you dance very well, but—"

"What is this, a compliment? From you?"

Kate ignored the interruption. "But you ought not hold her too close in a waltz. I have already warned you to minimize the damage your privateering will cause. You cannot come across as a rake, either."

Deverill's expression turned contemplative. "I'll wager some ladies are attracted to wickedness. Seduction may work as well as attentiveness."

"Perhaps, but you will likely have to win over her family and the arbiters of society. If you seem bent on seduction, you might attract the lady but her family will rush to shield her. But again, none of that is as important as sharing a more personal side of yourself."

For a moment, Deverill's thick lashes lowered to veil his eyes. Then he pushed away from the door frame and sauntered toward her. "How is this for sharing my feelings? Yesterday you left me in a painfully aroused state."

Kate lifted an eyebrow. "So *I* am to blame? *You* are the one who kissed *me*. I was doing my best to stop you."

"Hardly your best. Do you know what I did last night when I was lying alone in my bed, unable to sleep? I brought myself to pleasure with my hand. And I was thinking of you the whole time. In fact, I dreamed about you the entire night. Quite lustful dreams, I might add."

His explicit talk took her aback. But then Deverill had a notorious record for knocking her off balance.

"You will just have to control your lustful urges," Kate retorted.

"What about your urges?"

"I don't have urges."

"I'll wager you do."

Deverill stood before her, gazing down at her. "I think you are underestimating how large a role physical appeal plays in a courtship. In my experience, a woman wants to be wanted."

He wanted *her,* an underlying note in his voice implied. The notion was soothing to her vanity but made her pulse race.

When she had no quick riposte, Deverill sat on the bench beside her and gave her his blandest smile. Kate watched him warily. She didn't trust that look, yet she stifled the urge to leap up and retreat across the folly, determined to hold her ground.

"You are more desirable than any of the candidates on your list," he murmured.

"Thank you, but I am not interested in you in the least."

It was the wrong thing to say, judging from the intrigued spark in his eyes. No doubt he felt challenged by her resistance.

"Now that is a falsehood if I ever heard one," he said slowly. "Yesterday on your sofa was vivid proof."

"A momentary aberration that I already regret."

"Was it an aberration?"

"Yes. Not every woman lusts for you."

"I don't care about every woman. Only you. Confess, you want me."

He was goading her and tempting her at the same time—and against her will, Kate responded, "It is not unreasonable that I feel an attraction for you. I am human after all."

"Ah, yes. Very human. All woman. And I think you want a real flesh-and-blood man, not the tame, dull, idealized sort you profess to admire."

Reaching over, he grasped her hand and drew it to the front placket of his breeches, sending a shock of awareness rocketing through Kate. Beneath the fabric, he was very large and very hard.

"I am very much flesh and blood, sweetheart."

She fought the urge to snatch her hand back. Deverill was vigorously flouting her rules of proper behavior and pushing the boundaries of acceptable conduct, but she wasn't required to play his game.

"The condition of your flesh is not my concern," she said sweetly as she calmly freed her hand from his grasp.

Deverill eyed her, assessing. "You are cruel to leave me in such dire pain."

"And you are brazen and outrageous."

"You once admired brazenness. In fact, you once

were brazen and daring yourself. You seem to have forgotten how to be wild and adventurous. You are far too concerned about being a proper lady."

Kate winced inwardly. His charge was similar to the accusation Lady Dalton had made last evening about her prudishness.

It seemed Deverill was not finished with his observations, either. "For too long you have tried to restrain your lively, enchanting nature. These days you resemble a cold-blooded princess."

"I am *not* cold-blooded," Kate retorted with more vehemence than she intended.

"Then why are you so skittish? Is it because you are afraid you will enjoy my lovemaking too much?"

"I am not afraid, either."

"Then show me."

Kate summoned a frown. "I will do no such thing. You are a champion at baiting me."

"Am I succeeding?"

The amusement lurking in his eyes vexed and exasperated her, and she knew she was in trouble.

It was sheer idiocy to make this into a battle for supremacy between them, for Deverill was almost certain to win. On the other hand, she was tired of always feeling defensive. Moreover, she kept remembering the widow's stinging rebuke. The scandalous Lady X would never have been so concerned with violating propriety.

"I have no intention of becoming your lover," Kate said with less assurance than she would have liked.

"Why not? If you've enjoyed lovers before, what are you worried about?"

She glanced around the folly. "This is still far too public a place. Someone might catch us in a state of undress."

"There is no need for us to undress. I can make love to you fully clothed. In fact, I could bring you to climax with a minimum of touching, without either my hands or my mouth."

"I very much doubt that."

In answer, Deverill leaned closer, bringing his face within a breath of hers.

Kate drew back as far as possible. "What are you doing?"

"You issued a challenge."

"Not intentionally."

When she rose to her feet, he caught her hand. "Are you running away?"

At his provoking query, Kate planted her feet. "No, I am not running away!"

He looked skeptical. "I never took you for the craven sort."

The implication riled her. "I am not craven, Deverill!"

"Then prove it." When she was silent, he tugged on her hand. "Come closer, sweetheart."

"Why?"

He gave her a slow smile. "Indulge me."

She narrowed her eyes at him. "What are you about?"

"Showing you pleasure, what else?"

What else? It was clear he was set on seducing her to establish his mastery over her, and she was rising to his bait, devil take him.

It didn't help when he asked in a tone that was slightly taunting, "Haven't your 'marvelous' lovers ever brought you to pleasure with the barest stimulation? They must not have been very skilled or concerned about your satisfaction. I would never make that mistake."

The promise in his vow stroked her nerve endings.

Kate set her jaw. No one could get under her skin the way Brandon Deverill could. His smile alone was infuriating. He knew how devastating that smile could be. And his eyes . . . She saw both desire and tenderness in his eyes. Heaven help her. She was out of her depth, her own harried emotions spinning out of control. Worse, he had ignited a deep, desperate desire in her to surrender—and a deeper need to prove him wrong. She was *not* a coward.

She took a deliberate step forward, till their knees touched. "Now what?"

Gazing up at her, he spread his legs slightly. "Now I want you to mount my thigh."

Her eyebrows shot up. "Are you serious?"

"Utterly. It will be like riding a horse. You are an excellent horsewoman."

Defiantly, Kate hiked up her skirts several inches and eased her right leg over his right one. Then placing her hands on Deverill's shoulders for balance, she settled on his thigh and stared back at him. "Like this?"

At her rebellious gaze, he cocked his head. "Not quite. You are far too tense. Relax your body. As you said, this is not a battle."

Kate swallowed. There was a hypnotic force in his gaze. He was capable of stirring wicked fantasies with a mere look.

Sliding his arms around her, Deverill drew her close enough that her breasts pressed against his chest. Her heart picked up its pace, banging against her rib cage.

Then he moved his thigh slightly, lifting her up. The pressure on the sensitive core of her made Kate give a faint gasp.

"Now close your eyes," he commanded, his voice a seductive murmur.

When she obeyed, he leaned forward to plant a delicate kiss on her cheek. His lips were tender, coaxing, softly teasing her flushed skin.

"You said you didn't need to use your mouth," Kate complained in a ragged voice.

"So I did. But I want to kiss you, badly. I want to taste you and savor you and arouse you. . . ."

Again he moved his thigh against her mound, sending a shock of fire rippling through her. Her eyes still shut, Kate tightened her fingers on his shoulders, her breath stuck somewhere between her lungs and her throat.

"But I don't need to even touch you," Deverill continued in a softer voice, "to know what I would find.

I can imagine parting your thighs, finding your mound with my fingers, stroking your slick cleft. . . ."

The vivid picture he painted contributed to the sweet eroticism of his voice, while the friction he created incited a burning desire to press harder against his sinewed thigh. With an involuntary whimper, Kate began to move her hips, riding his flesh, relishing the play of musculature against the very center of her.

As if understanding her need, he reached down to grasp her buttocks, aiding her in finding a rhythm. Excitement melded with yearning inside Kate. Her fingers tangled in his hair, and she hid her face in his neck, panting at the incredible sensations coursing through her body.

Deverill's husky voice came to her through a fevered haze. "I can imagine how wet you are for me, how hot."

She thrust herself more urgently against his thigh, her pelvis undulating, her breath rasping.

"Easy, love. Go slowly. . . . The better to draw out our pleasure."

Slowly? What he asked was impossible. Her body was moving of its own urgent volition while he continued whispering against her ear.

"Just let yourself enjoy, Kate. Let me free you of all that rigid control."

But her resistance was instinctive. "I don't want . . . I can't—"

"Yes, you *can*. Use your imagination. Picture me

thrusting between your thighs . . . moving with you, loving your incredible body. . . ."

She could easily imagine her most potent fantasy come to life: Deverill making love to her, loving her . . . joining with her in perfect union.

Her eyes shut, Kate arched against him as the spiraling pleasure built relentlessly. "What . . . is happening to me? The heat . . ."

"I know, angel. Don't fight it. Just surrender."

She didn't want to fight it. She had no power over her body any longer, no power over the coiling tension.

Sensation swelled inside her, unbearably sweet. She rocked back and forth, her muscles clenching, her limbs tightening. *This is how a lightning storm feels* was her last coherent thought before heat and need exploded through her, so intense her lungs seized. Her keening cry muffled against his coat, she collapsed against Deverill weakly and buried her face in his shoulder as rippling shivers racked her.

For a long while, he said nothing, nor did she. She couldn't speak. Her breath was gone, her throat dry. She felt dazed, shaken, while her body thrummed with sensual pleasure.

Secure in his embrace, Kate was grateful for the time to cool her overheated senses and reclaim her wits. She didn't want to move. In truth, she didn't want anything to disturb the wonder of this moment.

At length, though, Deverill reached up to stroke a wayward tress from her forehead. "That was your first climax, wasn't it," he murmured, a statement, not a question. "You are still a virgin."

Kate kept her face hidden as embarrassment flooded her. Somehow he knew she had been fibbing. "How did you know?"

"Your startlement, for one thing. And you taste like innocence when you kiss. I thought you said you had known lovers before."

"I might have exaggerated a tiny bit."

His soft chuckle of disbelief made Kate lift her head to glare at him.

He traced a fingertip over her cheekbone, studying her with intent dark eyes. "Why did you claim otherwise?"

She ducked her head again, her cheeks flaming. "You are so experienced, I didn't want you thinking me a complete novice at passion. I do have my pride."

"Ah, darling Kate," she heard him say with a murmur of laughter. "You never cease to amaze me."

"I *knew* you would tease me mercilessly," she muttered.

"No, no, this is not teasing. I am exceedingly glad you are inexperienced." His tone was tender and amused. "Indeed, I am honored you chose me to educate you. It makes a man feel more manly to think he can give his woman pleasure."

She made a scoffing sound. "I have no doubt you can succeed on *that* score. But I am not your woman and never will be."

Not answering, he lifted her up to resettle her on

his lap and gathered her in his arms. Kate couldn't summon the will to resist. Instead, she laid her cheek against the fine wool of his coat, the pleasure lingering despite his amusement at her expense.

"You're incredibly responsive," Deverill added in a thoughtful tone. "I expected nothing less. That is a high compliment, by the way. I am taking your tutoring to heart."

He intended to use her own advice against her? Kate was about to protest when Deverill spoke again in a low voice. "You had no need to pretend experience with me."

Yes, she had. Her prevarication had seemed justified at the time. How did a woman explain her insecurities to a man, especially one as virile and masculine as Deverill? If she'd thought he hadn't wanted her six years ago, how could he want her now that she was older and practically on the shelf?

While she debated her reply, Deverill nodded to himself. "It makes sense now. Frankly I was amazed to think your brother would allow you to take a lover."

"Allow?" Kate repeated. "Ash has no say in the matter. I am no longer a child and his responsibility."

"Good. Then you can make your own decisions."

Pulling away, she raised her gaze to his. "What do you mean, 'good'?"

"I want to be your first lover."

The bold statement sent a thrill through Kate. She wanted that, too, so very badly.

"If you are so independent, you can choose for yourself."

Staring back at him, Kate felt a confusing mix of regret and desire. His offer was incredibly tempting. She wanted Deverill intensely . . . and yet not at the price she would have to pay. He might be interested in seducing her with his body, but his heart wasn't engaged and never would be.

"I won't be taking you or anyone else for my lover. I intend to save myself for my husband."

"Six years ago you were prepared to give yourself to me."

"I was mistaken."

With a faint smile, Deverill drew her head back down to his shoulder. "Perhaps it was best that I didn't make love to you then. Your brother would have shot me out of hand for taking advantage of you. At least now I won't have to deal with him coming after me with murder in his heart."

"He will have no reason to come after you. We won't become lovers."

She felt Deverill's lips press tenderly against her hair. "Why shouldn't you enjoy pleasure like a man can?"

At the absurd question, Kate's mouth curled. It was a long-held complaint of hers also, but there was an obvious answer. "You well know that an unmarried young lady cannot take lovers."

"Who says?"

"Society's rules."

"Rules can be circumvented. You weren't meant for spinsterhood. You are far too passionate to languish on the shelf. Too full of life. You need a man who can satisfy that craving in you. Admit it, you've lost your sense of wonder and adventure."

When she was silent, he bent closer to kiss her temple, then shifted across her face . . . her eyelids, her nose, her cheekbone, her throat. The feather touch of his lips on her throat held a tantalizing sensuality.

"I can teach you to be a woman, Kate, not just a society princess. Think of it. I could set you free."

She did think of it. The freedom to do as she pleased. The chance to enjoy pleasure as a man could, unshackled by the chains that society placed on women. Deverill could indeed set her free.

He had always treated her as an equal, not as an heiress, not as a weakling or some lesser creature, either. He made her feel like a person rather than a delicate object to be set on a pedestal and adored. He even appreciated her high spirits and never censured her sometimes tart tongue and rash temper. But there were so many things she wasn't allowed to do because of her gender and breeding.

"All that fire, all that bottled-up passion," he whispered, his mouth moving back to her face.

At his seductive accolade, Kate felt the spellbinding daze overcome her again. His lips were so arousing. The scalding heat of his touch made her forget how to breathe. She couldn't bear for him to stop.

Hang the man. This was precisely what he intended.

Her breath shamefully uneven, Kate extricated herself from Deverill's embrace and slid off his lap. Drawing the lapels of her cloak together, she glanced out the folly door at the garden. "The rain has stopped. We should return to the house. And before you accuse me of running away, I am not. I have considered your offer and choose to decline."

"A pity," Deverill said with an exaggerated sigh. Rising from the bench, he followed her to the doorway. "I trust I can eventually change your mind. Fortunately, I can be patient. As difficult as it will be, I will wait until you invite me to make love to you."

Looking up, Kate met his gaze. "You will have a long wait."

"We shall see."

The promise in his declaration unnerved her, as did the unabashed desire in his eyes.

That settled it, Kate decided as she plunged into the garden where the damp air felt cool on her flushed face. No more meetings alone with Deverill. Never, *ever.* Her pitifully weak willpower simply couldn't withstand it.

Chapter Eight

Kate woke the next morning feeling hot and achy and frustrated. Why the devil did she keep having such erotic dreams of Deverill?

A foolish question, obviously, considering the intimacies between them yesterday, the brazen liberties he had taken with her. She finally understood why carnal passion had such a powerful effect on lovers throughout the ages. There really was nothing quite like it—the spiraling heat, the starbursts exploding inside her body—and that was only a fraction of the pleasure Deverill promised. She had a great deal to learn about lovemaking and wished he could be the one to teach her.

Another singularly witless sentiment to add to the many others that have plagued you of late.

Giving a disgusted sigh, Kate tried to suppress both memory and fantasy as she rose from her bed and dressed. With a burst of fresh resolve, she went to work arranging for Deverill to meet Daphne Farnwell at the earliest opportunity, which, she learned to her disappointment, would not be for two more days since Daphne had prior obligations.

Meanwhile, Kate renewed her vow to avoid any private moments with him. She didn't trust herself to be alone with the man, nor did she trust him not to take advantage of her profound weakness for him.

Her plan, however, got off to an inauspicious start that evening when the Beaufort carriage collected Deverill for a musical performance at the King's Theatre. Upon entering the barouche, he took the seat beside her, close enough that his thigh brushed hers, reminding her how effectively he had used his thigh in the folly. Kate felt a flush of heat rise inside her. After returning his greeting, she kept her eyes fixed straight ahead and hoped the relative dimness of the interior hid her blush.

There were other moments in the course of the evening when she also felt a heightened awareness of Deverill: Upon arriving, when he removed her cloak and his fingers grazed her bare shoulders. When his gaze lingered on her during the splendid violin concerto, and again as a famous opera singer entertained the company with her remarkable soprano. At the first intermission when Deverill took her hand to help her rise from her seat.

Yet she single-mindedly kept her focus on her task.

During the intermission, she introduced him to one more candidate on her list, Miss Eliza Rowe. Kate was especially glad that conversing with the young lady kept him occupied and away from Lady Dalton, who, unhappily for Kate, was in attendance. When she spied the beautiful widow across the room, her jaw firmed with fresh determination.

As soon as she could politely extract Deverill from the discussion, she deliberately steered him in the opposite direction, which made his eyebrow lift in question. "Why such haste to return to our seats?"

"Lady X, if you must know. She is eyeing you like the cat after the canary. I don't want her sinking her claws into you. You can do much better."

To change the subject, Kate added, "That reminds me. . . . Our next engagement will be tomorrow afternoon at a garden party in Richmond. And the following evening, some family friends, Lord and Lady Perry, are holding a ball at their home. I particularly wish you to meet a newer friend of mine there."

For the remainder of the musical evening, Kate was rather proud of her composure whenever she was near Deverill, yet she was eager to have him woo Daphne and take the responsibility for his courtship out of her hands.

As luck would have it, though, another unpleasant encounter with Julia Dalton threatened her hard-won equanimity. During the second intermission, they happened to meet in the ladies' retiring room. When the widow voiced a snide remark under her breath about keeping Valmere on a short leash, Kate had had enough.

Grasping her rival's wrist, she led a startled Lady Dalton from the room and down the corridor, past milling theater patrons to a dim corner where they could be somewhat private.

Kate kept her voice hushed while throwing down the gauntlet. "I regret depressing your aspirations, Lady X, but Valmere will never fall for your wiles. I will make certain of it."

The look the widow returned was both amused and smug. "If I chose to pursue him, you could not stop me."

"Would you care to test your theory?"

"Indeed I would—and I shall do so at my first opportunity. I hear Valmere will be attending the Radcliffe garden party in Richmond tomorrow."

Kate could barely stop her lip from curling in disgust. "You are keeping a close eye on his social engagements, I see."

Lady Dalton smiled wickedly. "It is only shrewd. I will have my chance then, unless you are prepared to stand guard over him the entire time."

They eyed each other sharply before Kate realized she was getting nowhere. Would she do better to offer a truce of sorts?

She held up a hand. "Rather than quarrel with you, *I* would be shrewd to appeal to your sense of decency. Your current protector deserves your loyalty," Kate pointed out, referring to Mr. Edmund Lisle, who had supported Julia for the better part of two years. "From what I hear, Lisle adores you."

"Of course he does."

"Then instead of chasing after Valmere, perhaps you should be content with a bird in hand."

Lady Dalton's haughty look of disdain returned. "My affairs are none of your concern."

Kate's spine stiffened. "You made it my concern when you threatened the happiness of my family and friends. You well know that your treatment of my cousin Quinn was appalling, and now you want to add Valmere to your callous list of conquests. Moreover, you owe Lisle. You have spent years trading your beauty and sensual talents for his patronage."

"At least I *have* sensual talents, which is more than you can boast."

The cutting accusation stung, but Kate returned a cold smile. "I have no idea why Lisle fancies you so ardently, given your character. I should think that even among Cyprians there is a code of honor. Apparently you know nothing about honor, however—deceiving the gentleman who is keeping you in funds and providing for your luxurious lifestyle. Indiscretions are one thing, but a liaison with Valmere would be an outright betrayal."

Kate could tell she had struck a nerve when Lady Dalton winced and drew herself up to her full height. "I do *not* require lectures from *you,* Lady Katharine. Now, pray, excuse me. . . ."

It was the widow's turn to stalk off, leaving Kate marginally satisfied. She disliked lowering herself to

Julia Dalton's level, but it felt good to act instead of calmly accepting the insults that witch dished out.

Their little scene had attracted an avid audience, Kate realized, glancing around to see a dozen curious stares. The gossipmongers, too, would view their spat with glee—a Wilde causing yet another public spectacle. Yet she refused to tolerate Julia Dalton's scheming. On the contrary, she intended to shut down the beautiful widow's pursuit of Deverill before it bore any fruit whatsoever.

To that end, Kate used her powerful connections to arrange an invitation to the garden party in Richmond for Edmund Lisle—and hoped he would be intrigued enough to attend an exclusive social event at an elegant country estate on the River Thames. It was not underhanded to use Lady Dalton's protector to keep her in check, Kate believed. Merely a necessary step to save Deverill.

The next afternoon at the party, there were no more new bridal candidates for him to meet, but the grasping Miss Armitage was there and was clearly intent on pursuing him, a circumstance Deverill did not appear to relish.

Lady Dalton was present as well—and very quickly attempted to sink her claws into him.

Regrettably, Kate was waylaid indoors by an acquaintance while the scheming widow followed Deverill out onto the rear terrace, which overlooked the beautiful gardens and river. By the time Kate broke free,

Julia was hanging on his arm, fluttering her eyelashes, flashing him beguiling looks interspersed with little trills of laughter.

Much to Kate's relief, however, Lisle stepped through the terrace doors just then.

Edmund Lisle boasted a rather stocky figure but had handsome features, despite his thinning brown hair. Additionally, he was fairly wealthy, a prosperity he'd successfully augmented as an amateur gamester. To Kate's mind, he didn't deserve the various humiliations his mistress had dealt him, even if he and Quinn had once been enemies.

Lisle came to a dead stop upon spying Lady X. Clearly he was experienced enough to comprehend her aim in a single glance. But when she suddenly caught sight of him, Julia abruptly abandoned Deverill, as if scalded, and hurried over to Lisle. After an inaudible exchange of words, some clearly harsh and angry, Lisle turned away, making for the terrace doors.

Julia glared daggers at Kate and muttered what sounded like a curse, then picked up her skirts and ran after Lisle. "Wait, darling, please. . . ."

Making her way through the crowd on the terrace, Kate joined Deverill, whose gaze was following the disappearing widow.

"Did you have a hand in taking her off my scent?" he queried.

She chose to answer with the truth. "I am not ashamed to say that I did. I hoped to keep her too occupied to chase after you."

Deverill gave Kate a knowing glance that was part amusement, part respect. "I am all admiration—and I thank you."

Kate returned a smile that was less triumph than gratitude.

"Now that you have rid me of Lady Dalton," Deverill added, "you could save me from the Armitage chit."

"Apparently Miss Armitage has a tendre for you."

"Not for me. For my fortune and title."

"I warned you, Lord Valmere."

When he shot her a sour look, this time Kate replied with a genuine smile before turning away.

Deverill, however, reached out to grasp her arm, staying her. "Not so fast." When she turned back, his tone took on a mock pleading quality. "You wouldn't abandon me to the she-wolves, would you?"

"What? You need me beside you to protect you? Such a big, strong fellow?"

He flashed her a very male grin. "Perhaps I do need your protection." Taking her elbow, he pulled Kate toward the stone banister overlooking the gardens, away from the crowd. "I had not expected my bride search to be so disappointing," he continued in a low voice. "In fact, I am considering calling off the whole thing."

Kate searched his face in surprise. "But we have barely begun. Take heart, Deverill. I have someone in mind who could be ideal for you. The Honorable Miss Daphne Farnwell. You will like her, I promise. I will introduce you tomorrow night at the Perrys' ball."

He was silent for a span before saying lightly, "I think I should wed you instead."

Kate's jaw dropped momentarily—until she realized he must be joking. Giving a soft laugh, she replied in the same vein. "Because it would shield you from fortune hunters."

"It would also save me the bother of a courtship."

"I see," she said with amusement. "You hope to avoid the hard work required to find the right mate."

"Without a doubt."

"But you don't really want to wed me."

Tilting his head, he gave her a contemplative glance. "I am not so certain."

"I am. You are only considering me for convenience."

"You would hardly be *convenient*. I could think of few prospects more likely to cause me trouble and grief. You are not the comfortable sort—but that is actually a point in your favor. And in some ways, you would be the easiest choice for my bride. For one thing, you could effortlessly assume the role of my baroness."

"Any number of ladies could."

"But none who compare to you. You are the most desirable woman of my acquaintance. And I need a wife to fill my life and warm my bed."

His gaze locked with hers, making her feel breathless. Kate could barely contain her flush. Trying to ignore the fluttering warmth in the pit of her stomach, she looked out over the gardens. "But I don't want you for my husband."

"Why not?"

"You know why not. We are incompatible in the only way that counts: We don't love each other. And you have said you have no intention of changing."

"At least you already know my faults. Otherwise, we would make a good match."

"That would not be enough for me."

"You could try to mold me as you wish."

Kate laughed outright. "How gullible do you think I am? You would be impossible to mold to that extent." She shook her head. "No, we should keep to our original plan. For now . . . perhaps we should find Ash and Maura and take our leave. You know Maura dislikes leaving her young son for so long."

A short while later, they did quit the garden party, but Kate found that Deverill's impromptu proposal lingered in her mind long after they had dropped him off at his hotel.

What if she were actually to accept his offer of marriage? Even though he was clearly not serious, it was a ridiculously intriguing proposition. But no. She intended to hold out for her dream of true love, and she couldn't trust that Deverill would ever love her. By his own admission, tender emotions and feelings such as love were foreign to him.

But what if she could somehow *make* Deverill love her?

She quickly shied away from the question as an impossibility. Abandoning her standards was not an option, either. Her parents' marriage had been based on love and devotion and rock-solid trust, and she would settle for nothing less. Finding the same mutual heart bond was the only reason she would ever marry.

With thoughts laced with regret, Kate gave up contemplating what-ifs and turned her attention to the next evening—making certain that Daphne appeared in the best possible light.

Chapter Nine

The Perrys' ball was a grand, glittering affair, with over a hundred guests in attendance. As expected, when Kate presented two more candidates on her list, Deverill did not seem enamored of the sharp-witted Miss Dodd or the soft-spoken Miss Osborne.

However, her favorite choice, Miss Daphne Farnwell, was a different story altogether. For the first time, he seemed genuinely interested in furthering an acquaintance and immediately danced two dances with her.

Daphne, who was slender and elegant, with golden-brown hair and light blue eyes, contrasted appealingly with Deverill's powerful build and ebony hair.

Later, watching them laughing together, their heads close as he murmured in her ear, Kate unconsciously frowned—and then caught herself.

What was wrong with her, to be suffering pangs of jealousy toward Daphne? She ought to feel ashamed.

Likely she would find fault in any lady she'd arranged for him to inspect, because of her fondness for Deverill if nothing else. She harbored real anger toward Lady Dalton, but Daphne had no such glaring deficiencies and might be perfect for him.

In an act of will, Kate directed her concentration to her own dance partner. And yet a niggling dissatisfaction kept nagging at her. Had she perhaps made a mistake pairing him with Daphne?

When it came time for refreshments, she accompanied Maura and Ash to the supper rooms while Deverill escorted Daphne. Kate couldn't take her eyes off the attractive couple, a fact that Maura commented on once Ash stepped away.

"It seems Lord Valmere is getting on famously with Miss Farnwell."

"Yes, it does," Kate replied.

"You don't sound happy about it."

"No, I am very happy," she claimed falsely. "Not only will Daphne make a good match for him, she will be lucky to have him for a husband."

Maura knew her too well, though. "Kate, dearest . . . you are expending great effort to turn Valmere into an ideal husband for some other woman. Are you certain that is what you want?"

"I have his best interests at heart."

"What of your best interests? What of *your* heart?" Maura's dark eyes held real concern. "I have seen how you are when you are with him, Kate. Your whole being lights up. The sparkle in your eyes returns—the one that has been missing for years."

Kate made a face at the indisputable statement. Doubtless the fiery spark of attraction she felt every time Deverill looked at her, the bright jolt of energy whenever he was near, was evident to anyone who knew her well.

"I can't deny it," she said with regret.

"But you also harbor deeper feelings for him. I think you want him for yourself."

Unable to protest, Kate gave Maura a probing glance. "What if I do?"

"Then you should take action."

"Meaning?"

Maura smiled kindly. "It seems to me that you are giving up prematurely. The Kate I have always known and loved would never act so passively. She would go after what she wants with every fiber in her being."

It was similar to the advice Kate had given to many a friend, and Maura knew it, judging by her self-satisfied look.

"I am nowhere near as skilled a matchmaker as you," Maura added. "But if you resolve to have him, I will help you in any way I can. And you should act soon"—she glanced toward Deverill, who gave every appearance of wooing Daphne—"before they form a strong attachment."

Another sharp pang shot through Kate, and when her friend turned away to address Ash, she was momentarily left alone to consider a stark realization:

She'd been deceiving herself by pretending that Daphne was his best choice.

The truth was, she didn't want Daphne to have him. She wanted Deverill for herself.

It was a disturbing acknowledgment, one that sent Kate's thoughts churning. It took an intense effort of will to control her unruly emotions and finish supper before returning to the ballroom.

She went through the motions of dancing and conversing, but she was still stewing over Maura's admonition a half hour later when Deverill suddenly appeared before her and drew her away from the crowd.

"Where are you taking me?" she asked in puzzlement as he led her out of the ballroom.

"Out of range" was his cryptic answer.

Hoping he would explain, she accompanied him along the corridor and felt more bewildered when he glanced into the various rooms they passed. Finally he ducked into a parlor that was unoccupied and dimly lit by a single lamp.

"What is the matter?" Kate demanded a little breathlessly.

Crossing the room to the hearth, he pulled her behind a Chinese screen that protected a sitter from hearth flames. "Miss Armitage is on my scent like a bloodhound."

Kate couldn't help but laugh. "Are you *hiding* from her?"

"Yes. Pray, keep your voice down."

"Now who is being craven?" she whispered.

He glanced down at her. "Wretch," he said lightly. "You are too damned gleeful at my predicament."

Kate kept her voice to a murmur. "You should remain here for a while. Miss Armitage is a rank amateur compared to Lady Dalton, but she can still cause you trouble."

"I will, but you must remain here with me."

"Deverill, the ball is not over. I am promised to several more dance partners."

"I know. One poor devil after another is dangling at your shoestrings. But I dislike standing in line. Now tell me if we were followed."

Puzzled by his remark, she turned toward the screen to peer between the crack in the hinged panels. "There is no one out there," she whispered.

"Good."

To her surprise, she felt Deverill's arm slip around her waist from behind. Kate went still. "What do you think you are doing?"

"This is revenge for being amused at my expense."

"I am sorry for laughing at you."

"No, you are not."

When his fingers rose to the décolletage of her ball gown and brushed the swell of her breasts, she sucked in a breath. "Deverill, you need to release me."

"Not on your life. Since you have avoided me all evening, I had to create my own opportunity to be alone with you."

Kate shook her head in disbelief. He was constantly

confounding her, and in this case, he had an ulterior motive. "Why would you need to get me alone?"

"I mean to bring you to pleasure."

"Right *here*?" Her voice rose an octave and came out a squeak.

"Hush, sweetheart," he chided. "You don't want to be discovered in my arms."

In the distance she could hear the sounds of chatter and music, but the parlor was fairly quiet. If someone were to enter, she and Deverill could be heard.

"I advise you to keep silent," he repeated. "If someone finds us like this, there will be a scandal."

Craning her neck to look back up at him, Kate narrowed her eyes. "Are you trying to coerce me?"

His mouth quirked. "I can't imagine coercing you into anything you don't wish to do. But you will wish this, I promise."

He was serious, she realized. Shock rippled along her spine, along with an electric thrill.

When she tried to break away from him, Deverill prevented her by tightening his embrace. "Be still, princess. If you struggle against me, you will cause a scene."

His warning was abetted by her realization that she had no desire to struggle. In fact, she craved more of the pleasure he had given her in the folly.

What did that say about her wantonness? What did that say about his? Many of her ancestors had lived lives of scandal and passion, and this generation of Wilde cousins had unabashedly lived up to their name. But Deverill was every bit as outrageous as her family, bold and brazen and so very irresistible. No one had ever lured her into temptation the way he did, damn him.

Kate was trying to form a coherent objection when he cut her off. "I am not releasing you, so you might as well let yourself enjoy this. . . ."

While he spoke, he raised her skirts to bare her sex to the evening air. Then, very gently, he ran his palm along the front of her thigh. The erotic caress made her breath catch.

When his palm shifted farther left, stroking the satin of her inner thigh, Kate tensed and remained so when his fingers glided through the curls covering her woman's mound.

The unexpectedness of the contact stunned her. She felt light-headed and unsettled. Then his hand slipped fully between her legs, pressing against her cleft. At the searing heat of his touch, longing melded with insidious excitement.

Deverill must have been pleased to find the wetness there, judging by his sound of approval.

"See," he murmured in her ear in the lazy, husky voice that always made her hot. "You want me badly."

"How . . . do you know?"

"Your body betrays you. You've grown hot and wet between your thighs, and the bud of your sex is hard and swollen."

As if to prove his claim, his fingers slid along her slick flesh, grazing the nubbin secreted in her feminine folds. Even that slight pressure was like a jolt of lightning to Kate. Suddenly she lost the ability to think, to move, to breathe.

"Hold up your gown," he ordered softly.

He was asking her to participate in her own seduction? She knew better, and yet she obeyed.

"Ah, sweet Kate. . . ." His rough whisper was mesmerizing, increasing the sexual excitement inside her. "I remember how you looked climaxing the other day, how you felt, the little moans you made. . . . You can't moan now, though. You need to remain quiet, remember?"

When Kate gave another whimper of frustration, he hushed her by placing his free palm over her mouth. His right hand remained between her legs to continue his sensual assault, probing the delicate tissue, rubbing lightly. Kate strove to maintain control. He was as strong-willed as she was, and he was leaving her no choice but to submit to him.

"You are not . . . playing fairly," she complained in a muffled tone.

"No." She heard the smile in his voice as he drew his fingers along the crevice, stroking, parting her sensitive flesh.

"Open your legs for me, lovely Kate. . . ."

She gave in, closing her eyes, her head falling back against his shoulder.

The next moment he gently slid one finger inside her. Kate arched wildly against him, her heart racing with echoing thunder.

"Steady," he urged. Bending his head, he touched the frantic pulse in her neck with his lips while he plied her folds with his finger, gliding slowly, sinking just deeply enough inside to linger and tease before withdrawing again.

She was panting a little when he pushed her thighs farther apart and a second finger joined the first with a sweetly probing eroticism.

Kate whimpered again, her hands instinctively clenching at the silk fabric of her gown. She was suddenly a quivering, trembling jumble of nerve endings, and Deverill was encouraging her abandon with every caress, every provocative whisper.

Her hips began moving instinctively in a primitive, needful rhythm. He was wooing her senses, his wicked fingers sheathed in her pulsing warmth while his thumb attended the swollen nub and the throbbing knot of nerves there. She could feel the walls of her woman's passage stretching, heating, could feel her dampness grow, seeping and spreading from her core to her inner thighs.

"Lord, I want you. I have imagined what your lovemaking would be like, your lovely body coiled around mine. . . ."

He pressed his lips in the curve of her neck, feathering her skin with kisses, sending pleasure rocking through Kate as he stroked her with torturous intent. The heat rising inside her centered around the imprisoning caress of his hand, yet he made her whole body burn.

In another score of heartbeats, she was writhing. Suddenly, the pleasure was too keen to be borne. Her hips jerked, driving her sex against his fingers. Sensation tore through her, spiraling outward.

She gave herself up to the convulsive climax he urged upon her, her body shaking. The intensity of it stole her breath away.

Even when her spasms faded, Deverill kept his fingers where they were. Kate sagged back against him, her eyes tightly closed. If he hadn't been holding her, she would have slipped to the floor.

Eventually, though, he pushed her skirts down and, still supporting her, turned her in his arms. Then he tipped her face up and his lips found hers tenderly.

His slow, thorough, heart-stopping kiss devastated all her remaining willpower, rendering her utterly weak and helpless.

When at last he pulled away, Kate gazed up at him blindly. Once again he had left her dazed with pleasure. Even through her daze, however, one thought kept returning. She wanted more from Deverill than just pleasure. She wanted him to want *her* for more than just pleasure. She wanted him to love her.

So what do you intend to do about it?

Her sight clearing, she realized Deverill was gazing down at her with unmistakable desire. She refused to look away, but the heat generated by his look made her blood sizzle.

Then he drew her hand to the front of his satin breeches. "Once again you have caused me great pain," he accused, a spark of humor lacing the strain in his voice.

"It is your own fault," Kate rasped.

Determined to seize control back from him, she withdrew her hand from his grasp. But in that moment, she hit upon a plan.

She didn't want to lose Deverill—to that witch Julia Dalton or even to that paragon of bridal candidates, Daphne Farnwell. Therefore, she would heed Maura's wise advice to act.

She had no other choice, Kate reminded herself. The women in her family were not shrinking violets. No self-respecting Wilde lady would sit back and relinquish her gentleman to a rival, or worse, actively help the object of her affection find someone else to wed.

If she wanted Deverill, she needed to fight for him.

Making up her mind, she took a deep breath. She would answer "yes" to his marriage offer.

At least conditionally.

A betrothal would keep him safe from the likes of Julia Dalton and Phoebe Armitage for the moment. More crucially, it would give her time to see if she could change his mind about love . . . perhaps even the chance to make him love her.

Regaining a measure of her strength from her new resolve, Kate reached up and slid her arms around his neck. "I think you are right," she murmured, holding his surprised gaze.

She could tell she had caught Deverill off guard; she had shocked herself a little as well.

"How so?" he replied cautiously.

"I believe I will accept your proposal of marriage after all."

Chapter Ten

Savoring his stunned silence, Kate bit back a smile. It felt good to turn the tables on Deverill for once, to put *him* on the defensive. He was eyeing her skeptically, as if he couldn't credit her sudden change of heart.

She lifted a quizzical eyebrow. "Yesterday you said you might want to marry me. Are you already reneging on your offer?"

"No."

"Well then, I will agree to a temporary engagement."

He frowned. "Why temporary?"

"You said you wanted protection from the machinations of Lady Dalton and Miss Armitage. A formal arrangement will shield you from them and any other fortune hunters hounding you."

"You are suggesting we enter into a sham betrothal?"

"No, the betrothal will be entirely real. Whether the

wedding ever takes place is the question. During our time in France, we can come to know each other better. Just consider, Deverill. After being in close proximity for days or even weeks, we might be ready to murder each other. With a temporary understanding, we can easily call off the betrothal when we return to England."

Deverill shook his head in disbelief, although that distinctive look of amusement returned to his eyes. "I won't change my mind about wanting to wed you," he assured her.

"But *I* may. We have very different priorities. We need to see if there is any hope of us developing a deeper attachment. If you are still of the same mind then as now, there is no point in continuing a betrothal."

Sobering, Deverill curled his mouth. "So we are back to the matter of love."

"Did you expect otherwise?" When he was silent, Kate searched his face and found only skepticism written there. Determinedly, she made her dozenth effort to explain her deeply held beliefs. "You have made carnal desire the basis of our relationship, Deverill. I want much more in a marriage. Feelings and emotions are more important than any carnal attraction."

"For you, perhaps."

"That is precisely my point. The very notion of love is merely a game to you. You want to win for the sake of winning, regardless of your personal feelings. Indeed, you use passion as a weapon to render me witless, so you can get your way, whatever that might be. Do you deny it?"

His expression grew enigmatic. "I have been clear about wanting to free you from your inhibitions."

"Ah yes. You want to liberate me from prudishness and blind adherence to conventions. Well, you will have to cease your campaign. I am not willing to jeopardize my reputation for a few moments of illicit passion, even if you are."

As if debating his own thoughts, Deverill looked off into the distance, then softly chuckled to himself. "Do you realize how many women would leap at the chance to wed me?"

Kate smiled reluctantly. "I do. But those are my terms. I understand why they may be too onerous for you."

"I suppose," he said slowly, "there is another advantage to a betrothal. It will lend a measure of propriety to our journey. And we could be alone in the same room without raising eyebrows."

"Yes," Kate agreed, "but we must both behave with more circumspection from now on. As it is, we are courting scandal every time we are together. Our betrothal cannot be only about seduction. *You* may not care if we are caught in a compromising position, but I do."

Glancing back, he aimed his focus intently on her. "If you were compromised, you would have no choice but to marry me."

"I will always have a choice," Kate retorted. "You

could never coerce me into marriage. And you should know by now that I don't respond well to threats."

Meeting her gaze steadily, he seemed to realize she was not bluffing, for he smiled imperceptibly and nodded. "I do know. Very well, I agree to your terms."

The alacrity of his acceptance surprised her. Kate studied Deverill for a long moment, wondering what he had up his sleeve.

But he allowed her no more time for reflection. "If that is settled, I propose we move up our voyage to France. It will simplify matters greatly if we set sail next week."

"What do you mean?" Kate asked. "Mrs. Cuthbert's wedding is next week."

"We can leave directly afterward."

"So soon?"

"You want the matter of your parents' fate resolved quickly, don't you?"

"Yes, of course." She was very eager to afford them a proper memorial after all these years.

"And I will be glad to end these damned interminable social rituals," Deverill said almost cheerfully. "Searching for a shipwreck will be far more interesting. We should begin planning for the trip in earnest. I will arrange a meeting with Macky for tomorrow if possible."

Kate pursed her lips in thought. "I will have to advise my uncle Cornelius and aunt Rachel at once if they are to accompany us. I will write to them at Beauvoir first thing in the morning."

"Good. Then let us announce our betrothal now."

When Deverill took her hand to lead her back to the ballroom, Kate resisted. "*Now?* Tonight?"

"It will give notice to the fortune hunters that I am off-limits. And I am not allowing you time to change your mind, either."

She didn't intend to change her mind, Kate thought as she accompanied him from the parlor. And yet when they entered the crowded ballroom a few moments later, a panicky feeling welled in her stomach. A formal announcement in public would make a betrothal to Deverill all too real.

He made good on his plan, though, and proceeded directly to the orchestra. At the conclusion of the current dance, he commanded the attention of the guests by proclaiming in a proud voice, "Pray, allow me to share my good news. Lady Katharine Wilde has agreed to make me the happiest of men by consenting to be my wife."

Immediately the company broke into excited chatter, while Deverill punctuated his announcement by looking deeply into her eyes. Bringing her hand to his lips, he kissed her fingers. "I am fortunate to have captured the brightest star in the heavens," he said softly.

That tender, intimate expression was for the benefit of the company, Kate knew, yet she wanted so badly for it to be real.

Tearing her gaze from his, she glanced around her and found the reactions varied. She heard whispers about how romantic Lord Valmere's declaration was, but she could see that some of the younger ladies were visibly disappointed to have lost London's most exciting bachelor.

Maura seemed only a little surprised and, upon joining Kate, embraced her happily. Ash bent to kiss her cheek and murmur in her ear with cynical amusement, "So the preeminent matchmaker finally meets her match."

On the other hand, Lady Dalton, who had come late to the ball, gave her a malignant glare.

Kate flashed back a pointed smile of satisfaction. Lady X's goading had lit a fire under her, although her rival would be incensed to know it. She now intended to pursue Deverill herself.

Yet it would be the challenge of a lifetime, Kate had no doubt. He wanted a superficial relationship, a marriage of convenience based on mere passion, but she needed to make him want love.

Kate managed a moment alone with Maura to explain the plan for a trial betrothal and to thank her for her prodding. "You were right. I must be willing to make my own fate and fight for him."

Kate then spent the next quarter hour standing by her new fiancé's side, accepting felicitations and trying to will away the knots in her stomach. Events were moving so quickly, she felt a bit dazed.

For better or worse, she was now engaged to Brandon Deverill, Baron Valmere. And somehow, some way, she would attempt the daunting task of winning his heart.

* * *

Only after parting ways with the Wildes at the end of the long evening did Brandon acknowledge his keen feeling of satisfaction. He was now engaged to Kate, the first step in securing her hand in marriage.

Embarking sooner on the journey to France would likely aid in his goal. Different environs would give him better odds of proving their compatibility and allow them more privacy as well, without constantly being in the fishbowl of London society, and without having her entire family to contend with, especially her highly protective older brother.

It was not an auspicious sign, therefore, when Ash said he would call at Fenton's Hotel the next morning to discuss the temporary nature of their betrothal over breakfast. But for the time being, Brandon intended to savor his achievement.

After retiring to bed, he spent the interval before sleep recalling the moment he'd announced his betrothal to Kate—in particular his uncommon sense of pride that she had consented to be his, even if only under strict conditions. She had looked exceptionally striking tonight in a sapphire-blue gown that set off her creamy skin and fiery hair.

Yet her tantalizing beauty, her feminine grace, her silvery laugh were only a small cause of his possessiveness toward her. He couldn't help recalling the image of Kate at her most defenseless, when he'd brought her to passion not once but twice in the past several days. The flush suffusing her face, the dazed look in her green eyes . . . He would do well to forget those sensual memories during a visit from her brother, though.

When Ash appeared at his hotel room door promptly at nine, he began with a not-so-subtle warning. "I presume you remember that Kate is my sister? I am trusting you to safeguard her during your time in France."

"You know I will do my utmost."

"It's surprising that she even consented to a provisional betrothal," Ash mused. "If I recall your manner toward each other years ago, you sometimes quarreled yourselves into a standstill."

"Perhaps that was a large reason I couldn't forget her during all the time I was away," Brandon admitted. "In truth, I primarily returned to England in order to claim her."

Ash seemed at first relieved, then amused. "You ought not tell her you mean to claim her."

"I won't. I know better than to get her back up."

"That's our Kate, independent to the bone."

"I intend to convince her that we make a suitable match. For me, she is the most ideal candidate by far, and I believe I am the same for her."

"I suspect so."

"Then I have your blessing to wed her?" Brandon asked.

"Yes. Frankly, I would be grateful if you would," Ash replied. "Kate is much too alone, especially now that the rest of us have wed. Someone with her nature is not meant to be alone."

"Indeed," Brandon agreed wholeheartedly as he led the way down to the hotel dining room.

"How do you plan to succeed where so many others have failed?"

"I hope that finding your parents' shipwreck will go a long way toward winning her favor."

"You already have her favor. It is her heart you must win. I doubt she will marry without love."

"So she says."

Ash smiled. "As long as you realize what you are up against, you stand a chance. You can count on the family's assistance if you need it."

"Thank you. I very well may call on you."

He was under no illusions about the difficulty of his challenge—to change Kate's mind about mutual love being a condition for their marriage, so that she would accept him just as he was, closed heart and all.

To that end, he intended to alter his strategy. Passion was not likely to convince her, he'd learned over the past few days. So he would woo Kate as she wanted to be wooed—with "emotions and feelings," as she was so fond of saying. No more seduction, at least of the physical kind. Instead, he needed to share more of himself, to curb his conquering male instincts and follow her rules of proper behavior for a change.

It would be a novel approach, pursuing her with the intent of winning her heart rather than only her body. Women had always come easily to him, but he would have to work hard to win Kate. He could also help his case by showing that he belonged in her family, and that he had their support.

Settling at a breakfast table with her brother, Brandon recalled a long-ago moment when the Wildes were partaking of a picnic by the lake at Beauvoir. Kate was in her element, surrounded by her loved ones, her laugh filled with life and joy.

She was much more guarded now, and he was largely to blame. He could see through her sophisticated social mask, though. Could sense her vulnerability beneath her confident, independent demeanor.

He was counting on that vulnerability to aid him when he embarked on a real courtship. If she wanted romance rather than passion, then he would endeavor to provide it.

Chapter Eleven

To plan for the journey, Brandon set his meeting with Beau Macklin at his cousin Trey's house that afternoon. It would be a reunion of his former fellow Guardians—almost like old times. Additionally, the location would allow Kate the opportunity to meet another auburn-haired beauty—Trey's wife, Antonia.

Macky was already present when Brandon arrived with Kate. Once the introductions were made, Antonia graciously invited them to stay for tea after they finished the business of their visit: Determining the date and details of the voyage, preparing to visit the pauper's grave where Lady Beaufort was buried, and finally, developing a strategy to deal with the pirates they would likely encounter while attempting to locate the shipwreck. Trey sat in on the discussion to offer his counsel and volunteer his expertise if needed.

Macky began by reporting the findings of his investigation some months earlier, repeating for Brandon's benefit his conclusions about Lady Beaufort's demise and the explosive fire that had occurred on board the ship, the *Zephyr,* over a dozen years ago upon its attempted return to England. Then he laid out maps of Aquitaine and the southwestern coast of France.

Watching them pore over the maps together, Kate remarked, "It appears as if you have done this before."

Brandon smiled, remembering the many clandestine missions the Guardians had planned while he was a member. "We have."

Macky indicated a location on one map. "From what we can surmise, the *Zephyr* sailed from the river port of Bordeaux, here, heading for the Bay of Biscay. Shortly before reaching the seaport of Royan on the Gironde estuary, the ship was rocked by an explosion and fire. The *Zephyr* attempted to turn toward shore, then drifted into one of the coves that dot the shoreline where it floundered and sank somewhere near the village of Saint-Georges-de-Didonne, here. Flotsam and debris ended up on the neighboring beaches, but since the incident occurred so long ago, no one I spoke to could identify the exact location of the wreck. Somehow Lady Katharine's mother survived and washed ashore also, downstream of St. Georges. She is buried here, on the outskirts of Royan."

When Kate's expression grew shadowed, Brandon knew she was contemplating her mother's sad fate.

"Additionally, St. Georges is a den for pirates,"

Macky continued after a moment. "The inhabitants are mostly poor fishermen, so they augment their incomes by raiding foreign vessels and storing their contraband in the grottoes and caves in the chalk cliffs. But they know every cove and inlet along the coast. They also control the commerce in that area. If you intend to search for a shipwreck, you will have to deal with them. Once you arrive, you could perhaps hire them to search for the site and salvage any sunken treasure."

Trey chimed in then. "Can pirates be trusted to turn over any valuables they find? I understand the de Chagny jewels were considered priceless."

Macky answered. "That depends on how much supervision you plan to give and how many of the jewels remain."

Kate spoke quietly. "Most were already removed by the saboteur before the *Zephyr* sank, and recovering what remains is secondary to my mind. The jewels belonged to my aunt's French family who were guillotined during the Revolution, and so hold little personal meaning for me or my family. The only item of personal significance is my father's signet ring, which no doubt will be impossible to find. It will be enough to properly bury my mother. And if we find the sunken ship, I would like to hold a ceremony to honor the dead, including my father and Aunt Angelique and Uncle Lionel."

"Were you able to meet with any of the pirates?" Brandon asked Macky.

"Yes. Their leader—a man by the name of Jean Louvel—captains a brigantine."

"Louvel?" Brandon said sharply. "A large, swarthy man with a scar on his left cheek?"

"Yes."

Brandon frowned. "That might present a problem. I have tangled with him before, in America."

Kate gave him a puzzled look. "Do you mean not all French pirates aided the Americans during the war?"

"Most did, Louvel included. His crew joined our fight against England. But my conflict with him was personal."

"So you are adversaries?"

"You might say that," Brandon replied, recalling his clash with the pirate had been over a woman. "The last time we met, we exchanged sword blows."

Kate gazed at him in consternation. "Will your relationship affect our ability to find the *Zephyr*?"

"Perhaps," Brandon said honestly. "Kate, you chose me to accompany you to France because I was most likely to be on good terms with the pirates there. But that strategy is in jeopardy now. I will do better dealing with Louvel alone."

She frowned as realization dawned. "You mean to leave me behind?"

"I don't want to risk your safety. You should remain here in England and trust me to carry out your task."

Her expression turned earnest. "Of course I must

accompany you." Brandon could hear the quaver in her voice in addition to the rising concern. "You wouldn't deny me the chance to bury my parents, would you?"

He hesitated, then offered another argument against her involvement. "If I recall, you said you have a dread of sailing."

"I can't allow that to stop me. Please, Deverill . . . I must go."

Brandon nodded slowly. If he refused to escort Kate, she would merely go on her own. And he was still the best person to protect her, notwithstanding his hostile former association with Louvel. Furthermore, his main objective was to convince Kate they were a good match, which could only happen if she accompanied him. "Very well, but as a precaution we should develop an alternate strategy to deal with Louvel should our first go awry. Trey, I may ask for your assistance."

"I'm happy to serve in any way I can," his cousin said.

Macky interjected a question. "Will you need someone to translate for you? Only some of the villagers there speak English."

Kate rallied enough to volunteer. "My French is fairly fluent. Aunt Angelique taught me from a young age, and later my governesses and teachers at boarding school drummed grammar and vocabulary into my head."

"I know a little French also," Brandon added.

For another half hour, they discussed more details about the enterprise—including the salvage calculations and equipment design recently made by Kate's cousin Quinn—and finally made plans to meet with the captain of Brandon's ship on the morrow.

Later, when they went to the drawing room for tea, Trey said in an aside to Brandon, "I presume Lady Katharine knows nothing about the Guardians."

"No, and I don't plan on telling her until we are wed."

Trey nodded. In accordance with the charter, members were sworn to secrecy, and only spouses could be told about the real purpose and history of the elite organization that was centuries old.

Brandon was glad that if necessary he could call on support from the Guardians, since he now had an uneasy feeling about this mission. Given his bad blood with Louvel, successfully resolving the issues of the shipwreck was not only less likely, but walking into this particular pirates' den could prove dangerous for Kate, and even put her life at risk along with his own.

Yet as he had promised her brother, he would do everything in his power to keep her safe. And as he had promised himself, he would use the opportunity to convince Kate that her future was with him as his wife.

The final week before their departure was a whirlwind of activity for Kate. Planning the final details of the journey, preparing for Nell's wedding to Mr.

Horatio Underwood, wrapping up social engagements, and saying farewells while pretending to celebrate her own betrothal occupied her every waking moment.

The biggest surprise, however, was the change she noticed in Deverill: He matched his circumspection in private with his circumspection in public. There was nothing risqué or untoward in any of his actions, and no physical contact whatsoever.

Not that she trusted his apparent conversion. He might be making an attempt to behave, yet he couldn't change his intrinsic nature. It was only prudent to question his motives. And regardless of his restraint, the attraction between them was still there in spades, sizzling beneath the surface. Merely a look from Deverill still made Kate's stomach flutter and her pulse race. Indeed, now that she knew the sensual pleasure he could give her, she craved his touch even when she knew her desire drastically weakened her willpower.

Ironically, she couldn't quell her discontent at this softer, tamer, more gentlemanly version of Deverill.

Take, for example, his initial meeting with her uncle Cornelius and aunt Rachel when they arrived in London for the wedding. Deverill was the epitome of a perfect suitor, not only conducting an overt courtship for their benefit, Kate observed, but appealing to her scholarly uncle's intellect and thoroughly charming Rachel, who had only become a member of the Wilde family last year, and who was wary of most noblemen because of her difficult past with her brute of a late husband. By week's end, both her uncle and aunt were clearly enamored of Deverill.

On the day of the wedding, the weather cooperated and sunlight filled the church. Plump, middle-aged Nell looked beautiful, dressed in a pale blue gown with an overskirt of ivory lace while beaming with joy. And Mr. Underwood was clearly besotted with his bride. Kate found herself weeping happy tears as she watched their vows being spoken.

Sitting beside her, Deverill silently handed her his handkerchief. "Why the devil are you crying?" he murmured as the bride and groom walked together down the aisle, accepting felicitations from the guests.

"I don't really know," Kate said, sniffing. "I suppose because Nell's first marriage was arranged against her wishes, and during her widowhood, she struggled financially. She is truly a good person and deserves the best life has to offer." Kate wiped her eyes. "I am wildly happy for her, even if I am sad for myself at losing her as my companion. I will miss her terribly."

"You should be pleased that you matched them. Even I can see how much in love they are." Deverill gave a soft chuckle. "I confess, it has a charming appeal. I am not accustomed to weddings where the bridal couple is in love."

"A pity," Kate replied before being struck by a sudden realization. Deverill was making an effort to share his feelings, just as she had asked of him. Perhaps she was being too quick to suspect him of insincerity, or worse, some sort of furtive calculation. Perhaps, after all, he was striving to be the suitor she wanted, without any hidden purpose in mind.

The wedding breakfast after the ceremony was held at the Beaufort mansion in Grosvenor Square. When the guests had assembled in the drawing room, Kate had a moment to speak to Daphne, who shared a secret with Rachel, although few people besides the Wildes knew of it.

"I wish to apologize, Daphne," Kate said in a low voice. "You must think me a grasping dunce for trying to pair you with Lord Valmere, only to become engaged to him myself the same evening. It was unkind of me to raise your hopes."

Surprisingly, Daphne gave a laugh. "Not at all. My hopes were never raised. Valmere made it clear from the first that he had his sights set on you."

Kate glanced across the room at Deverill, who was conversing with her brother, Ash. "He did?"

"Yes, indeed. I took his hints as a warning not to assume too much regarding his attentions. It is you he wants, Kate, not I."

Maura joined them just then, in time to overhear Daphne's last remark. When Daphne left, Maura gave Kate a sober look. "If he wants you that keenly, I hope it is for the right reasons. I know you said this betrothal was temporary, Kate, but I worry that you might lose your heart to him irrevocably this time and invite an even worse case of unrequited love."

Kate took a deep breath. "I promise I won't," she vowed. "I well know the dangers."

Yet Kate knew Maura was right. She couldn't let her longing for love with Deverill make her blind to reality or expose her to fresh pain.

The trouble was that barely two hours later, directly after the company had partaken of a grand wedding feast, Deverill approached her with a small velvet box.

"I have a betrothal gift for you," he said, opening the box to display a pendant on a delicate gold chain. "St. Nicholas is the patron saint of sailors. This medallion is supposed to keep you safe at sea. You can wear it on our voyage."

Kate felt her heart melting. "It is lovely," she murmured, accepting the box with delight and awe. Deverill had remembered her morbid fear of sailing and wanted to reassure her and buck up her confidence.

"Turn around. I will help you put it on."

When she complied, he draped the necklace around her neck and fastened the clasp.

The light brush of his fingers against her nape sent a jolt of sensation through Kate, yet for once she didn't think it was a deliberate ploy on his part to gain physical mastery over her. Deverill had not tried to get her alone. On the contrary, they were standing in a crowded, noisy room filled with wedding guests and servants.

Turning back around, Kate gazed up at him. "Thank you. It was extremely thoughtful of you."

Deverill smiled. "You wanted a romantic gesture.

This small token of affection is something a proper suitor would give the lady he is courting."

Trying to keep the moment light, she gave him a smile in return. "There might be hope for you yet."

And yet . . . she was conscious of a distinct need to remain on guard with the new Deverill. Chances were, this was his more devious way of winning her over—with tender, intimate displays of kindness. He might have left off trying to seduce her body, but now he was intent on seducing her heart, which could be even more dangerous, Kate thought, recalling Maura's warning.

She wished he could have meant the gesture as a token of his love, but she would be wiser to count his gift as just another step in his plan to compel her surrender.

And unlike six years ago, this time she was determined to be wise.

Chapter Twelve

Gray skies threatening rain seemed a poor omen for a voyage when Kate arrived at the bustling London docks with her uncle and aunt the next morning. The din of activity did nothing to soothe her anxiety at the prospect of boarding a ship, either.

With her stomach in knots, she searched the throng for any sign of Deverill. The quay teemed with drays and wagons transporting merchandise and produce to and from the numerous boats and seafaring craft anchored on the River Thames, while odors of tar and fish accompanied the raucous cries of seagulls.

Miraculously, though, Deverill somehow found them in the crowd and ordered their luggage transferred to his ship by two strapping sailors. Then, taking Kate's arm, he escorted her toward a sleek, schooner-rigged vessel. Negotiating the gangway, she wanted to turn and flee, but Deverill swung her down the last step, onto the polished wooden deck, before assisting Rachel and Cornelius.

"Welcome aboard the *Galene,*" Deverill said.

Her scholarly uncle's ears pricked up. "Named for one of the Greek sea nymphs, the Nereides, I presume?"

"Exactly."

Deverill then introduced them to the ship's captain, Benjamin Halsey, a weathered but jovial-looking fellow.

"You couldn't be in better hands," Deverill claimed, no doubt to reassure Kate.

Kate felt slightly comforted. She had to remember that Captain Halsey was an expert seaman, as was Deverill himself. The crew also looked supremely efficient as they scurried over the ship, checking lines and raising sails for the three tall masts.

Shortly, Deverill led them down a ladder to a lower deck and along a companionway to the cabins assigned to them.

"You are in luck. The *Galene* is a passenger vessel rather than a merchantman, built by my shipping company for speed, not cargo. You will have your own quarters, albeit small and spartan."

He opened a door for her uncle and aunt, then indicated the next door for Kate.

Preceding Deverill into her cabin, she saw that it was sparsely equipped with a narrow bunk, a washstand with commode and basin, a rack of pegs for hanging clothing, and a cabinet for storage.

Kate went directly to the porthole window, however, and bent to look out.

"Not luxurious," Deverill added, "but adequate enough I trust."

"Yes, thank you. It is more than adequate."

"Our voyage to France will only last two days and nights, three at most," he reminded her as if he understood her phobia about being trapped on a sinking ship.

That is two days too many. Scolding herself, she took a breath, trying to steady her nerves.

"Would you care to remain here and settle in?" Deverill asked.

Kate turned back to him. "I would rather go above deck with you. It feels a bit oppressive here, as if the walls are closing in on me—although I suppose they are properly called bulkheads."

He flashed her an encouraging smile. "I commend you on knowing the correct terminology."

"Quinn spent the last year designing a sailing ship powered by steam, so I took it upon myself to learn about his passion. He hopes to launch it this summer."

"Your brother told me about your cousin's venture. I certainly would like to see it." Putting a hand at her back to guide her from the cabin, Deverill suggested lightly, "Feel free to indulge in a fit of hysterics if you wish."

"I am sorry," Kate said, flushing. "I am not usually the hysterical sort."

"You needn't apologize. And I know very well what sort you are."

They collected Rachel and Cornelius on the way topside, and Deverill deposited them at the railing on the foredeck, out of the way of the crew, who were preparing to weigh anchor.

"Excuse me, I shall return shortly," he said with a polite bow.

Kate regretted his departure at once, even though her relatives were standing right beside her.

For a while they said little as they watched the crew at work and listened to the unfamiliar sounds: Captain Halsey's firm commands, the creak of timber and mooring cables, and finally the snapping of sails overhead as the canvas caught the wind.

Feeling the ship begin to move, Kate clenched her fingers. In response, Cornelius put one arm about her shoulders, and the other around his wife.

Kate sent him a grateful smile. Her middle-aged uncle boasted a tall, refined build and aristocratic features, but his thinning silver hair and spectacles gave him the vague air of a bookworm. Rachel was shorter but slender, elegant, and still a beauty, despite her pale complexion and the ample gray streaking her dark hair.

Kate noticed that Rachel didn't appear much more at ease than she did.

"I am no better a sailor than you are," Rachel confessed. "I am too susceptible to seasickness."

"At least you have a valid excuse." Kate glanced at

her own white knuckles where she gripped the rail. "Aren't we a pair?" she asked with a weak attempt at humor. "I regret putting you both through this. If not for chaperoning me, you would not have to take this journey."

Cornelius shook his head. "No, no, this was my decision as well. I want to find my brother's resting place as much as you do."

Some time passed before the *Galene* had threaded a path between other ships and was sailing down the Thames toward the English Channel. Gulls swooped in low circles about the bow while the breeze that blew in Kate's face carried the scent of brine. As the canvas spread, she felt the schooner leap forward.

Almost immediately, Rachel professed queasiness from the rising and falling motion of the ship. "I think I should lie down," she murmured, looking a bit pale.

"Shall I go below with you?" Kate asked with concern.

Instantly Cornelius grew worried also. "No, I will escort her below."

Kate watched as, with great care, he guided his wife toward the hatch. His love for Rachel was blindingly obvious, in no small part because they had been separated for decades before being reunited by Skye.

Kate disliked being alone and so counted herself fortunate when Deverill appeared at her side. "I have made a hundred voyages and I am still in one piece," he remarked as if he could read her thoughts.

"That is gratifying to know," she said with little enthusiasm.

"You should look upon this as an adventure."

She fingered her medallion of St. Nicholas that he'd given her. Normally she craved adventure, but the possibility of drowning scrambled her rational mind. "I have been abroad only once. Our family accompanied Jack to France when he went to meet his royal father for the first time. If not for my dislike of sailing, I would be eager to see other parts of the world, yet I cannot help imagining what my parents went through in their final hours. . . ."

Realizing she was close to babbling, Kate bit her tongue.

"It is understandable," Deverill said, "that you are not comfortable sailing when you've had so little experience on board a ship. The first time I climbed the rigging, I was terrified."

She couldn't picture him being terrified of anything. He looked in his natural element, with his easy stance on the swaying deck and his raven locks ruffled by the wind.

When she didn't respond, he tried another tack. "What is this? The intrepid Princess Katharine admitting to weakness? I must say your fragility is unexpected. You are usually quite fearless." He gave her a teasing smile. "The Kate I know would never let a little apprehension stop her. Remember the ruins when you risked your life to save an injured lad?"

"That was different. That was dry land."

"Not so very different," he countered. "You resolved then not to let fear rule you because there were larger goals at stake. Just think of the end results of this voyage. You will give your mother a proper memorial and perhaps your father and other kin as well."

"I suppose you are right."

"Of course I am right. I always am."

When that didn't elicit a rise from her, he arched an eyebrow at her. "This is a twist I relish. You require me to coddle you."

With that charge, Kate bestirred herself to retort. "You are mocking me."

"Never," he replied with a straight face.

She returned a weak smile. "Perhaps you should toss me overboard now and put me out of my misery."

"Don't think I won't, if you become too much of a burden."

Kate managed a small laugh. Ribbing her was Deverill's way of easing her fear, she knew. He was trying to buck up her courage, and for that she was grateful. She hated feeling so craven.

"Why don't I tell you about my shipping company?" Deverill asked. "If you intend to wallow in your apprehension, the least I can do is attempt to distract you."

"Yes, please do," Kate said fervently.

"As you may know, my family owns a fleet of merchant ships, all built to our designs, headquartered in Virginia. Richmond, to be precise. . . ."

For the next hour, Deverill entertained her with tales about his business endeavors. Surprisingly, Kate found herself diverted enough that she didn't mind when the schooner tacked out of the sound into the wind-driven rollers of the Channel. She was even growing accustomed to the rhythmic pitch of the deck as the bow of the ship carved purposefully through each successive wave.

Holding on to the railing, Kate glanced overhead at the forest of masts and billowing white canvas. She could see two men in the rigging, swinging from the yards without any trace of uncertainty or fear.

Still, the motion reminded her of her aunt.

"I should go below and check on Aunt Rachel. I hope her nausea is not too severe."

"I will have our cook make her some ginger tea."

"You have ginger tea on board?"

"An ample supply," he said dryly. "My mother is a poor sailor and insists on being well stocked."

"I could help prepare it," Kate offered. "I would like to stay busy."

"I will take you to the galley, then."

They left the foredeck for the waist of the ship. When they reached the galley, Deverill turned her over to the cook, who fired up the iron stove to boil water.

When eventually Kate carried a mug of steaming tea to her aunt's cabin, Rachel still looked pale but not entirely indisposed. Instead, she was sitting up in her bunk, attempting to concentrate on reading a book.

"My seasickness is not as extreme as I feared," she told Kate.

"Then perhaps you should return outside. The fresh air could do you good."

"I am better off here, my dear. I believe you should have time alone with Lord Valmere."

Kate's instincts went on alert. "Should I? Are you trying to matchmake, Aunt?"

Her suspicions were confirmed when Rachel and Cornelius shared a guilty look. When Kate narrowed her gaze disapprovingly, her uncle cleared his throat and scurried from the cabin.

"Have you only been pretending to be ill?" Kate asked her aunt.

"Not in the least. Lying down truly helped relieve my nausea." When Kate appeared skeptical, Rachel flushed. "You should not be put out if we wish to give you more privacy with Valmere, my dear. You know that we only want what is best for you. I can see the strong attachment between the two of you and think you should nurture it."

Kate couldn't repress a faint smile. "Your machinations are worthy of my own, although I would never have expected Uncle to act as your romantic accomplice."

Rachel's cheeks grew warmer. "In truth, he is just as eager as I to see Valmere's suit prosper. Perhaps because we were separated for years. Cornelius and I wasted so much time, Kate. You don't want to live with our same regrets."

Kate gave a sober nod. Almost everyone believed longtime bachelor Lord Cornelius to be a boring, staid aberration in the Wilde family, and that, because he eschewed social interactions in favor of his ancient tomes, he hadn't inherited the legacy of passion the rest of their clan claimed. But "almost everyone" was mistaken. Last year had come a startling revelation even for his family—that Cornelius and Rachel were former lovers and that Daphne Farnwell was their daughter, the product of their illicit affair two decades earlier.

Looking sad at the memory, Rachel searched Kate's face intently. "If you think Valmere is your true mate, you should do everything in your power to make your union come to pass."

Kate refrained from commenting. She wanted to trust that her long-held beliefs about love and passion and romance were real. That Deverill could someday feel as deeply for her as she could feel about him. That he could learn to let down his guard and open his heart to her.

For now, however, she simply wanted to survive the Channel crossing.

After keeping Rachel company for a time, Kate went above deck again. And once again, her uncle chose to flee rather than be taken to task.

Kate was reassured by Deverill's presence, though, when he returned to her side. She felt safer when she was with him. When the ship rose and fell on a high swell, she gripped the railing. Deverill never budged, but instead braced his legs naturally and swayed to the ship's roll. But of course, he was accustomed to life on the high seas, impervious to waves.

As the day wore on, they partook of a light luncheon in the galley. Afterward, Kate returned to her station near the bow to watch the gray waters of the Channel race past. She could see land in the distance. The schooner was heading south and west now, she knew. Tomorrow they would reach the even more dangerous seas of the Bay of Biscay. For now, though, her anxiety began to ease.

But then dusk started to fall, and her nerves returned, despite her best efforts to tamp them down. Her aunt and uncle joined her and Deverill in the galley for a simple dinner, but then retired to their cabin. Kate lingered, reluctant to be alone.

In fact, she wanted Deverill to take her mind off her fear of drowning. To her shame, her hands started to shake. Her hands never shook.

"You are cold," he murmured. Rising from the table, he shed his coat and draped it around her shoulders.

His body heat was still in the fabric, which comforted Kate a measure, enough that her lips formed a wincing smile of self-ridicule. "Not cold exactly. More lily-livered."

Deverill chuckled. "Clearly you require something stronger than tea. I have a fine brandy that I've been saving for a special occasion."

Turning, he rummaged in a cupboard and brought out a bottle, then poured an ample amount into a mug for her and sat beside her on the bench once again.

"Here, drink up," he ordered.

Swallowing a gulp, Kate felt the burn down her throat, then eyed the depth of the liquid with skepticism. "If I drink all this, I will get foxed."

"Being a little foxed could be the best thing for you."

Replying in his same spirit, she tried to jest. "See, this is another way we are incompatible. I wouldn't make a good wife for a magnate whose company builds ships."

"No, but you will make a much better baroness than I make a baron."

"True." She was an expert in ballrooms, while he was expert in bedrooms and at sea.

Deverill was contemplating her with sympathy. "I promise I won't let anything happen to you, Kate."

She appreciated that he was willing to indulge her irrational trepidation, but shook her head. "You know you can't promise any such thing. You cannot command nature."

Taking another swallow, Kate recalled a memory of her cousin Quinn. "I realize now how Quinn felt. He once told me he'd designed his steam-driven ship because he hated being powerless to control fate. For years we all believed that if the *Zephyr* had been a steamship, it could have outrun the storm that sank it. As it turned out, the culprit wasn't a storm but an evil man bent on greed and revenge. I still suffer nightmares about my parents sinking," she admitted in a low voice.

Deverill reached out to touch the back of her hand where it rested on the table. "You are not alone, Kate. I have bad dreams of the recent war."

She looked up at him. All day she had been selfishly thinking only of herself. Giving herself a mental shake, she determined to do better. "I am sorry. What kind of dreams trouble *you*?"

His jaw hardened, and he drew back his hand. "I dislike talking about it."

"I cannot imagine what you went through," she murmured.

For a moment, he made no reply. "Most people cannot. Particularly your British aristocracy."

"It is your aristocracy now also," Kate reminded him gently.

"True." Deverill heaved a sigh. "Regrettably, I had loyalties to both sides but had to choose between them."

"Why did you elect to fight when you could have safely remained in England?"

"My American countrymen needed me. It would have been cowardly to think only of my own safety." His voice lowered an octave. "The worst part was visiting destruction on my own kin. Having to turn against my friends and colleagues like my cousin Trey and Macky and Hawk."

Kate fell silent. She hadn't often thought about the sacrifices Deverill had made, carrying out what he believed was his duty.

Looking down at the table before him, he became strangely introspective. "War is not glamorous or exciting. Indeed it's often senseless and idiotic. But in this case it was necessary. Your navy was vastly in the wrong to make slaves out of our seamen."

"They justified their actions by claiming the greater good. They needed to keep the navy strong to battle Boney."

"It was still wrong."

She felt his suppressed intensity. "Perhaps so," she allowed.

"There was too much killing and blood and pain," he added quietly.

Wanting to take his mind off his grisly memories, Kate steered the subject to his former service. "To hear Hawkhurst talk about it, serving in the British Foreign Office as you did was a noble calling. What did you do for the F.O.?"

"Many things. And I often supplied ships for our missions. There were always villains to vanquish—despots, local tyrants, Napoleon Bonaparte. We were able to make a real difference when Boney was threatening to take over the world."

"You also aided Aunt Bella some years ago, didn't

you? She said a number of her Foreign Office friends mounted a rescue when she was abducted by a Berber sheik."

He shook his head. "I was in America by then so I wasn't part of the rescue."

Kate thought back on Deverill's reasons for leaving for America. She had to admire him for fighting and risking death for what he believed in, even if his choice had taken him away from her.

"I am very glad you weren't injured, or worse," she said softly.

Deverill shrugged. "I rarely talk about it. I dislike even thinking about it." His smile was grim when he raised his gaze to hers. "See your influence? I've never before told anyone how I felt."

"Not even your family?"

He gave a mirthless huff of laughter. "Especially not my family. They didn't share my reservations, probably because they didn't have the close ties to England that I did. My father mainly sought retaliation for the losses of our ships and crews. My mother was angry that it disrupted her social routine. My younger brother was far too eager to hear about my adventures." Deverill smiled again, a bit sadly. "I once was adventurous. I loved the sea . . . until the war."

At his confession, a deluge of thoughts and feelings swamped Kate. "I am glad you told me. It isn't good to keep things like that bottled up inside you."

His gaze was level. “If you care to know why I don’t let myself feel, it’s because of the war.”

It surprised her, Deverill letting her see this darker, hidden side of himself. The deeper, conflicted man inside. But she was grateful.

His confession tugged on her heartstrings and made her reconsider. She’d been wrong to pressure him to feel, Kate reflected. There were good reasons he was detached and dispassionate. She’d wondered what had shaped him into the man he was, and now she better understood. Warring against his former friends and colleagues had scarred him. And he had no loving family to confide in, as she did.

At her new awareness, something sharp pierced her chest. If Deverill couldn’t feel tender emotions such as love, it was for his own self-protection.

She ought not try so hard to change him, Kate realized. Instead she should try to help him forget his violent past. She still believed if he was to learn to love, he had to open himself to healing emotions, not grim ones of war and death. But for now, he seemed to have had enough of introspection.

“The hour is late. You should get some sleep.”

“I suppose so,” Kate said reluctantly.

He had succeeded in distracting her from her own dark thoughts, but now they returned full force. Taking up a lantern, Deverill walked her to her cabin and preceded her inside.

After showing her how to properly secure the lantern on a shelf, he accepted the return of his coat and hung it on his arm.

As he turned to leave, though, a panicky feeling gripped Kate. "Deverill?"

"Yes?"

"Would you . . . would you please hold me for a moment?"

He raised an eyebrow. "You are the one who set the rules about no embracing."

"I know, but . . . this would not be an embrace exactly."

He hesitated, then crossed the small cabin and slid his arms around her, taking her in a light but protective grasp.

Gratefully, Kate buried her face in his chest. She could feel the steel warmth beneath the cambric fabric of his shirt.

When a short while later he reached up to smooth her hair tenderly, she let out a sigh. She felt safe with Deverill; she always had. She wished he could stay here with her all night long. She needed the sense of security he gave her. But of course they couldn't spend the night together without the benefit of marriage.

For a time he simply held her. Then pressing a light, chaste kiss on her forehead, Deverill stepped back.

When she looked up at him regretfully, he reached up and gave a featherlight blow to her chin with his knuckles. "Buck up, sweetheart. If you need me, I will be close by. Only two doors down from yours."

The calm timbre of his voice was reassuring, so

Kate forced herself to let him go. When the door closed behind him, she took a shaky breath.

She had to be brave. Even a fraction as brave as Deverill had been when he went off to fight a war he had never wanted.

Still, she knew it would be a very long night.

Chapter Thirteen

Leaving Kate in distress like that was hard, but protecting her reputation was more important, Brandon decided.

Falling asleep was also hard, he shortly discovered. The moment he shut his eyes, memories assaulted him—brutal recollections of hostilities against various British warships. *The explosions of cannon fire. The stench of gunpowder and smoke and blood. The agonized cries of wounded, dying men.*

All dredged up during his confessions to Kate this evening.

Confessions that were unfamiliar and foreign to him in their intimacy. Merely the fact that he'd disclosed his own nightmares to her was frankly remarkable.

He hadn't always been so closed off. The change had begun with his homecoming after his first successful battle at sea. With blood on his hands, he hadn't wanted or deserved the hero's welcome he'd received. Neither had he expected his family's macabre relish at his defeating the enemy so soundly. His father had been triumphant, his mother gleeful, his younger brother excited.

At least his brother's naïveté came from being fed tall tales of glorious naval victories during his sheltered and pampered youth. But, Brandon acknowledged, he should have predicted his parents' responses. His father had always been reserved and dictatorial, his mother proud and aloof. Both were possessive and vengeful when it came to preserving their dynasty and business investments.

Locking his jaw, Brandon rolled over in the narrow bunk and punched his pillow. For certain, he never wanted to become like his father, nor would he ever want a wife like his mother.

An image of Kate leapt into his mind. The contrast between the two women was so stark. His mother was cold and selfish while Kate was warm and generous and passionate.

Kate reveled in emotions—and was trying her damnedest to draw them out of him, despite his resistance.

Since the war, he'd forcibly constrained his emotions. Deliberately focused on forgetting the dark memories. Purposely avoided the pain that any sort of feeling brought. Yet tonight, for the first time in years, he had truly lowered his defenses.

Just as astonishing, sharing his feelings with Kate had felt . . . good. Strange but good.

Tonight Kate had also made him aware of something else: For a long time he had felt alone. Alone and incomplete and empty. As if a part of him was missing.

His heart, perhaps?

If so, could she help him find that missing organ?

It wasn't beyond the realm of possibility. Kate invoked his protective instincts—mightily—yet he sensed she had something *he* badly needed: That comforting feeling of sharing. Of togetherness. Of completeness.

Even more profound, the elusive prospect of joy that was genuinely alien to him.

He would never be the kind of man to let his emotions rule, Brandon knew, but more and more of late, he felt sensations bubbling up from the dark crater where he had long ago buried them. Something resembling hope.

Another realization struck him: He could try to become the man Kate wanted him to be. Not only to win her hand in marriage, but for his own sake as well.

If he could let himself feel, perhaps he could banish the emptiness inside of him. More crucially, perhaps he could fulfill the promise of a future with Kate that even now seemed maddeningly out of reach.

Kate passed a restless night, starting awake every time the schooner sank in a deep trough. When she dragged herself out of bed the following morning, she dressed and immediately went topside, preferring to be in the open air rather than trapped in the bowels of the ship.

The sight that greeted her, however, made her temporarily forget her own phobia: High above her head, Deverill was clinging to a yardarm, apparently securing a sail. Braced against the wind and rock of the ship, he looked as much at home challenging death as she did confronting a haughty society matron in her own drawing room.

Alarmed for him, Kate watched with bated breath as he finally climbed down.

"Whatever are you doing, risking your life like that?" she demanded when he reached her. "Cannot your crew see to the rigging?"

With a wave of his hand, he brushed off her concern. "I like to keep busy. You look pale," Deverill remarked, scanning her face.

Remembering her own difficulties, Kate forced a smile. "I will be very glad when we reach land."

"Only one more night, although I suspect we may be in for some rough water before then."

When he pointed to the gray clouds on the horizon, Kate felt her stomach tighten.

She forced herself to concentrate on the present moment, asking Deverill about his ships, his life at sea, and the network of commerce his family's company had built to export and import goods between America and Europe. But all the while she remained on edge.

Fortunately, that bout of foul weather chiefly bypassed them and the seas grew calmer. Late in the day, however, she could see another storm approaching. The skies grew dark again, while lightning flickered in the distance.

When a gusting wind spawned swelling waves flecked with whitecaps, her aunt and uncle retired to the comfort of their cabin. Soon the thunderheads grew more ominous and the increasingly choppy motion of the schooner made balance difficult.

With a strong wind whipping through the rigging, Captain Halsey sent sailors aloft to "reef the main topsail," Deverill explained. "Likely it is merely a squall, but to be safe, Halsey will trim the sails even farther, leaving only enough to steer the ship."

An hour later a pelting rain began. Deverill ordered Kate below and would brook no argument. "It isn't safe for you here," he added emphatically.

She had to agree. Despite clinging to the rail, she was already in danger of losing her footing on the pitching deck. Yet she went reluctantly, not wanting to stay below where she would be trapped if the ship capsized.

Kate negotiated the hatch and ladder, then staggered and groped her way along the dim companionway. She stopped at the first door to check on her aunt, and discovered that Rachel had been so miserable with nausea, Cornelius had given her a dose of laudanum to make her sleep.

Kate hated being alone just now, yet there was little room for her there, so she went to her own cabin. After carefully lighting a storm lantern and turning down the flame, she sat huddled on her bunk, striving to tamp down her fears. She was even more worried about Deverill and the crew, exposed as they were to the raw elements above.

Shortly the storm struck in its full fury. High waves battered the wooden hull of the ship, the thuds accompanied by creaks and groans of the schooner from the buffeting wind. Alarmed, Kate fought to maintain her courage while being bombarded with images from her worst nightmares.

Just then she heard a faint knock on the door. When it swung open, Deverill stood there wearing an oilskin, his face and hair streaming wet. The relief she felt at knowing he was safe was indescribable.

"I brought you a cold supper," he said quickly, crossing the short space to her. "Bread and cheese and meats. We can't risk a coal fire in the galley stove."

"Thank you," Kate replied, accepting the knapsack from him, even though she had no appetite. "Won't you stay and take supper with me?"

"I must get back. The crew is struggling, and Halsey needs all hands on deck managing the sails and bailing water."

"Please . . . take care."

Deverill flashed her a grin. "I will. I promised I

would escort you to France, and I always honor my promises."

Just then the schooner gave another eerie groan. When Kate flinched, he hastened to reassure her. "Those are only normal ship noises in a storm."

Kate nodded but shivered. Before she could say another word, Deverill bent down and pressed a light kiss on the top of her head.

He must have noted her damp hair and cloak, for he stood back and frowned at her. "Change out of those wet clothes at once before you catch a chill," he directed, then left as quickly as he'd come, shutting the door firmly behind him.

Kate complied with difficulty, bracing herself against the pitches and yaws of the ship as she shed her cloak and gown and corset and donned a serviceable gown of brown kerseymere, then pulled the pins from her hair and combed the damp, unruly mass with her fingers.

Still shivering in the chill air of the cabin, she settled back in the bunk and wrapped her arms around her knees, striving to maintain a semblance of composure. She had wanted to throw her arms around Deverill and keep him safe and have him keep *her* safe, but she'd had to let him go while she stayed behind to battle her waking nightmares alone.

When he returned to her cabin two hours later, Brandon found Kate much as he expected, shivering and wan and utterly unlike her usual vibrant self.

After stripping off his soggy oilskin and coat and boots, he sat beside her on the bunk, his back against the bulkhead, and gathered her close.

Weakly, Kate pressed her face into his shoulder, a docile response that had him worried.

"The worst is over," he assured her.

"How . . . do you know?" she asked in a small, hoarse voice.

"Years of experience."

The ship was steadier now. The howling wind had lessened, as had the lashing torrents from the night skies, although the rain kept up a steady, drumming beat.

Kate seemed oblivious to the improvement, however. "Please, stay with me. I can't bear to be alone any longer."

The tremor in her voice stabbed at his heart. "I will," he said gently. Now was not the time for teasing. She was chilled through and through. Indeed, she was shaking.

Shifting their positions, he stretched out on the narrow bunk, then pulled her close and wrapped himself around her. For a while he held her. Just held her . . . pressing his body against hers to warm her flesh. Yet he was keenly aware of how powerfully she affected him, how hard and aching his loins were.

This wasn't the moment to feel such stark lust, Brandon warned himself. He should merely want to take care of Kate, to comfort her.

When she stirred against him, he drew back to survey her. Her complexion still looked very pale, but the deep auburn of her hair shone like fire in the glow of the lantern. She was so damned beautiful with the curling tresses spilling around her shoulders.

She raised her face to his. "Deverill . . . kiss me . . . *please.*"

Brandon froze. He badly wanted to comply, but he'd vowed he wouldn't succumb to his intense desire for her. *Comfort,* he repeated. *You are only here to comfort and warm her.*

Kate had other intentions, apparently. "Won't you even kiss me?"

One kiss couldn't hurt, could it?

Reluctantly he bent his head, covering her mouth with his, warming her cold lips, brushing the pliant surface. Kate responded with a fierceness that took him aback. Her kiss was urgent, almost desperate.

Breaking off, he rested his forehead against hers. "Sweetheart, we need to stop now or in another moment I won't let you go."

"I don't want to stop. I don't want to die a virgin."

Her leap in logic surprised him. "You aren't going to die at all."

"I might. Fate is so uncertain."

Pulling away, Kate stared back at him earnestly, her green eyes haunted. "Please . . . make love to me. *Please.*"

Brandon remained silent, yet he knew she could see the battle waging inside him. Outside the cabin, the rush of wind and rain continued, rolling the schooner like so much flotsam.

Kate clearly couldn't conquer her trepidation. "I despise being afraid," she said, her voice a plea. "Make me forget my fear, Deverill."

Something in his chest tightened. "Kate . . ." he warned, although without as much conviction as he should have. "We should be married before I bed you."

"I don't care. I want you. I *need* you."

He suspected that offering herself to him—acting before thinking—was her way of taking control of her life, her fear.

He could certainly understand her need to seize the initiative. He lay there fighting himself, struggling with his conscience, trying to summon his better instincts, just as he had six years ago. That time, he had taken the honorable course and rejected Kate's virginal advances. And yet, an insistent voice argued, honor wasn't the issue this time since he planned on wedding her regardless.

When she raised one arm to encircle his neck and sought to kiss him again, he tried to hold her away but realized he had made a decision. He would stake his claim on her in the most irrevocable way possible, and after becoming her lover, there would be no going back.

"Easy, love . . ." he murmured, feeling the hungry press of her lips against his jaw. "We need to go slowly your first time."

"What should I do?"

"Undress, to begin with. We have on too many clothes."

Untangling himself, he rose from the bunk and helped her up, then drew back the sheet and blankets that covered the bunk.

Kate had started to remove her gown, but when he made to assist her, she allowed him to undress her, remaining mute during his ministrations. He could have hurried, but instead Brandon drew out the moment, trailing light kisses over all the alluring places he uncovered . . . the column of her neck, the curve of her shoulder, her upper arm.

Her corset came next, so that she was left standing in her chemise. Holding her gaze, Brandon reached up to cup her breasts, feeling their fullness beneath the cambric. When he stroked his thumbs gently over her pebbled nipples, Kate inhaled a shallow breath and shut her eyes briefly in surrender.

He knelt at her feet then, to remove her slippers and stockings, and finally rose to pull her chemise over her head.

Kate remained totally still as he took her in. The sight of her nude body, so pale and beautiful, brought all his vivid dreams to life, yet Brandon determinedly banished them from his mind. This time was about Kate. Her awakening. Her pleasure. Her desire.

Stepping closer, he bent his head to taste her lips and lingered there to savor her before teasing a delicate path across her cheek and lower, beneath her ear.

When he pressed his lips into the soft skin, she gave a sigh but shivered.

"Are you cold?" he murmured.

"No . . . you make me hot. . . ."

Just that simple admission set his blood on fire.

Brandon drew back to study her. "Are you still certain?"

"Yes. I have never been more certain of anything." Her voice was firmer, her gaze entirely steady. "I want you, Deverill. . . . Please."

In response, he led her to the bunk and pressed her down. Reclining there on the mattress, she watched wide-eyed as he hastily shed his own garments.

In short order he stood before her, his aching member pulsing and erect. Barely holding his savage need in check, Brandon stared down at her nude form, taking in her ripe breasts, slender waist, gently flaring hips, and long, shapely legs. Beautiful didn't begin to describe her. The potent sensuality of her body called to everything male in him.

He had left her medallion around her throat, and the delicate gold disk reminded him of his task. The time had come for him to claim her. More crucially, he would make her forget her nightmares and replace the dark images with pure pleasure. Despite her professed certainty, she seemed especially vulnerable just now, even beyond her instinctive reaction to the storm. Brandon sat beside her on the bunk, determined to reassure her.

"I have pictured this. You wearing nothing, your

glorious hair down, spilling around your incredibly lovely body."

As he spoke, his fingers began making a slow, circular motion around the tip of her breast. The mere contact made Kate shiver, yet this time he knew it was from heat, not cold.

Leaving her breast, he slowly swept his hand down her length, drifting over her silken skin to her flat belly, pausing at the juncture of her thighs. When she stiffened instinctively, he returned a soothing murmur.

"Let me touch you, sweetheart. I need to make your body ready to receive me. Arousal will make it easier for you to take me inside you."

She bit her lower lip but nodded trustingly.

Probing, Brandon found the small kernel of her sex already slick with moisture. The discovery sent a surge of fire rocketing through him.

Heaven help him, he wanted her. Her body made him burn from the inside out. But he forced himself to remain tender as he stroked and caressed her.

Eventually her eyes grew hazed. Bending, he covered her lush mouth with his own. As her tongue met his, he felt an emotion akin to triumph. It was beguiling, the ardor in her kiss, the excitement, the tender searching.

He tangled his fingers in the rich fullness of her hair and drank of her sweetness, showing her how to respond, to give, to take. She was making small sounds of pleasure by the time he moved between her thighs.

When she tensed automatically, he spoke softly. "Try to relax, love."

She nodded, gazing up at him, still trusting.

Bracing his weight on his arms, he slowly, slowly entered her. He felt her wince when her fragile barrier rent, but Kate made no sound beyond a faint gasp. Brandon held himself still, letting her grow accustomed to his penetration while feeling the gentle kisses he was pressing over her face.

Finally, he paused to brush back a tendril of hair from her cheek. "Better now?"

"Yes." She looked more at ease, as if her discomfort was fading. After another long moment, she even stirred her hips tentatively, testing.

He feathered another kiss at the corner of her mouth as he fought the urge to drive himself into her more deeply. He heard her sigh as her eyes fluttered closed.

Brandon tightened his embrace and intensified their kiss, claiming and wooing. All he could think about was burying himself inside her wet, tight heat, yet he commanded himself to go slowly, sinking farther with great care, until he was fully embedded inside her.

He remained that way for a score of heartbeats. Then wanting her to respond with passion, he began to move, deliberately advancing the pace, coaxing her with his body and mouth and hands as well.

She seemed to accept his increasing urgency, welcoming him. Moments later, Kate whimpered feverishly, her nails digging into his shoulders as she instinctively matched his rhythm, a sign of the hot longing he knew was clamoring inside her.

When soon she bucked and writhed against him, Brandon clenched his teeth, striving for control, trying desperately to keep his savage need in check.

When her release came suddenly, however, it was too much for him to fight. A great shudder moved through his frame as at last he let himself fill her with the hot desire that he'd felt for Kate since his very first moment of meeting her.

It was quite some time before Brandon regained his senses. Breathing heavily, he tried to ease his weight off her, but Kate tightened her arms about his neck, as if never wanting to release him.

He peered down at her, wondering what to expect. She was gazing back at him steadily.

"Are you all right?" he asked, his voice husky with passion.

"Yes. That was . . ." She paused, as if searching for the right word. "Magical."

"It was indeed."

The shy smile she gave him touched him even more than her praise of his lovemaking.

Yes indeed, Brandon repeated to himself, shifting to one side and gathering her against him. When he pulled the covers up over them both, Kate gave a contented sigh and nuzzled her cheek in the curve of his shoulder and neck. They lay twined together, listening to the ebbing storm, their arms and legs braided.

"Thank you," she finally murmured.

"For what?"

"For making me forget my fear of sinking in the ship. I am not afraid anymore."

Brandon pressed a kiss against her forehead. "I should be shot for taking advantage of your panic."

"If I recall, I gave you little choice."

"That is hardly an excuse for claiming your innocence."

Pulling away, she pushed herself up on one elbow. "You are not to blame. You said you would wait to make love until I invited you. Well, I invited you. And I don't regret it for one moment."

Her eyes were bright, raw with feeling.

A man could drown in the light in her eyes.

Brandon raised his hands to cup her face, drinking in her beauty. Her hair was rich and unruly, her skin like gleaming ivory, her lips damp and passion-bruised.

Pushing his hand gently through the fiery cloud of her hair, he brushed some errant curls back from her face with his thumbs and drew her down to him. His lips found hers tenderly before he settled her beside him once more.

As Kate lay curled against him, he let himself relax into her warmth. The urgency in his body, the hard ache in his loins, had subsided, yet he didn't want to let her go. On the contrary, he wanted to remain just like this for hours, nestled with her, luxuriating in her warmth, her scent, her special glow.

Absently he stroked her bare arm beneath the

covers, his thoughts drifting. He had taken Kate as if he had the right. And as far as he was concerned, he did have the right. She was his wife-to-be.

His *wife*. The title gave him an extraordinary feeling of satisfaction. He'd had other lovers, but this time was somehow different. And more dangerous. The rigid control he'd kept over his emotions had fallen away.

A remarkable change in so short a span—although perhaps it was not so short after all. This moment had been seven years coming, since his first glimpse of her.

In truth, he was more shaken than he cared to admit. Their lovemaking had been unique in his experience. He'd felt joined to Kate, as if she were a part of him. *Complete*.

Again that particular word came to mind, along with "possessiveness." And his powerful feeling of possessiveness had been accentuated by a burgeoning well of tenderness, a sweet ache coming from deep inside him.

More profoundly, he had the sense that everything had changed. There was no longer any question in his mind. Kate would wed him now, regardless of her fanciful notions about love, Brandon vowed. He would make certain of it.

Tomorrow he would present his case to her uncle and aunt. He'd already had one private discussion with Lord Cornelius. In the morning he would have a second and persuade them to let Kate continue the journey alone with him, so he could pursue his courtship without restrictions.

He could count on their support, he suspected. They already knew he was fiercely protective of Kate, that he would never willingly let any harm come to her, and that he intended to win her hand in marriage.

The way to win her hand, however, was not through passion, he'd learned. Somehow, he would have to keep his hands off her—a supremely difficult task after tonight. He wanted Kate to hunger for him, to want him for far more than solace, but he was determined to woo her properly, without seduction.

More than merely wooing her, though, he had to prove a deeper bond was possible beyond mere carnal pleasure. He had to make her realize that no other husband would do for her. And most of all, he had to show her that he was committed to becoming her chosen mate, love or no love.

Chapter Fourteen

Kate woke to the gentle surge of the ship plowing through much calmer waters. Blinking at the bright sunlight shining through the porthole window, she glanced around her small cabin. There was no sign of Deverill. He had left her bed sometime during the night, to spare her reputation, no doubt. But as she lay there, his scent lingered on her skin—and in her mind.

She couldn't regret her rashness last night in pleading that he take her. Her fierce yearning to be with him was initially driven by fear—she had craved the vital, life-affirming intimacy of his lovemaking. She had known their joining would be remarkable, but she'd vastly underestimated how wonderful, how intensely glorious it would be. After the first moments of physical discomfort, there was only overwhelming pleasure, and not just of the physical kind. Kate hugged herself as she thought back on those precious hours with Deverill. The incredible feeling of intimacy—the bond they had shared—had felt deeper than mere carnal relations.

Yes, she ought to have heeded the nagging voice warning to protect her heart. It would have been wiser to wait until she could be assured of winning *his* heart. But she'd been following blind instinct.

A rush of warmth washed through her now as she remembered his tenderness, his sensuality, his skillful, careful arousal of her uninitiated body. This morning not only were her breasts swollen and the hollow between her thighs keenly sensitive, she felt a sweetly aching awareness in all the places he had touched.

Briefly she closed her eyes as memories cascaded through her. His powerful body moving over her, pressing into her . . . bringing her alive, setting her on fire.

For years she had built implausible fantasies around Deverill, but he had lived up to every single one. He hadn't just made love to her; he had joined with her on some deep unspoken level. And she couldn't help but believe he, too, had wanted, even needed, that perfect closeness between them.

Bestirring herself, Kate rose to wash and dress. As she began pinning her hair into a chignon, she recalled how his hands had tangled lovingly in the abundant mass.

Lovingly. Wishful thinking, perhaps?

Yet this morning it was easier to rekindle her hope for the future that she'd once envisioned with Deverill. The hope that passion could someday spark the flame of love.

She tended to believe that only one person in life was your soul mate. Whether or not that was a fallacy, last night she had felt as if she was *meant* to be with Deverill. And she longed to fill the same need for him. Perhaps now that she'd been given a privileged insight into his life and the reasons for his determined detachment, she stood a genuine chance of making her dreams come true.

Kate smoothed her gown and took a steadying breath, preparing to face him with renewed resolve. First, however, she needed to check on her aunt Rachel.

Cornelius answered her soft rap on their cabin door. After greeting her in hushed tones, he said with concern, "Rachel did not fare well last night, but she is sleeping soundly now."

Kate nodded regretfully. "Is there anything I can do for her?"

"Not at the moment. The sooner we reach land, the better."

"I will let Deverill know."

Feeling more urgency, Kate climbed the companionway ladder. When she stepped through the hatch, the sea air that greeted her was cool and crisp, washed clean by the storm. The crew was hard at work mending canvas and overhauling the rigging, but otherwise the schooner appeared back to normal: tall, raking masts swaying in rhythm against the June sky, sails billowing gracefully on the breeze. On her port side, the coast of France was much nearer than expected.

The only trouble was, her plan to remain composed splintered the instant she spied Deverill across the main deck. He was speaking to Captain Halsey, but he looked up and froze when he saw her.

Was she imagining it, or was his look more tender than ever before? More admiring? Was the faint smile that touched his lips a sign of welcome or self-directed irony? Was he feeling an inkling of the renewed warmth that flooded her and made her limbs weak?

At his intense look, she felt uncertain, awkward, shy . . . which was absurd. She had seldom experienced shyness in her entire life.

Suddenly vexed with herself, Kate shook off the uncommon sentiment and went to stand at the railing. Deverill shouldn't have the power to make her feel skittish as a day-old filly. His scrutiny shouldn't turn her breath ragged.

Yet she was very glad he was occupied with the captain, and that by the time he did join her, she had herself under control.

"You survived the night, I see," he murmured.

Instantly Kate felt herself blushing. So much for being in control, she thought, remembering his naked body. "Yes, thank you."

"It was my pleasure. Have you breakfasted yet?"

There was an underlying warmth in his words, but his manner was amicable, easy.

Kate decided it best to emulate his lead and act as if

nothing had changed between them. She wanted to give no reason for her family or his crew to suspect she had spent the night in Deverill's arms.

"Not yet. I thought I should check with you first to discuss the plans for the day."

"You have ample time. We should reach the port of Royan in a few hours. See the break in the coast there up ahead? That is the Gironde estuary."

Kate's gaze followed to where he was pointing. She could indeed see the mouth of the estuary where the Gironde River flowed into the sea. The *Zephyr* had tragically sunk near there after sailing from Bordeaux farther upstream.

"What happens when we reach Royan?"

"Our priority should be to settle your aunt at an inn where she may rest comfortably. After that, I plan to hire a carriage to convey us around the district for the next week or two."

"Good. Aunt Rachel will likely be too ill to travel any farther today."

"I also want to track down Louvel this afternoon and perhaps open negotiations to search for the shipwreck. But I presume you would first like to visit the church and see the site where your mother is buried."

Kate suddenly felt as if a shadow had passed over her, depleting her previous warmth. But it was time to turn her attention to the real purpose of their voyage.

Squaring her shoulders, she glanced up at Deverill. "Yes. Will you come with me?"

"Of course, if you wish."

"I do wish it," she said solemnly.

She couldn't help feeling more able to face her mother's grave site because Deverill would be by her side.

The morning proceeded much as he predicted—and as a fair wind propelled the schooner into the estuary, the scenery surrounding Royan matched what Kate expected.

Sheltered from the harsh Atlantic gales, the coast was sprinkled with wooded, rocky headlands and sandy coves, while a castle fortress guarded the entrance to Royan's harbor. The climate here was far warmer than England, she'd been told. And like many coastal seaports, the town boasted buildings of light-colored stone with red-tiled roofs, accented with pine trees and splashes of newly budding bougainvillea.

As Kate watched from the railing, they sailed into the harbor, which was dotted with vessels of various sizes. Dazzling sunlight reflected off the white sails and blue water so intensely that she had to shield her eyes.

Shortly after Captain Halsey dropped anchor, a rowboat ferried out to the *Galene,* carrying the harbormaster, who boarded and conferred with both Halsey and Deverill. Within the hour, Kate was settling her weary aunt into rooms at a local inn while Deverill hired a carriage from the nearby livery stable.

Rachel felt too weak to accompany them to the church but urged them to proceed without her. But, of course, Cornelius wouldn't leave his wife's sickbed.

Instead, he decided to wait for their valises to be delivered from the ship, professing that he would be satisfied to have Kate report back to him about the condition of the grave.

Kate was anxious to begin. She and Deverill ate a quick luncheon, and soon he was driving her to the ancient church on the southern outskirts of town.

The elderly priest had anticipated Kate's arrival, due to several recent correspondences with the Wilde family. After kindly welcoming them, he showed them to the cemetery at the rear of the property, then led them through a squeaky gate into an overgrown section—where paupers were buried, he apologized in French and broken English.

"We felt certain," Father Ramonde explained, "that your *maman* came from a good family since she wore a gold locket with a crest etched on the face. But we had no way of learning her identity. She spoke only her given name before succumbing to her injuries."

Proceeding down an unkempt, grassy path, he halted before an aged wooden marker bleached gray by years of sun and rain.

Kate hesitated, feeling her throat constrict. It had been many weeks since her family learned the truth about the *Zephyr*'s sinking—and of Lady Beaufort's brief survival after washing ashore, half-drowned and in great pain. In that time Kate had obsessively focused on finding her mother's burial site. Now that the moment was at hand, however, she braced herself for the blow.

The priest quietly withdrew, providing privacy for her and Deverill. Clenching her hands together, Kate stepped forward, staring down at the simple wooden marker. She could barely make out the name carved there.

"*Melicent,*" she whispered. Her voice was tight with tears while her eyes stung. Behind her, Deverill brought his hand to rest lightly on her shoulder.

Conscious of his silent offering of comfort and strength, she bowed her head. She was profoundly grateful for his presence, for she hadn't wanted to brave this emotional moment alone.

"She died far too soon," he murmured.

"Yes . . ."

Suddenly swamped by the old grief, Kate began to cry softly, which made little sense. How could she hurt so badly when it had been many years since the tragedy?

In response, Deverill pulled her close, wrapping an arm around her and pressing her head into his shoulder, as if to absorb her pain. Desperately wanting the solace he offered, Kate leaned into him and let the tears come.

Even after her sobs lessened, he continued holding her. She stood there pliantly—until she felt the light pressure of his fingers on her cheek and heard his sympathetic voice. "I can only imagine the sorrow you suffered, losing both parents you loved."

Feeling the sharp ache again, Kate blindly lifted her face and locked her mouth on his. Her kiss must have caught him off guard for he tensed. When she wrapped her arms tightly about his neck and tried to intensify their kiss, Deverill stopped her and pulled back.

"This isn't the time or the place, sweetheart," he said gently.

Kate stared up at him. There was something unbearably intimate in his dark gaze, as if he could see past all her defenses.

Suddenly she felt oddly vulnerable and exposed and embarrassed by her lapse. As she searched in her reticule for a handkerchief, she forced a watery laugh, trying to make light of his rejection. "I know. This is getting to be a burdensome habit—you consoling me when I act like a weakling."

The slight scoffing sound he made held only a little humor. "I'm well aware your weakness is only temporary, but I won't take advantage of it again as I did last night."

"You didn't take advantage. I offered myself to you."

His jaw flexed, as if he was about to contradict her, but he settled for saying brusquely, "When you want me for more than comfort, pray let me know."

She thought she understood his unspoken message. He wanted her, perhaps even badly, but not when she was so emotionally fragile and vulnerable. She needed to be willing and eager and fully in control of her faculties, not driven by fear or sorrow.

"Meanwhile," Deverill continued, "we still have a

great deal of work to do this afternoon. At the moment, we should return to the church and speak with Father Ramonde."

"Yes." Chastened, Kate swallowed and used the handkerchief to dry her eyes. She should be glad Deverill had given her direction, stability, focus. And she resolved to be stronger in the future. A man like him most certainly wouldn't want a sniveling watering pot for his bride. If she hoped to win his love, this was not the way to go about it, and she very much wanted to be the kind of woman he could love.

As they retraced their path to the church, however, all thoughts of love and romance fled Kate's thoughts, for Deverill was all business when he outlined his intentions. "We need to discuss delivery of the headstone you had commissioned. And more pressing, I want advance information about Louvel and advice on approaching him. I don't want to give him any warning about our arrival."

Kate nodded in agreement. Questioning Father Ramonde was more prudent than making inquiries about town, since a priest would be less inclined to be in league with pirates and could better be trusted to keep confidences.

They met with the priest, who provided answers to many of their questions.

"*Oui, Capitaine* Jean Louvel is headquartered nearby in St. Georges, several miles south of Royan. But perhaps it is unwise to walk into a pirates' den, given Louvel's unsavory reputation?"

When Deverill acknowledged his concern, the priest gave specific directions.

Kate was also able to question him about a subject more dear to her. "Might there be a way for me to recover the locket my mother wore?"

"*Je ne sais pas*—it has been such a long time. I believe it was sold to pay the physician's cost to care for your mother's injuries. I shall make inquiries."

"Thank you," she said gratefully.

In all likelihood the crest on the locket belonged to the Marquesses of Beaufort and not some other noble family, and finding it would prove beyond any doubt that her mother was indeed buried there in the pauper's grave. Yet Kate knew in her heart that their suppositions weren't wrong.

Shortly afterward, they took their leave. Once in the carriage, she wondered why Deverill turned the horses back the way they had come rather than toward St. Georges. "We are returning to Royan?"

"Temporarily. In addition to the element of surprise, I want an armed escort when I confront Louvel. I arranged with Halsey to provide several of his best men who are skilled in hand-to-hand combat."

Kate frowned. "Do you expect violence from Louvel?"

"No, but it would be unwise to underestimate him. Our last encounter was less than amicable."

"What happened?"

"He believed, falsely, that I had stolen the affections of his lover."

Her eyebrow shot up. "Your conflict was over a woman?"

Deverill grimaced. "Regrettably, yes. She approached me, though, and when I rebuffed her advances, she grew vindictive and claimed I had violated her. Louvel and I ended up fighting a duel with swords, which is how he obtained the scar on his cheek."

During the first part of the drive, Kate quizzed him about his plan to meet Louvel, and Deverill explained.

"I could hire men and boats in Royan, but it's better to involve Louvel and secure his collaboration than have him as a certain enemy. If we can come to terms, I intend to stay in St. Georges to supervise the salvage effort. He is fairly honorable as far as pirates go, but given our history, I don't wholly trust him. As for you, I want you to remain in Royan."

"You must be jesting."

"Not in the least."

"I did not come all this way to be useless or play a passive role. If you think to leave me behind—" Kate began, only to bite her tongue as she realized a sweeter tone would go further to change his mind. "Only a short time ago you challenged me to become more wild and adventurous. Well, this is a prime opportunity."

"I was speaking of carnal adventures. And I never meant to encourage more risk-taking at the price of your safety."

Kate eyed him in consternation. "You expect me to let you face danger alone? When you are acting on my behalf? What kind of coward do you take me for? No, don't answer that," she hastened to add, remembering how she had quailed during the storm.

For a moment she sat there debating what to say. She was very grateful that Deverill had taken on her mission to properly lay her parents to rest, and even appreciated that he was willing to fight her battles for her. A part of her relished the fact that he wanted to protect her.

Yet she wanted to protect him as well. More crucially, she simply could not allow Deverill to risk danger for her sake while she remained safely out of harm's way. She would never forgive herself if something happened to him.

"You aren't certain Louvel will respond with anger," Kate finally said.

"I would lay odds on it."

"Have you considered that I might actually be of some use in negotiating with him? I have a great deal of experience handling difficult men."

"And you could be a liability as well. Louvel could see you as the means to enact revenge on me."

"If so, then we will deal with it. In any event . . ." Kate's jaw firmed. "I am *not* remaining behind."

Their argument lasted for the remainder of the drive. Deverill was one of the few men whose force of will matched her own, but in this instance, she was adamant. And by the time they reached the inn, she had convinced him that she would go to St. Georges on her own if he refused to take her.

As she descended from the carriage, Kate heard him muttering under his breath about stubborn females.

While Deverill saw to horses and weapons for Halsey's men, she went upstairs to repack her valise for an extended stay in St. Georges and to confer with her aunt and uncle.

Perhaps because she refrained from mentioning the possible danger, they were not averse to the plan. Uncle Cornelius agreed to have her mother's headstone delivered to the church while she was away.

Just as surprisingly, Rachel made no objection to letting her niece accompany Deverill unchaperoned. She herself was still too ill to travel but hoped to recover enough by tomorrow to slowly stroll the sandy beaches, saying that the sun and warmth would do her good.

Not for the first time did Kate suspect her aunt of exaggerating her condition so that the engaged couple could have more privacy. And Kate was certain of it when Rachel sent Cornelius away to see to the luggage and handed Kate a small silk bag. "This is from your aunt Isabella."

Puzzled, Kate opened the drawstring. Inside were several sponges with thin strings attached, and two small vials of liquid. "What is this?"

"The means to avoid getting with child. You must soak a sponge in vinegar or brandy and place it deep within your woman's passage."

Kate didn't know whether to feel embarrassed or not. Before she could reply, Rachel continued.

"Isabella and I both wished to prevent you becoming enceinte in the event you and Lord Valmere became lovers. She felt certain it would be needed. I would say she was right. You are lovers, are you not?"

Kate felt a blush heat her cheeks. "Is it so obvious?"

"Only to me. I don't believe Cornelius has an inkling." She paused. "I do not mean to judge or criticize, Kate. I simply don't want you to follow my path." A look of sadness crossed Rachel's face. "If I had known of this method, I could have been spared great heartache, having to abandon my daughter to my brute of a husband."

She shuddered, then steeled her spine as if drawing on some hidden strength. Visibly shaking off her bad memories, Rachel smiled kindly. "I know how difficult it is to resist a handsome man when your heart is wholly engaged. I was in love with Cornelius, just as you are with Valmere."

Kate gave a start. "I am not in love with Valmere," she protested.

"Well, if you are not, you soon could be, given a proper environment for fostering love. A sojourn alone with him could be just what you need. Isabella is of the same mind, but she wants you to be prepared."

Kate might have continued the discussion, but settled for a simple thank-you and returned to her room to fetch her pelisse and bonnet.

As she waited for Deverill to return, she thought about her aunt's sage advice and realized that she actually held a similar conviction. Bearing a child out of wedlock was out of the question. She would never force the label of bastard on a child. Which meant that becoming "enceinte" would take the choice of marrying Deverill out of her hands.

You should have considered that before demanding that he make love to you last night, you ninny— Was it only last night?

Her body answered for her. Her feminine places were still tender, her senses still overly reactive. Deverill's mere *look* felt more intimate now, not to mention his touch. The lightest brush of his fingers on just her hand elicited an electric response in her body that was far outsized than was reasonable.

But worse, her thoughts were filled with him. And her feelings—Well, her feelings were a chaotic muddle, ranging from tenderness to triumph, from despair to hope and back again.

But the essential, irrefutable truth was, Kate realized, if she was not in love with Deverill yet, she easily could be. And a sojourn alone with him could push her completely over the edge. Now that they had made love, Deverill would undoubtedly return to his normal, irresistible methods of seduction, and she would have few defenses.

But perhaps she should welcome his passion. Perhaps after all, physical intimacy could inspire emotional intimacy, which could lead to love.

And if she wanted his love, she couldn't worry so

much about protecting her own heart. Instead, she had to focus on winning his.

Four brawny sailors, mounted and armed, accompanied them to St. Georges. Adhering to directions provided by the priest, they took the coastal road, which afforded occasional glimpses of the sea beyond thickets of pine and scrub bush.

During the drive, Deverill told Kate his plan for when they reached the pirate's headquarters. "When we encounter Louvel, let me do the talking. And I will address you as Miss Wilde rather than Lady Katharine. We'll likely be bargaining with him, and revealing that you are a wealthy noblewoman would only give him leverage."

Kate nodded. "You would know best how to deal with him. It seems an improbable coincidence that you are acquainted with the very pirate I wish to hire."

"Not too improbable," Deverill countered. "Most corsairs in this region are Basque, but there are also Frenchmen who were drawn to America's war with Britain by the lure of riches. Privateers made a very good living harrying the British fleet. The most notable was Jean Laffite in the Louisiana territory."

"It is unfortunate that you are enemies with Louvel."

Deverill grimaced. "Highly unfortunate. But he has always been driven by greed. I expect he can set aside his wounded pride if the reward is large enough."

They then discussed what to offer Louvel for his

services. Kate had brought ample funds with her, primarily in gold guineas, but had left it behind on the *Galene* since pirates might be inclined to take her money and provide nothing in return. Similarly, they had not written in advance, since knowledge of the shipwreck might inspire Louvel to conduct a search of his own before they could arrive to supervise the salvage.

"Some of your aunt's jewelry may be recoverable from the wreckage, is that correct?" Deverill asked.

"Yes." The villain who had blown up the *Zephyr* had absconded with most of the de Chagny treasure, but several of the priceless jewels were still missing and thought to be at the bottom of the estuary with the shipwreck. "Why?"

"If you are amenable, any items of worth we find could be additional payment for Louvel's efforts. The prospect of finding treasure will serve to motivate him further."

Kate frowned in contemplation. "It is probably too much to hope that I will ever see my father's signet ring again."

"Probably," Deverill agreed.

Kate shrugged. "It doesn't matter. Locating the wreckage is all I truly care about. I will be satisfied if we can just find proof of the *Zephyr*'s identity." Her voice lowered. "It seems a bit morbid to search for treasure among wreckage where so many people perished. Reportedly there were a dozen crew and passengers on board the *Zephyr*."

Deverill made a scoffing sound. "Trust me, Louvel and his cohorts won't be put off by a ship's violent end."

The seaside village of St. Georges was pretty and prosperous-looking, no doubt because fishermen supplemented their meager incomes with piracy. When they reached a certain street, Deverill drew the carriage to a halt and pointed. "That must be Louvel's residence."

In the distance, against a backdrop of blue sky and even bluer water, stood an elegant, storied mansion, built of beige stone with the ubiquitous red-tiled roof but obviously home to someone of stature and wealth.

Deverill ordered their entourage to wait there, in view of the house. If he hadn't emerged in half an hour, they were to ride up to the door in a show of strength. Then, urging his pair of horses forward, he continued down the street, turned onto a sweeping gravel drive, and halted near the carriage house.

As he helped Kate down, a warm salt breeze caressed her face but did little to quell the prickling of her nerves. Not knowing what to expect, she held her breath when Deverill rapped lightly on the door. A few moments later an elderly female servant admitted them and, without much curiosity, showed them into a perfectly genteel parlor that overlooked the sea.

The splendid view from the tall French windows first caught Kate's eye, but then her attention was quickly drawn to the couple sitting on a sofa, sipping wine.

It was a surprisingly domestic scene for a pirate, Kate thought—one that could have taken place in any refined home in England. The woman was a blond beauty, stylishly dressed, perhaps a few years older than herself. The tall, muscular man wore more casual attire but was exceptionally handsome in a swarthy kind of way. The scar marking his left cheek stood out against his bronzed complexion and suggested his identity was none other than Jean Louvel.

At the entrance of guests, Louvel glanced up politely but froze when he caught sight of Deverill. "*Vous! Ce que le diable?*"

With a scowl darkening his face even further, Louvel suddenly leapt to his feet and bypassed the tea table in a single bound. Lunging across the parlor, he unsheathed a rapier from its scabbard, then spun and advanced toward them, holding the blade up menacingly.

Chapter Fifteen

Kate's heart stopped in her chest. Before she could even think what to do, Deverill caught her elbow and yanked her behind him, shielding her with his large body.

Louvel halted before them, aiming the deadly point of the rapier at Deverill's throat. Repeating his curse, the pirate growled, "*Pourquoi êtes-vous ici, Anglais?*" which Kate interpreted as "Why are you here, Englishman?"

The two men were of a similar height and build, but Louvel clearly had the advantage with his weapon raised ominously, his fierce expression suggesting that he still bore a grudge after all these years.

In response to the threatening act, however, Deverill calmly responded. "Clearly you want to run me through, but you should think twice. It would be a pity to ruin your elegant furniture and carpets with blood—either mine or yours."

Ignoring the pirate's incredulous sputter, Deverill glanced across the parlor. The beauty had risen also, a worried look on her face, her concern evidently as great as Kate's.

"Pray, will you introduce us to your lady?" Deverill added.

"Introduce you!" Louvel exclaimed in a heavy French accent.

Tension was thick in the small parlor. Waiting anxiously for the pirate's reply, Kate held her breath while digging her nails into her palms. Deverill had taken a big risk, leaving himself vulnerable like this. She questioned the wisdom of his nonchalance—although having grown up with two brothers and a male cousin, she understood that showing any weakness toward a man such as Louvel would only invite more belligerence and earn contempt rather than respect.

Louvel stared back at Deverill and finally shook his head. "*Incroyable.*"

"What is incredible?"

"You, appearing at my doorstep unarmed."

"Why do you assume I am unarmed?" Casually opening his jacket, Deverill drew a pistol from his belt and made a show of examining the priming. He was issuing a challenge in return, quite obviously.

Grinning unexpectedly then, Deverill brushed the rapier point aside with a forefinger and lightly cuffed Louvel on the shoulder while adopting a disarming tone. "I have missed you, you hotheaded hulk."

A disbelieving bark of laughter escaped Louvel. "Me,

I cannot credit you. You were always too courageous for your own good."

"But I am not stupid. I once thought that of you, however. You acted the imbecile, accusing me of besmirching your honor and insisting that I fight you. I told you then, I had no interest in your lover. You didn't believe me and nearly did me in."

"Hah! It was you who gave me this scar," Louvel countered gruffly, rubbing his cheek.

"I merely acted in self-defense." Deverill looked pointedly at the rapier. "I did not come here to reenact our duel."

"Then for what reason *did* you come?"

"To pay you a courtesy call. I have business in these parts, and by all reports, you control much of the enterprise hereabouts."

Louvel's eyes narrowed in suspicion. "What business?"

"I will gladly discuss it with you but not while we are engaged in a standoff. Shall we call it a draw?"

"Oui."

Though still scowling, Louvel lowered his weapon and stepped back. The blond-haired woman gave a sigh of relief, as did Kate.

"Permit me to make introductions," Deverill said then. "This is Miss Katharine Wilde. I wish to locate a shipwreck on her behalf. Some fourteen years ago, her parents and uncle and aunt were on board a ship when it went down in this vicinity."

Louvel was studying Kate. "What, has she the tied tongue? Can she not speak for herself?"

Kate, who was not tongue-tied in the least, answered for Deverill. "Indeed she can, Monsieur Louvel." But she said it sweetly and offered a soft, submissive smile to take the sting out of her words, suspecting that Louvel would not be pleased to be contested by a mere woman. "Forgive me for nearly swooning. I am unaccustomed to being greeted in such a violent fashion or threatened with a wicked sword blade."

Catching the amused gleam in Deverill's eye at the notion of her swooning, she went on quickly. "Mr. Deverill told me that you were a charming gentleman, monsieur, and that you two were once friends and compatriots. I very much hope that you are willing to let bygones be bygones, instead of remaining enemies."

"Even though he sought to kill me?" Louvel retorted, glaring anew.

"Had he truly wanted to kill you, I imagine he would have succeeded," Kate said with another winsome smile.

Louvel stared at her, but after a moment, his glower eased a measure. "*C'est vrai.* Very true. He allowed me to vent my anger without carving out my liver. But did this dog also tell you that he gave me this scar?"

"A scar that only makes you more intriguing to the ladies, no doubt."

His jaw remained stubbornly set, but his resistance

was weakening, Kate could tell. In a further sign that she had managed to defuse his anger, Louvel shook his head as his lips twisted in a grudging grin. Fleetingly, he even eyed her with new respect before giving a low, rough laugh.

She didn't trust that oily laugh, or care for the way the pirate was ogling her, his dark eyes raking her contemplatively from head to toe.

Neither did the blond lady, judging by her expression.

She had made herself Louvel's target, Kate realized. And although that was far better than having him attack Deverill in retaliation for an imagined offense that occurred many years ago, she didn't want to make an adversary of the woman from the very start.

Moving close to Deverill, Kate slipped her arm in his. "Darling," she said lovingly, "we should petition Monsieur Louvel to assist us. I am certain he could be an immense help."

"Perhaps." Deverill covered her hand possessively and addressed Louvel. "I want to hire a crew to search for the shipwreck, and you are the logical choice to lead the effort."

Louvel's look turned calculating. "For what reason should I assist you?"

"Because it is a highly lucrative proposition. Fifty guineas as surety, quadruple that amount if the wreck is located and salvaged in the next fortnight."

The pirate rubbed his jaw thoughtfully, then nodded.

"I am willing to consider your proposition. Will you join us for refreshments so we may review the details?"

The beauty, who was introduced as Mademoiselle Gabrielle Dupree, greeted them warily, then left to fetch more wine. Before getting down to bargaining, Louvel questioned what was known about the shipwreck.

Deverill explained about the explosion and fire and how the *Zephyr* had turned toward shore near St. Georges before sinking. In turn, the pirate pointed out the difficulty they would face in finding the site after so many years. Additionally, the depth of the water would greatly affect the chance of success, limiting the light by which to see and the air to breathe. And salvage would be impossible if the pressure was more than a man could withstand while diving.

"Yet the wreckage could be in shallow enough water," Deverill said. "The floor of the estuary here is said to be from three to six fathoms deep—feasible for experienced swimmers."

Since a fathom equaled six feet, Kate judged the maximum depth to be thirty-six feet, which Louvel conceded was achievable.

"Furthermore," Deverill continued, "Miss Wilde's cousin has engineered a diving apparatus designed to extend breathing time. As for divers, my own shipmaster can supply two such seamen as well as nets and longline hooks to drag the seafloor. However, my schooner is too large to maneuver easily in these waters. So from you I would need several smaller sailboats and crews."

Just then Mademoiselle Dupree returned with a young male servant, who carried a tray laden with wine and two more glasses. She poured the wine while Louvel sought to increase the payment.

"For the commission, I require four hundred guineas, half now."

Deverill countered, "I could agree to four hundred, but you'll get a quarter now in gold. Another quarter if you locate the correct ship, and the final half upon salvage."

A sly glint flickered in Louvel's eyes. "What is this? You believe that I would cheat you?"

Deverill flashed a slow grin. "Any self-respecting brigand would attempt it."

"C'est vrai," Louvel admitted.

"But you heed your own code of honor, so I'll wager I can trust you."

"That is also true."

When still Louvel hesitated, Kate chimed in. "There may have been other treasure on board the *Zephyr*—jewels belonging to my French kin. If so, you may claim it all. I only want a signet ring that belonged to my father, if it can even be found. For sentimental reasons, you understand, since it is not especially valuable."

The glint in the pirate's eye deepened at the mention of treasure. "Very well, *Anglais*, I agree to your terms."

"We should begin in the morning," Deverill said. "I presume we will establish a grid pattern to map our search, so we don't miss any possible locations."

"*Oui.* It will take a day, perhaps two, to gather the proper equipment and to employ the best seamen." Louvel followed with a grin of his own, his teeth flashing white. "My compatriots are better suited to *causing* wrecks than salvaging them."

His quip was hardly reassuring to Kate. And even though she and Deverill had succeeded with the first step, her anxiousness abated only slightly when they all drank a toast to their newly formed partnership.

When eventually they got around to discussing accommodations, Deverill asked about finding nearby lodging for himself, Miss Wilde, and four seamen. The closest inn was in Royan, too distant for his needs. Moreover, Louvel balked at letting any of his rival's men stay in St. Georges, evidently wary of relinquishing a vastly superior numerical advantage of employees. Miss Wilde, however, would be welcome as a guest in his home while Deverill could lodge with his crewmen elsewhere.

Deverill replied with a hint of warning in his congenial tone. "If you think to make a play for *ma chère femme,* I would advise against it."

Seated beside Kate on the sofa, he casually slipped an arm around her to cup her breast. Although startled by his bald act of possessiveness and being termed his "woman," she managed to tamp down her reflexive inclination, which was to box his ears. Undoubtedly his show of ownership was a notice to Louvel to keep away, and she hoped the pirate understood the message.

Unexpectedly then, Mademoiselle Dupree suggested a solution in halting, heavily accented English, saying that her friend's cottage was available since she had gone to care for an ailing parent.

Kate suspected the offer was spurred by jealousy rather than generosity since Dupree was most likely Louvel's mistress. Clearly she was not happy with the thought of Kate living in the same house as her protector.

Deverill again made clear his own position, laying claim to Kate as his lover. "Miss Wilde will reside with me. Given our past history, Louvel, you will understand if I prefer not to let her out of my sight."

Louvel appeared to bristle. "You accuse me of having wicked intentions?"

"Let us just say I would not put it past you to retaliate and try to win her allegiance."

While the two men stared each other down like wolves, Kate bit her tongue, not wishing to add fuel to the feud.

Thankfully, Louvel backed away from an overt conflict by nodding, as if settling the matter in his mind. "You may both reside in the cottage, but Mademoiselle Wilde will provide company for Gabrielle here while we search for the wreckage."

The beauty did not look pleased with that prospect, either, but she said in a subdued voice, "I will take you to my friend's cottage. It is not far."

Apparently she was eager to get Kate out of the house and away from Louvel. After Deverill arranged a time to meet in the morning, Gabrielle led them out the front entrance to collect his carriage. His men were waiting outside, just as instructed, so Mademoiselle Dupree directed him two blocks down a side street, to a cottage with a blue door, then set off with Kate while Deverill saw to the horses and spoke to his men before sending them back to his ship in Royan.

Glad to have time alone with the other woman, Kate quickly reverted to French and did her best to seem disarming and self-deprecating while trying to show that she had absolutely no interest in stealing the pirate's affections.

"I sincerely thank you for your hospitality, Mademoiselle Dupree. It means a great deal to me to be able to lay my parents to rest."

Her shrug was stiff, although not overtly hostile, so Kate turned the conversation to more mundane matters.

"Is there a market or farmhouse nearby where we can purchase food for supper?"

"I will send supper to you by one of the servants," Gabrielle said rather grudgingly.

"Thank you again. Our arrival cannot be welcome to you. It is clear that you worry about what mischief we will stir, or even what danger we present. I promise you, though, Deverill is not a threat to Monsieur Louvel. He only hopes to put their contentious past behind them."

Dupree's suspicious look was tempered when Kate gave a small laugh. "Men can be such simpletons sometimes, always fighting over minor matters and wounded pride. If we women ruled the world, we would be far more civilized, is that not so?"

When her comment surprised a faint smile from the beauty, Kate continued in the same vein. "We should help them to get along so they don't kill each other. I do not want to lose Deverill, just as I am certain you do not want to lose Monsieur Louvel."

"Very true, Mademoiselle Wilde."

"Please, will you call me Kate? It seems unnecessary to stand on formality when I may be underfoot for some time."

"Yes, if you will use my name, Gabrielle."

Kate followed with a friendly question about her relatives. "Does any of your family live nearby?"

More soberly, Gabrielle explained that her parents were gone, both claimed by illnesses, and so was her older brother, who had perished at sea.

"Then you understand my grief at losing my own parents," Kate said quietly.

"Yes, to my regret."

Shortly they arrived at a charming little house covered with ivy and accented with newly flowering bougainvillea, and Gabrielle located the key to the front door beneath a clay pot. Kate accompanied her into the cottage, and found herself in a pretty parlor adorned with white lace curtains and vases of dried flowers.

Kate removed her cloak and hung it on a peg as she praised the interior. "We shall be quite comfortable here. Again, I am exceedingly grateful to you and your friend. We will gladly pay for our use of her home."

Gabrielle nodded with her own look of gratitude. "My friend will put the funds to good purpose."

After that, she unbent enough to provide a thorough tour of the cottage. Besides the parlor, there were three other rooms—a kitchen, bedchamber, and workroom for mending fishing nets and canvas sails—all immaculately kept. At Kate's request, Gabrielle devoted particular attention to how to stoke the iron stove and how to draw water from the well at the side of the house, while Kate gently probed about her background and history.

"You must be lonely when Monsieur Louvel is away."

"Indeed, very much so. I dislike it when Jean sails away for long periods. I fear for him."

"I fear for Deverill also." Kate paused. Her goal was to cultivate the beauty's trust if not friendship and turn her into an ally of sorts, and the surest way was to confide her feelings for Deverill. "It is a cold fate, being left behind to wait for our loved ones to return safely." She gave a deliberate sigh. "No doubt I am foolish to pine for a man and wish to win his heart."

"I do not consider it foolish in the least," Gabrielle replied staunchly.

With further discussion, Gabrielle eventually admitted that she came from a good family, but without any means of support she had traded on her looks to become the mistress of the most powerful man in the district. Yet it was not purely a monetary arrangement. In truth, she had become extremely fond of him.

"I suspected as much," Kate said with sympathy.

"Is my fancy so very obvious?"

"Not especially. I have an overly romantic disposition and a fondness for helping couples find happiness and even love. Forgive me, but I have seen how you look at Louvel. You would like for your ardor to be reciprocated, is that true?"

Gabrielle ducked her head rather shyly. "Yes."

"How long have you been with him?"

"Two years. But he is not inclined to marry."

"In my country I am known to have skills as a matchmaker. Perhaps I could help you in some small way. And if you have any advice about how I can secure my lover's affections, I would be grateful to hear it."

When Gabrielle took her leave, Kate thought she had made progress establishing a basis for goodwill rather than enmity.

She had inventoried the pantry by the time Deverill arrived with their valises and reported on the instructions he'd given his armed men. "I sent them back to the *Galene* to fetch the salvage equipment. We should be out of jeopardy for a few days."

"Why do you say so?"

"It's in Louvel's best interest to proceed with the salvage for now. Until we find the ship and determine if there is any sunken treasure to fight over, he will likely honor our collaboration."

"Are you worried he will eventually strike against you?" Kate asked.

"I don't trust him not to try. He gave in more easily than expected. He appears amiable enough now, but he's a cutthroat at heart, and he's not one to relinquish a grudge." Deverill sent her a penetrating look. "I confess, I don't like the way Louvel lusts after you."

"Nor do I. But did you have to claim that I was your *chère femme*?"

"Yes. He needs to know that you are mine. He will be more inclined to keep his hands off you if he thinks you are warming my bed."

Kate hesitated. "Perhaps I should mention, there is only one bed."

"Is there? Where is the bedchamber?"

"There, to your right."

Turning, he carried the valises into the room. Kate followed and watched as he set them on the floor in one corner.

However, he merely glanced at the bed, which was wide enough for two and covered with a blue-and-yellow quilt patterned with flowers. While shedding his jacket in favor of shirtsleeves, he made no mention of the sleeping arrangements, leaving her uncertain about what the night had in store and wondering how they would pass the time until then. He spoke as if reading her thoughts. "Let us go outside where it will be cooler."

Kate was more than happy to oblige, since the cottage was a trifle warm. As she led him to the kitchen, she asked, "Would you like something to drink? There is ale in the pantry, along with several bottles of wine."

"I'll have an ale, thanks."

"Gabrielle will send supper within the hour."

"You are on a first name basis already?"

"I don't want her as an enemy. In fact, I hope to win her confidence and make her an ally."

"I noticed your effort to make Louvel an ally. He lapped up your flattery. Little did he know your show of acquiescence was a sham."

"I had no choice. He would have hated to have his masculinity challenged by a woman."

Deverill's mouth curved. "Make yourself useful and serve me an ale, woman."

Kate shot him an arch look. "You are enjoying my pretense of submissiveness far too much. Don't expect it to last."

Deverill chuckled. "I won't. I know better."

Kate poured his ale while he opened a bottle of wine for her. They carried their glasses through the parlor and out the rear door to a portico shaded from the bright sunshine by a sloping roof and pine trees.

A wicker table and chairs provided a comfortable spot from which to view the sea behind the house. The Gironde estuary boasted sandy beaches similar to the southern Atlantic coast of France but with warmer water and much calmer waves.

Taking a deep breath of the fresh air, Kate listened to the waves washing upon the shore below. The temperature was extremely pleasant, as was the next hour. Indeed, she couldn't remember a more relaxed time with Deverill, which bolstered her hopes for the next few days. Sharing the cottage like this, alone together without the hovering presence of family or servants, could only increase their chances of becoming acquainted on a deeper, more intimate level.

Her hopes were fulfilled for the first part of the evening at least—an amiable, almost domestic intimacy spent learning little details about each other. As pledged, Gabrielle sent a servant with supper in a basket: a delicious roasted chicken, potatoes in a cream sauce, a medley of vegetables, and a loaf of warm bread.

Eventually, the sky grew pink and gold, then turned to dusk, promising a beautiful summer night. Kate drank in the spectacular view of the moonlit sea, with the soft thunder of the ocean tide as a musical backdrop.

Some half hour later, Deverill rose. "I'm for bed. Would you care to join me?"

His gaze locked with hers. She couldn't tell what he was thinking, but surely he intended for them to share the bed.

"Yes," she murmured, accepting his assistance in rising.

They carried their dishes into the kitchen. While Kate saw to the remnants of their meal, he lit a lamp.

He took her elbow, sending a tingling shock down the length of her arm, and escorted her to the bedchamber, where he began to undress. First his cravat, then his boots and stockings, then his shirt.

Kate stared a little breathlessly at the hard-muscled chest on display in the lamplight, but she tore her gaze from the snug fit of his breeches before he shed those as well.

A moment later he called to her. "Kate, love . . ."

Her heart gave a lurch in her chest when she caught sight of his naked splendor. Deverill had the dark, dangerous good looks that made women go weak, and she was certainly no exception.

The look in his eyes, too, made her recall the night of the storm, his magnificent lovemaking, his amazing body moving over her, between her thighs.

Stop ogling him at once, you moonling. The last thing she needed was Deverill knowing how much his nudity affected her—but apparently her goal was hopeless.

"Come here, sweetheart."

When she complied, he slowly bent his head. His lips were tender, soft, as they found hers . . . but apparently he was only teasing her, for instead of embracing her, he stepped back.

"Now your turn," he commanded softly.

He leaned a shoulder against the door frame and watched as she removed her own clothing. His naked body was distracting her, all bronzed skin and defined muscle, but judging from his scrutiny, he seemed to enjoy the distraction she provided as well.

The last of her garments was her shift, and when she stood completely nude before him, Kate felt unsure and exposed. For a long moment, he spoke not a word. Her blush deepened as his gaze lingered on her, admiring her bare breasts, the thatch of curls between her thighs.

Her awareness and tension built, until she was hot with anticipation. "Now what?" she finally asked.

"What indeed?" His eyes knowing, he smiled sweetly—and even that taunting smile was sinfully appealing.

He moved closer, close enough that she could feel the heat of his body, another way of tempting her, she suspected. Every nerve in her body jangled at his nearness.

Kate stared at his mouth with yearning. The need to feel his sheltering arms again made her ache.

Then abruptly, Deverill turned and sauntered over to

the wardrobe and pulled out a blanket, which he spread on the carpet.

"I will take the floor."

His declaration startled her. "What do you mean?"

"I mean, I'll allow you to have the bed."

"You needn't be so chivalrous," Kate protested.

"It is not chivalry but self-preservation. The temptation will be too great if I must sleep beside you."

She felt marginally better, knowing she was tempting him also. "We have already been intimate. We might as well continue."

"That is not a good enough reason."

Her brow furrowed. "In the graveyard, you'd said I must want you for more than comfort. Well I do."

"I am delighted to hear it. But I've taken a vow of celibacy."

"I beg your pardon?" Kate stared, taken aback. "Whatever for?"

"First, there is a small matter of honor."

Kate stifled an exasperated sigh. "I don't understand. In England, you made numerous attempts to seduce me. Now you have grown a conscience?"

"But here, without the benefit of marriage, we would be living in sin."

That would be nothing new for her family, Kate thought. The Wildes were accustomed to sinning. The corner of her mouth curved sardonically. "Even my aunt Rachel did not object to an affair between us. In fact, she gave me some special sponges to prevent me from getting with child."

"Did she, now?" Deverill's eyebrow shot up at that revelation, but he shook his head. "My answer is still no. I decided you are right. We need time to create a deeper bond, without carnal desire clouding our judgment. Which entails keeping physical contact at a minimum."

She was speechless. How could she win his love if he refused to touch her?

At her silence, he flashed her a faint smile that was rather infuriating. "You set the conditions for our betrothal, remember? You wanted to see if a deeper attachment was possible beyond the carnal."

"Yes, but I thought since we made love last night . . ."

"You wanted to be wooed with romance, not seduction, so I will do just that."

"But I no longer want only romance."

"Well, I want our betrothal to be permanent, without conditions."

"You know why I cannot agree to that."

"So we are at a standoff. A pity. The floor looks rather hard." He glanced down at his makeshift bed before contemplating her thoughtfully. "If you were to agree to wed me without qualification, I would gladly make love to you."

Kate's gaze narrowed. "What is this? Coercion?"

"If you care to see it that way."

There was no other way to see it.

She had been concerned by his resistance, wondering why he wasn't pursuing her with an inkling of the same intensity as before, now that he'd enjoyed her body. But evidently he was waiting for her to agree to wed him.

She folded her arms over her chest. "I won't beg you to make love to me, Deverill."

"Good, since I don't know how much willpower I can summon."

She pressed her lips together. She had a good notion to shake him and make him see reason.

As if reading her thoughts, he gave a warm chuckle.

Without speaking again, Kate marched over to her valise. Flustered and vexed, she found her nightdress and drew it on. Then she climbed into bed, snuffed the lamp, drew the covers up, and turned her back to Deverill.

She expected to hear him making his own bed on the floor, but silence filled the small room. After a moment, she felt the mattress give way as he joined her beneath the covers.

Before she could react, he inched up her nightdress to her hips, then slid his arms around her and pulled her back into the cradle of his body.

At the shock of heat against her skin, Kate caught her breath. "What are you about, Deverill?"

"I have reconsidered."

"You said you wouldn't make love to me."

"I won't. I am making you ache, just as you've done to me. Let's see how well you handle temptation while I sleep beside you."

Kate clenched her teeth. He was fully aroused, his member swollen and hard against her buttocks, and he was making her equally aroused—no doubt to remind her of what she was missing by refusing to wed him.

"Sometimes," she stated in a barely restrained voice, "you can be the most irksome, contrary man of my acquaintance—which is saying a great deal considering the men in my family."

"I won't argue with you." He brushed aside her hair and pressed a kiss in the curve of her neck, eliciting a responsive shiver from her. "Now go to sleep, love. We have a long day ahead of us tomorrow."

His tone was easy but resolute. She wouldn't sway him, she knew he was saying. Until she gave in, he would sleep in the same bed with her but go no further.

More infuriatingly, she was pitifully glad he had relented even that much.

Despite his advice to sleep, Kate remained awake for a long while. The wash of sexual heat flushing through her body made her restless and on edge, while images of them together naked and wicked and intensely passionate kept assaulting her.

Eventually his body relaxed and his breathing slowed. Kate lay there, listening to his heartbeat. The undercurrent of tension kept her senses tinglingly alive, yet it felt so good to be here with Deverill, sweeter than the sweetest wine.

No doubt such enforced celibacy would be beneficial to the growth of their relationship, but she didn't like it at all. Not when she wanted to melt into his arms, to savor his hard strength, to explore the explosive magic that he'd only given her a taste of before. Even with the frustration of unfulfilled sexual arousal, though, lying in Deverill's embrace was far, far better than sleeping alone.

And that realization was the most infuriating of all.

Chapter Sixteen

When Brandon woke at dawn's first light, he lay next to Kate, burning. He relished sleeping with her, but sharing her bed, being unable to satisfy his fierce desire for her, was sheer torment.

Indeed, last evening had strained his willpower to the breaking point. He'd spent much of the time fighting his natural inclination to overwhelm her with passion. He could easily imagine kissing her awake now and arousing her silken body, guiding her to unlock her wildest self. He craved feeling her body respond with ardor.

Even so, he was fully committed to winning Kate—which meant striving to romance her as she wanted, without relying on physical seduction. He needed to show her what it would be like to be his wife, the simple pleasure they could find together.

Even more than pleasure, he wanted to make her happy. Thus for her sake he would try to be the man she wanted him to be, Brandon vowed. If it meant having to explore his long-buried feelings, well then, he was willing to concede.

Just then Kate rolled over onto her back. When her thigh brushed his swollen cock, the contact sent a jolt of pure pleasure rocketing through him.

Sucking in his breath, Brandon raised himself on one elbow to gaze down at her. Her disheveled auburn hair glowed richly in the rays of sunlight filtering through the lace curtains.

He brushed some errant curls from her face, marveling at the effect she'd had on him in the short weeks since his return to England. Already he could feel his emotions softening, his rigid guard dropping. He was losing his strict detachment. And the restless dissatisfaction that had gripped him had eased significantly. Even better, the sharp emptiness he'd known for years was gone entirely.

Kate had given him a taste of an intimacy he'd never known, a tenderness he'd never thought he would experience. Without question, the prospect of creating something deeper didn't alarm him as it once had, nor did building the kind of bond he'd always avoided. Perhaps with time he could even permit himself to feel stronger emotions, like love.

If anyone could show him how to love, it would be Kate.

The thought lingered on his mind as she stirred awake and slowly became aware of her surroundings. After a moment she turned her head and focused her warm, sleep-drugged eyes directly on him.

When she offered him a soft smile that was part shyness, part siren, the sharp pleasure of it stabbed him in his midsection, in his loins.

Brandon swore under his breath and determinedly reined in his baser instincts before they bolted. He couldn't lie here any longer, though, with Kate firing his blood. Nor could he possibly touch her and remain unmoved.

So he planted a light kiss on her temple and slipped from the bed. A bracing bath in the sea would help temper his explosive lust.

"I am going for a swim," he announced, bending to pick up his breeches. "My absence will allow you some privacy."

She blinked at the suddenness of his decision, but without waiting for her to respond, he gathered up the remainder of his clothing and quit the room.

When Kate recovered from her speechlessness, she stretched languidly. She'd been having the most pleasant dream, indulging in the fantasy that Deverill was her husband, her lover. It was quite a delicious feeling, waking to the feel of a hard, very male body beside her. And the sight of his nude form—so tanned and solidly muscled—made her recall how he had made love to her the night of the storm. At the memory, she could feel her nipples harden.

Painfully aware of her breasts and the hollow between her thighs, Kate bestirred herself to rise.

As she washed with water from the basin, she longed for a bath herself. Gabrielle had shown her the small copper tub in a closet off the kitchen, but there was likely not enough time to build a fire in the stove and heat enough bathwater. And most certainly she didn't want to be caught naked when Deverill returned from his swim.

After dressing, she brushed her hair and wound it back into a tidy knot, then went to the kitchen to consider what could be prepared for breakfast.

She had her longings under better control by the time Deverill entered by way of the back door, but her resolve to appear casual instantly deserted her. He was clad in only breeches, his torso glistening with moisture, hair slicked back from his face. Her mouth went dry at the sight of so much warm, bronzed skin, and she was glad when he announced his intention to dress and shave. With a shadow of stubble darkening his jaw, he looked ruggedly handsome and more than a little dangerous, like the pirates he meant to consort with today.

While he disappeared, Kate busied herself putting together a breakfast of bread and jam and slices of ham from the loin stored in the pantry cooler. She craved a cup of hot tea, but settled for cider.

Deverill appeared a short while later and joined her at the kitchen table. When he complimented her resourcefulness, Kate demurred. At Beauvoir in Kent where she had grown up, she commanded an enormous staff, and a smaller one at the mansion in London, but she had learned enough to get by in a pinch.

"I should go to the market and purchase food," she said. "And perhaps I can hire a servant to help with the cleaning and cooking."

Over their meal they discussed the plans for the day.

"From the beach you can see the small harbor of St. Georges," Deverill told her. "Louvel's men will gather there to begin the search while he and I interview the villagers who witnessed the *Zephyr* go down, according to Macky's investigation."

"I wish I could accompany you," Kate said, "but Louvel and his fellow pirates will not appreciate my tagging along. And my time will be better spent cultivating an acquaintance with Gabrielle."

When a companionable silence followed, Kate once again was struck by the simple domestic scene and couldn't help wondering if this was what their marriage would be like.

All too soon, however, the peaceful interlude ended, for Deverill gave her a pistol to carry in her reticule, as well as a sharp-bladed dagger, reminding her how serious their situation was, facing a band of potential cutthroats. She and Deverill would need to work together and keep their wits about them if they hoped to prevail without major consequence.

When they were finished eating, Deverill retrieved the horses and carriage from the local livery and delivered Kate to the pirate's house. Before they parted ways, she managed to divulge her misgivings. "I admit I am worried for you."

"I am more worried for you," he replied. "I don't like the thought of leaving you alone—although I suspect you can fend for yourself," he quickly added. "I know better than to question your courage."

That dredged a smile from her, as she knew he'd meant to.

Kate stood watching with Gabrielle as the men departed, then began asking questions. The Frenchwoman explained the layout of the village and led her outside at the rear of the house, which afforded expansive views of the sea. When she pointed out the harbor in the distance to their right, Kate could just make out a number of fishing vessels—sailboats and skiffs and dinghies—tied to the jetties. Along the coast to their left, Gabrielle said, were ample caves and grottoes and pretty beaches.

Afterward, they returned inside to the parlor, where a tea tray had been delivered. When the conversation broadened, they both lamented having to remain at home while men did the real work.

"Regrettably, it is the lot of women everywhere," Gabrielle remarked. But then she described her situation, and it became clear that the Frenchwoman had far more freedom than English girls of similar station. The village of St. Georges was fairly poor but lively, and except for her lack of family and husband, she cherished living there. Furthermore, her position as Louvel's mistress was seen as practical rather than shameful.

"I confess I am envious," Kate said honestly. "In my country, a genteel young lady must strictly adhere to propriety or risk causing a scandal."

From there the conversation turned to more mundane matters, beginning with care of the cottage. Gabrielle offered to accompany Kate to the market that afternoon, and to supply a servant to help with the chores. When Kate confessed that she was unaccustomed to boiling water for a bath, Gabrielle shared some welcome news.

"There is a Roman bath not too distant from here. Since it was built many centuries ago, much of the building is in ruins. But the pools are supplied by a hot spring and are quite enjoyable. You might want to visit."

"That sounds heavenly," Kate admitted.

"I will draw a map for you with the direction."

All the while, Kate kept up a gentle probing of the Frenchwoman's life and her relationship with Louvel. Additionally, she shared some of her own romantic history with Deverill. Confessing the humiliation of his rejection years ago went a long way toward gaining Gabrielle's trust and convincing her to divulge her own confidences.

"I fear to press Jean on marriage," Gabrielle eventually admitted. "He is not the romantic sort in the least."

"Do you think he loves you?" Kate asked.

A wistful look entered her eyes. "There are times when I believe so, but I cannot be certain."

"It would help if I could see the two of you together, to judge how he feels about you. We would be better able to determine a plan of action then."

Gabrielle sat more upright, looking eager and optimistic. "But yes. The opportunity could arise if you and Monsieur Deverill were to dine with us. Perhaps tomorrow evening? In the interim, I will seek Jean's permission. I dare not invite you without it."

"I understand," Kate assured her. "Dining together is an excellent idea."

"I will begin tonight." A surprisingly impish gleam shone in Gabrielle's eyes. "The boudoir is a prime place to persuade him. There, I have been able many times to sway Jean to my wishes."

Kate couldn't help but smile. "What is your secret?"

"Seduction of course." Gabrielle studied Kate thoughtfully. "Perhaps you should plot a seduction of Monsieur Deverill. Lust can prove a powerful incitement."

Her smile turned to a frown. It was no more than she had advised many of her would-be matches, but even so, it would present a daunting challenge. He was an expert at seduction while she was a novice. "If I were to try, I could not be overt about it. I failed miserably once before. . . ."

Yet seduction might be her only means of making him abandon his vow of celibacy.

Kate bit her lip in contemplation. It would be supremely fitting if she could drive Deverill wild with lust, as he was so clearly set on doing with her. She would derive great satisfaction from making him yearn for her, from making him want her madly. But far more important, by stoking Deverill's desire, she stood a better chance of winning his heart.

By the time they finished their tea, a plan was beginning to take shape in Kate's mind. And by midmorning when they prepared to visit the market, her spirits had lifted significantly. Like Gabrielle, she felt more optimistic than she had in a great while.

Now all she needed was to take the first step.

As it happened, Deverill created the opportunity for her that very evening. Kate was waiting at the cottage when he returned from the harbor. Over supper, which she had prepared with the aid of two servants, he reported their progress—how they had assembled the necessary boats and equipment and sailors, and outlined a map of the area where they would initially concentrate the search on the morrow.

Afterward, Deverill invited her for a walk on the beach.

The day was fading as they made their way from the cottage along a sandy path flanked by scrub bush. Depositing a blanket and a bottle of wine in the sand, they removed their shoes and stockings and strolled along the shore.

Much to Kate's satisfaction, Deverill took her hand to help her over a clump of seagrass and never relinquished it. It was a perfect summer evening, with sunlight painting the water a rose gold and the music of nature serenading them: the call of seagulls, waves rushing gently at their feet, a soft breeze dancing over them.

Dusk had fallen when they returned to their chosen spot and settled on the blanket. With a rising moon silvering the water, Kate thought the scene enchanting.

"The view is lovely," she said with all sincerity.

"Yes, it is," Deverill responded while gazing directly at her.

Kate had begun to wonder what he was thinking, when he spoke again. "It might have escaped your notice, but I am making a romantic gesture, just as you wished. I still hope to persuade you to make our betrothal a permanent union."

And I hope to persuade you to love me, she thought.

Aloud, she said, "It will take more than one romantic evening to convince me."

"But I haven't begun to use all the weapons at my disposal."

Kate cocked an eyebrow at him. "Weapons? I did not realize it was a battle between us."

"Securing your hand in marriage is indeed a battle."

Determined to keep the conversation light, she refrained from commenting.

A moment later he proposed a swim, then removed his shirt. When he stood and began to unbutton his breeches, she was pressed into asking, "You mean to swim naked in public?"

"Certainly. There is no one here to see us. Come and join me." When she hesitated, Deverill's lips curved. "You are showing your craven side again."

Wisely ignoring his baiting, Kate politely declined. "I already washed at the cottage this afternoon, and the sea is a bit chilly for my taste. In fact, I would rather utilize a Roman bath. Gabrielle says there is one nearby, fed by a hot spring."

"We can explore it some other time. Meanwhile, we have the beach all to ourselves." At her silence, he prodded her further. "You wanted to become more adventuresome, did you not? I am only thinking of you, of broadening your horizons."

"How very obliging of you," Kate said sweetly. "Thank you, but I will remain here and enjoy the view."

"As you wish."

He stripped off his breeches, but instead of leaving, he remained standing before her, entirely naked. Kate found herself studying him, thinking how bold and daring he was, how magnificent his body was—

She brought her thoughts up short. No doubt Deverill was taunting her in an effort to rouse her desire, displaying himself in so brazen a fashion.

Kate sent him a frown. "You are trying to tempt me, admit it."

Deverill shrugged, oozing innocence. Not answering, he turned and strode away.

Without volition, she watched as he waded out a short distance, then dove into the dark waves and became lost to sight. Making a scoffing sound, she shook her head at her own frailty. As usual he had succeeded in making her blush, turning her entire body warm.

But two could play that game. In truth if she had any hope of seducing him, she had to make him just as hot as she was. Recalling what she'd planned, she removed her gown and corset, leaving only her muslin shift. Then she poured herself a glass of wine and sat there sipping. A delicious anticipation crawled up her spine as she waited for Deverill to return.

After a time, she spied him wading back toward her. Even in the semidark, she could make out his form. Ordinarily she was not easily awed by a man, yet she found herself riveted by the sight of a Grecian god striding from the water—broad shoulders, narrow waist, rigid belly, lean hips, long, sinewed legs . . . A god, indeed. His build and physical prowess set him apart from other mere mortals and he put the classical statues to shame.

And when he drew close she could see his stark beauty: his curling locks wet with seawater, the clean strong lines of his face, the sheer power of his body. The display left her breathless.

Her only satisfaction was that she seemed to have caught him by surprise with her own state of undress.

His bold eyes skimmed over her before he threw himself down on the blanket beside her.

Yet he made no move to take her in his arms, or even to kiss her. Instead, he poured some wine for himself and with a casual disregard of his nudity, propped himself on one elbow to drink it.

Still, he was watching her with a warm intensity that was unsettling and flattering. Kate was exquisitely aware of Deverill by her side.

"Aren't you the least chilled?" she finally asked to break the silence.

"No. The evening is fairly warm."

Perhaps it was. Certainly her body was, as she contemplated her next step.

Taking a breath, she slowly pulled down the straps of her shift, then the bodice.

Deverill's eyes seemed to flare as the peaks of her breasts were revealed, but he instantly stopped her. "That's far enough, sweetheart."

Kate paused but sent him a disapproving look. "I don't understand why you still refuse to make love to me. You yourself taught me that we can enjoy pleasure without actual coupling."

"You know why. It is my best leverage."

"I doubt that is your only reason."

"Oh?"

"I think you are afraid."

"Of what?"

"That you could never live up to the lover of my dreams. You are afraid to even try."

That amused, tender look was back in his eyes. "I am not afraid."

She arched a challenging brow at him. "Then prove it."

After a moment he murmured two words that made her pulse race. "Come closer."

Setting her glass in the sand, she obeyed, inching her way nearer until he could touch her.

Holding her gaze, he lifted a finger and stroked lightly, masterfully, down the column of her throat, then lower, to her right nipple. Even that barest contact sent a jolt of awareness shivering along her skin, a feminine reaction that heightened all of her senses.

But again, he was only teasing her, for he soon dropped his hand.

Kate let out an exasperated sigh. "You delight in vexing me, don't you?"

"Quite."

The laughter in his voice made her want to laugh and grind her teeth in return, but she managed to calm herself in favor of plotting her revenge. Raising an eyebrow, she contemplated him. "If I really set my mind to it, I doubt you could resist me."

"Is that so?"

"Yes."

Deliberately, she reached out to brush his flat belly just above his loins. The instant she touched his skin, his stomach muscles clenched.

He stared at her with that knowing look, comprehension gleaming in his eyes. "You're a handful, aren't you?" he accused, his voice deep and amused.

"I intend to be."

At his chuckle, Kate took heart. She was no femme fatale who could bring a man to his knees—at least not *yet*. But she was eager to learn. Admittedly the prospect of having Deverill on his knees, pleading for release, was a delicious thought.

"Do your worst, then," he invited.

She took his glass from him and set it aside but kept her gaze focused solely on him. "Lie back," she ordered.

"No, you will have to make me."

Easing closer, she knelt directly beside him. Then leaning forward, she pressed her hands against his shoulders. Surprisingly, her effort was met with only token resistance. Deverill rolled onto both elbows and lounged back against the blanket, letting her look her fill.

Kate spent another moment admiring his physique. She had never been so keenly aware of his body, so hard and strong, of the virility in his broad shoulders.

With her palms, she urged him to lie fully on his back. He offered greater resistance this time, but she pushed harder, until she was pinning him down. The coiled strength beneath her palms was unmistakable. He could shake her off with barely a flex of his muscles, she knew. But for now he indulged the pretense that she was in complete control. Lightly she ran her hands over the expanse of his chest, feeling smooth, hot flesh over corded muscles, dusted with silken hair.

Then her gaze drifted lower, to his taut belly, the powerful sprawl of his thighs, the swollen, jutting erection that reached almost to his navel. Her breathing turned shallow.

"If I knew what to do, the contest would be more fair," she murmured. "You need to tutor me. . . . Teach me how to pleasure you."

"I suppose I could do that much."

Reaching up, he cupped her breasts, using his thumbs to prod her nipples. Excitement swept over her, but she tamped it down.

"No. You need to show me how to pleasure *you*. This is not showing me."

Anticipation glimmered in his eyes. "Perhaps you should begin by stroking me with your hands."

"Yes."

She shifted her palms lower. His expression never changed, but when her exploring hands travelled to his belly, she felt a tension quiver inside him.

Bolder now, she moved her hand even lower to touch his swelling manhood. It jerked involuntarily, making her breath catch. Kate bit her lip. She could imagine having that engorged length inside her. . . . Fresh excitement spread through her body at the thought and made her breasts ache.

Deliberately she trailed her hand lower, letting her fingers curl around him. When his breath drew harshly between his teeth, she looked up, caught by the hypnotizing heat of his eyes.

His hot vitality seemed to thrum through her.

"*Show me,*" Kate repeated in a husky murmur.

His hand wrapped around hers, guiding her. Keeping a light grasp of her fingers, he coaxed her to fondle him, letting her cup the heavy sacs beneath his arousal, tracing the blunt, velvety head, until finally he curled her hand around his full length. Demonstrating how to give him pleasure, he began moving her hand slowly up and down, stroking.

"Harder, princess. . . . You won't hurt me."

"Like this?"

"Yes, exactly like that. . . ."

His hips arched in response. A shameful thrill raced through Kate, kindling her senses. She was inflamed by the feel of him, by the lazy passion glowing in his eyes. And yet . . .

"Isn't there more?" she asked with curiosity.

"A great deal more. You are welcome to use your imagination."

She could only follow her instincts. Bending down to him, she breathed in the scent of warm sand and salt and his own essence, the clean, masculine fragrance of his skin.

Holding her breath, she tasted him with her tongue.

"I am all admiration for your inventiveness," he said in a hoarse voice.

"But I have barely begun," she warned with a smile.

She pressed her lips along his shaft, tasting the

marble-smooth skin. He jerked when she kissed him there, and when she ran her tongue upward, a shudder ran through him, igniting a sense of power in Kate. It was a heady feeling, knowing she could evoke such a response from Deverill. It was thrilling, exhilarating, to think she could torment him with her caresses the way he did her. He was blatantly aroused now, the rigid rod thrusting high.

Her tongue began stroking rhythmically, his head fell back. And when she began to suckle him, he inhaled as if fighting for control.

Encouraged, she explored him with her mouth and tongue, tasting the slick, velvet contours, making love to the most intimate part of him.

Finally, though, he grasped her shoulders to lift her mouth away. "That is far enough," Deverill rasped. "Just hold my cock in your hand."

When she complied, he went back to guiding her strokes. As he increased the pace, she glanced up at him. His face was taut, the skin flushed. His jaw locked as their fingers kneaded harder, sweeping up and down in short, rough motions.

His breath was harsh and uneven by now, his fingers clenching around hers. But the moment before he exploded, he released her hand and cupped his own around the head of his shaft.

Kate held still, watching the last throes of his climax. It was incredibly erotic for her, giving him such pleasure. His eyes were shut, but when he opened them again, they were so dark they were almost black.

Now was the moment to press him, she knew. She held his gaze intently.

"Deverill, please . . . won't you make love to me?" she pleaded in a low voice. "You are right. I need to become more adventurous. I want to truly live, not merely exist. We are alone here, without chaperones or family to interfere or watch over me. And we should make the most of this opportunity."

Kate paused, her nerves stretched taut while she waited for him to respond.

It was quite some time before Deverill gave a sigh that was part surrender, part celebration. "Finally you acknowledge what I have been telling you all along. I would relish making love to you, sweetheart, but you deserve a more romantic setting than a gritty beach. Let us return to the cottage first."

"Yes," she said, her heart swelling.

She pulled up the bodice of her shift while he donned his breeches.

As they gathered up their belongings, he delayed long enough to drop a soft kiss on her lips. Another surge of breathless excitement and anticipation hit Kate.

She cherished the intimacy of their joined hands as they followed the sandy path. When he helped her over a grassy dune, she gazed up at him, admiring how moonlight played over the planes of his face.

Deverill looked down at just that moment and captured her gaze. Attraction sizzled between them, igniting the rise of heat inside her, along with a renewed sense of hope: He seemed confident that he would win this battle of wills, but she had a plan, too. He could teach her about passion, but she would teach him to love. She knew in her heart that lovemaking could be intimate and wonderful, not merely a physical expression of desire. To her mind, the very essence of romance was learning to love.

She badly wanted to help him overcome his resistance to loving, to draw him out of his self-imposed prison. Accordingly, she needed to stir in Deverill the soul-deep longing that she was beginning to feel. And she had to let it occur naturally rather than force him to have feelings for her.

He kept her close until they reached the kitchen. There, he lit a lamp before leading her to the bedchamber.

They parted in order to undress, but Kate was burningly aware of him a short distance away as she drew off her shift.

Feigning nonchalance, she went to her valise and drew out the pouch of sponges. "Are you familiar with these? I have never used them before. You will have to show me what to do."

"Gladly."

When she turned and found him watching her, the promise in his smile made her heart pound. Suddenly the memory of heat and desire and naked need hit her with breathtaking force.

Kate felt her knees go weak as Deverill crossed

to her. His bare arm encircling her waist, he pulled her close, his thighs brushing hers, his chest pressing against her breasts. He reached up and slid his fingers behind her nape, then bent his head.

The pure power of his kiss bolted through her body. He was a marvelous kisser, sure and possessive and incredibly sensual. A telltale shiver racked her.

As if he knew the cause, he lifted his head, and his gaze locked with hers, smoldering and intent.

"You want me. That is why you're flushed and hot."

He was right. She felt hot enough to make her thighs quiver.

His hands moved to cover her breasts, his palms cradling their weight, his thumbs pressing against her nipples. His smile was intimate, and so were his eyes.

At the ache of her breasts inside his gentle grip, Kate felt heat shimmer through her. "Deverill . . . tell me what I should do."

"Leave it to me, love. My masculine pride is at stake."

Bending again, he kissed the hollow of her throat, then let his lips trail lightly over her skin as he murmured in a husky voice, "I mean to satisfy you, to pleasure you, to make your body sing. . . ."

He was issuing his own challenge, Kate knew. Just thinking about what was in store made her breathing go wild.

Stopping his caressing mouth from exploring her

body further, she pulled his face back to hers and wrapped her arms around his neck.

"Enough talk," she replied, urgently raising her lips for his kiss. "If you expect to prove your skills as my dream lover, I demand action."

Chapter Seventeen

They woke the next morning, tangled in each other's arms. Sleepily Kate gazed back at Deverill, luxuriating in a rich sense of repletion and satisfaction. She'd spent the night learning him, savoring the strength of him, the sheer maleness of him. He hadn't just made love to her; he had *claimed* her.

And now, when he slowly eased over her and took her mouth, it wasn't a mere kiss, it was a *possession.*

That sensual encounter was the beginning of a magical time for Kate in the week that followed. She felt as if they were living in another world inhabited by only the two of them—feverish, romantic, enchanted—with both finding the spell impossible to break.

During long walks and late nights, they came to know each other better, their spirited sparring interspersed with laughter and quiet moments, and of course, pleasure. Boundless pleasure.

If she was bent on seducing him, he was doing the same to her. Indeed, the entire sennight became a tantalizing battle for supremacy between them, with Deverill daring her to become more adventurous, often alternating between provoking her and calling her bewitching and captivating.

She was the one who was captivated, though. His dark gaze left her feeling seduced and desirable. She who never got lost in a man's eyes regularly felt breathless and dizzy at his nearness.

And yet, regrettably to Kate's mind, most days they were required to engage with the real world.

That night they dined at Louvel's house. For a pirate, Jean Louvel seemed quite civilized and gentlemanly and welcoming as a host. Despite his proper table manners, however, his treatment of Gabrielle left something to be desired. Although he seemed genuinely fond of her, his behavior toward her bordered on arrogant and demanding, as if he considered her his property, Kate thought.

She observed their interactions carefully, and when the women retired to the drawing room, leaving the men to their port, she was able to question the beauty at some length.

Clearly Gabrielle was far more enamored of Louvel than he was of her. She truly loved him, but while he unquestionably bore a passion for her, his affection didn't indicate the prospect of marriage or family. Gabrielle wanted children—legitimate children. A place at his side as his wife, not just a mistress to warm his bed. But by her admission, her plan to seduce Louvel into proposing had borne little fruit thus far, nor did she expect it to.

"Have you spoken to him about marriage?" Kate asked her. "Does he know how you feel about him?"

"I have been too afraid to press him for fear he would cast me out. If that occurs, I would have no livelihood and no place to live. As the spurned lover, I would likely be compelled to move away, to leave my home, my friends."

"But even as his *chère femme*, you should have certain rights," Kate argued. "What if you were to give him an ultimatum? Demand marriage as payment for continuing with him? Sometimes men only need a little push in the right direction to come to their senses."

"If he refuses, then where would I be? I would have nowhere to go. And I have no leverage to sway him."

Kate considered Gabrielle thoughtfully, wondering whether to encourage her to risk being left with nothing. It was often the way of the world, where men held all the power and women were but chattel or, at a minimum, impotent supplicants. But if it was only a matter of money . . .

"Let me think on it, and I will try to devise a plan. Meanwhile, I am grateful for all the help you have given us since we arrived in St. Georges."

They went on to discuss how the search for the shipwreck was proceeding. And the next morning reminded Kate of the benefits of cultivating Louvel's good graces. With his permission she went with Gabrielle to the harbor to watch as a half-dozen vessels sailed away. The searchers began upstream of St. Georges and worked their way along the estuary toward the Atlantic, but there had been no sightings thus far. Over and over, their nets and hooks came up empty, with very little to show for their dredging efforts.

Midweek found Kate pondering more on her progress with Deverill. She thought he might be responding to her unspoken encouragement to be more open with his feelings. Undoubtedly an undercurrent of deeper emotion ran beneath the playful tone of their sexual encounters.

He never again spoke about the war, nor did she ask, but each time she saw the stark scar on his back beneath his shoulder blade, she felt a powerful urge to touch that old wound, along with an intense anger at whoever had hurt him. And she knew that having to fight his former friends and colleagues had scarred him more deeply than his flesh wound ever had.

He did talk about his family sometimes. At her instigation and his own, he shared a few fond memories of his younger brother, Griffith, during happier times, and less often, his conflicted feelings about his parents.

Kate knew she might be indulging in wishful thinking, but she couldn't help hoping that Deverill's frozen heart was slowly thawing, making him less resistant to the possibility of love.

As for passion, he was most definitely broadening her horizons as he'd promised. Two afternoons later, he returned early from the search and took her to explore the Roman bath that Gabrielle had mentioned.

The ancient buildings, which had been erected in a small cove with a spectacular view of the sea, had long ago fallen into ruin, but there were three fairly large pools made from slabs of stone, fed by a natural hot spring swirling from the depths. The water was fresh and clear and partially shaded by overhanging branches of tall willows that had sprouted between the cracks in the rock.

It was a perfect place for lovers, Kate thought: the aquamarine of the sea behind them, the waves washing upon the shore below, the surface of the heated pools dappled with sunlight that wove through the sheltering leaves above.

No sooner had they reached the edge of the largest pool when Deverill drew her close.

Under the pretense of kissing her, he raised the hem of her gown and slid a hand up her stockinged calf to slip one finger inside her. When she gasped, he drew back. His dark eyes seared her, conveying the promise of mindless rapture. "You're so wet for me. So hot and tight. Let me pleasure you, lovely Kate. . . ."

They both knew how this encounter would end—in her seduction. But vowing again that she would not make it easy for him, she danced away.

"All in good time," she said, flashing a teasing smile.

After undressing, she scooped up a cake of soap, then carefully descended a flight of stone steps and slipped into the pool. The water was pleasantly warm, the surface a little higher than waist deep.

She had begun soaping herself by the time Deverill shed his own clothing and stood on the bank, preparing to enter. She stared, enrapt. He looked like every woman's most wicked dream.

Out of self-preservation, Kate turned away. She heard a slight splash as he joined her. Then he came up behind her and slid his arms around her.

When his thighs brushed hers, she could feel the firm, purposeful nudge of his swollen manhood against her buttocks. Heat surrounded her. Her breasts felt heavy and full and throbbed for his touch.

"We are supposed to be bathing," Kate managed to say rather weakly.

"I know. Allow me to help you, angel."

The caress of his voice was so enticing, she could almost taste the pleasure he promised, could almost feel his lengthy shaft gliding between her feminine folds.

She protested no further when he took the soap from her. With a delicate touch, he soaped her breasts, then her belly. The drift of his slick hands on her bare skin felt so divine. . . . She was already breathless by the time he reached her woman's mound. Kate leaned back against him as he continued, closing her eyes against the exquisite sensations in her breasts, in her loins.

When he finished washing her front, he attended her back, then rinsed her entire body. To her surprise, he drew her toward the edge of the pool, then tossed the soap upon the ledge and turned her to face him. He was staring at her breasts, she realized—like a man hungry for a taste of her.

Her hands rose to press against his chest, yet she didn't really want to stop him. She could feel the hardness of his corded muscles beneath her palms as he bent down to trace one areola with his tongue. When his lips closed over the pebbled nipple and suckled, Kate responded with a revealing whimper that spoke of desire and want and need.

For a long moment he aroused her that way, licking and laving and savoring her . . . before apparently deciding it wasn't enough. With his hands at her waist, he lifted her to sit on the stone ledge and stepped between her thighs.

"What do you mean to do?" Kate asked.

"You'll see."

How he managed to invest so much beguiling promise in so few words, she couldn't begin to comprehend. And his gaze . . . His half smile reflected in his intent gaze, capturing her completely. He knew she couldn't look away.

Those eyes held hers, hot and dark and bright with challenge as his fingers parted the folds of her sex to lightly stroke. The erotic caress made her breath catch.

"Sit back, sweetheart. Just relax."

Biting her lip, Kate obediently braced her hands behind her, suddenly needing the support.

To her disappointment, his fingers moved away from

her thighs—but not far. As his hands began to work a wicked sorcery over the rest of her body, sensations flooded her, leaving her trembling and weak. He touched her everywhere, teasing, seducing, kneading, pulling at her sun-warmed flesh, plying her nipples with his fingers.

His gaze returning with relentless precision, he pressed her thighs wider, baring all her secrets. Then positioning her as if she was there strictly for his pleasure alone, he lowered his head.

When she felt his warm breath stir the damp curls at the juncture of her thighs, Kate quivered at the erotic shock of it.

Then his mouth moved closer to kiss her there. The caress shuddered through her. And when he found the taut bud of her sex with his tongue, her hips arched.

"Easy . . ." His voice was low, vibrant, stroking her like rich velvet.

One more tender lash of his tongue, and her head fell backward. His hands held her steady, anchoring her while he continued his tender assault with his mouth. He went on tasting her, tormenting her, his tongue probing her folds. Then he drew the swollen bud into his mouth as his middle finger slipped inside her.

The sensation was incredible—his hard finger sheathed in her flesh, his scalding mouth working its spell on her sex.

With a moan, Kate reached down to grasp his sable

hair. His mouth was magical, and so was his touch, but she wanted more of him.

"Deverill, I need . . ." she whispered urgently.

"I know." His own voice was a smoky rasp.

He was waiting for her sighs, her little cries, her signs of surrender, she knew. And soon Kate complied. She trembled violently, her whole body coiled unbearably tight. She lost touch with everything but her own frantic heartbeat.

He wasn't willing to permit her release just yet, though. Instead, he urged her to join him in the water, drawing her against him, her legs wrapped around his waist.

"Tell me what you want, Kate. . . ."

"You. I want you. . . ." Her fingers clutching his hair, she strove to get even closer, overwhelmed by the sheer, overpowering need to be one with him.

"Then you shall have me."

He watched her steadily, knowingly, as he lifted her slightly, then lowered her onto his shaft. It was the most glorious sensation. Kate relished every slow inch, the bliss of having him fill her so utterly and completely.

The power in his arms intensified her sensation of thrilling weakness. She gave another moan, full of awe at her own helplessness as she clung to him.

Yet she wasn't the only one affected. His dark eyes hot with need, Deverill gripped her buttocks. In response she ground herself against him, writhing helplessly against his delicious impalement. The frantic heat burned through her nerve endings. She was hot and only he could cool her; only he could satisfy the burning need inside her.

As if seared by the same heat, he captured her lips and kissed deeply, his tongue penetrating her mouth like his shaft was doing.

The taut, savage need was blazing between them now. Want had become craving, and Deverill's own rough excitement was matching her frenzy. She welcomed the hard thrusting of his body as he took her, his tongue plunging in the same demanding rhythm as he filled her again and again.

In the next instant a low, rough groan burst from his throat. His control snapped, shattered, while she ignited with fiery urgency. His lips drank in her wild moans, and they came together in a firestorm of passion.

When at last it was over, Kate collapsed bonelessly against him, their breaths rasping in harsh gasps.

It was a long while before she felt Deverill lift his head and sensed him watching her. Aware of how wanton and thoroughly pleasured she must look, she raised her gaze to find him looking flushed and pleasured also.

Furthermore, he seemed as exhausted as she felt.

With effort, he lifted her onto the ledge again, then leveraged himself up and sprawled beside her on the warm rock.

Having no energy remaining, she crawled into his arms and curled against him.

With the soft breeze flowing over them, the splintering sunlight shining through the trees to glisten on their wet bodies, she felt a perfect sense of peace.

It was a very long time before Deverill spoke. "I am waiting for your concession," he said weakly.

"Concession?"

"That I have proven my mastery. You consider me a splendid lover, admit it."

Kate gave a muffled laugh against his shoulder. "What shameless arrogance."

"It is not arrogance if it's true."

"Your vanity knows no bounds, I see. But since I would not want to puncture your inflated male self-esteem, I suppose I must agree. You are a splendid lover."

The accolade was indisputable, Kate thought lazily. Deverill had reduced her to a quivering thing, begging, pleading. . . . And it was past time for her to attempt the same thing with him.

Rousing herself, she slid one leg over his thighs so that she lay astride him. "Now it is my turn to test the skills you have taught me," she murmured against his neck.

He huffed in a weak chuckle. "I don't know if I can survive any more pleasure."

Kate raised her head to survey him. "Do you mean to cry pax, then?"

"Not on your life."

The challenging glint in his eye belied his claim of weariness. Grasping her hips, he lifted her up, then lowered her again, easing his way into her cleft with superb skill. Kate bit back a soft moan at the fullness of his penetration. He had only been waiting until her nearness could make him hard and ready again, she realized.

Impaled on his hardness, she gazed down at him. Desire was thick and raw and powerful between them once more.

Then his hands reached up to cup her breasts, and Kate caught her breath. When his fingers tightened on her nipples, the arousing caress sent renewed spasms of pleasure shuddering through her—and just like that, she was blazing hot again.

Naturally, Deverill recognized her need. Still joined at the loins, he rolled over with her, pressing himself more deeply into the sensitive depths of her body. Then he bent to kiss the swollen tips of her breasts, sucking each throbbing nipple in turn, making fresh desire twist inside her.

"Deverill . . ."

"Hush, love. I want you panting and mindless beneath me," he murmured.

"I thought," she said hoarsely, "this was *my* time to arouse *you*."

His tongue licked a slow, tormenting path up her throat to her ear. "Oh, you *will* arouse me, my sweet witch, believe me. This is merely something new to add to your repertoire."

His lips tugged suggestively on her earlobe. "What you require is a lesson in self-control," he whispered, devil soft. "The delay will make the consummation all the more stunning, I promise you. Now pay close attention. . . ."

The remainder of the week sped by for Kate. Deverill seemed determined to set her free, to make her into the passionate lover he claimed she could be.

On her part, Kate knew that the heady, intimate passion was changing her. She'd become addicted to his touch and scent; she *craved* him. She wanted to touch him a hundred times a day. Indeed, she had only to look at him and her body responded. The desire he ignited inside her was like wildfire, fierce and hot, and that left her unable to breathe.

As for Deverill, sometimes he was driven, intense, as if he couldn't get enough of her. At other times playful. He would pretend to be tamed—or allow her the *illusion* that he had let her tame him. He also acted as if he was set on learning all her secrets, yet shared few of his own.

Kate was thrilled to be wanted by him. His obvious ardor was highly gratifying to her own self-esteem. And yet she yearned for so much more.

That was doubtless why at week's end, when Deverill returned to report that the searchers had discovered the wreck of the *Zephyr,* she was not as gladdened as she should have been. She had hoped the endeavor would take longer, to allow her more time with Deverill in the temporary paradise they had made together.

"How do you know it was the ship that belonged to my parents?" she asked.

"Because we found the name emblazoned in the wood. I swam down to verify it myself."

The wreck, he told her, was located partway across the estuary, within sight of the shore, in water no more than twenty feet deep so that there was enough light to aid in excavation. Some large sections of the hull were still intact, with pieces of burnt timber and iron half buried in the sandy floor.

"If you would like to visit the site, you can sail out with us in a day or two," he added.

"Yes," Kate replied quietly. "I would like to see it eventually."

She couldn't bring herself to ask just then about the remains of the passengers and crew. But as the divers began bringing up various artifacts in the following days, they found several skeletons amid the debris.

Deverill spared her the gruesome details. In fact, it was impossible to tell if any of the victims might have been her father or aunt or uncle. But now they had enough proof to plan a symbolic burial.

On his orders, the divers gathered up the bones, to be placed in a casket that would be interred in the churchyard, a show of reverence for all who had perished.

In the days that followed, a sadness weighed heavily on Kate. Not merely the lingering grief of a daughter who'd lost cherished family members, but also regret that the magical interlude she had treasured with Deverill was almost over.

The time to make him love her was running out.

Those were the moments when she felt overly fatalistic. Perhaps she should accept that Deverill might not ever change, Kate reflected. If so, she should end their betrothal before she irrevocably lost her heart to him.

There were also moments, however, when she was certain that she ought to see her dream to completion. When she believed that Deverill was fated to be her husband, that she was meant to spend the rest of her life with him.

Something about him drew her so powerfully, and always had. She wanted to fill that same need in him. She wanted to bring happiness to his life, to be part of something special. To find the magic that her parents had known.

She wanted a husband who adored her as her father had adored her mother. She wanted Deverill to look at her with hunger, not just for her flesh but for her heart and soul.

She would have to decide very soon whether she was willing to give up on her quest, Kate knew. And with the discovery of the *Zephyr,* the question of ending their betrothal was becoming ever more urgent.

Chapter Eighteen

The excavation of the sunken ship continued for several more days, a task made difficult by layers of sediment covering the site, a lack of light, and restrictions on breathing. Since it was often too dim to see inside the wreckage of cabins and companionways, much of the exploration had to be done by feel. More crucially, the divers could stay underwater for only a few minutes at a time, even using an apparatus designed to trap air near the seafloor to periodically spell their lungs.

Several small casks and wooden boxes were unearthed, but no jewels were found, much to Louvel's regret, and eventually, Deverill judged it time to conclude the search.

When Kate agreed with his recommendation, they discussed how to handle final payment for the pirates' services, and additionally, how to help Gabrielle. The best option, Kate contended, was to deposit some three hundred guineas—the gold remaining once she made the final payment to Louvel—in a Royan bank in the Frenchwoman's name.

When Deverill questioned the wisdom of interfering with Louvel's romantic affairs, Kate replied emphatically, "I want to do this for her. Besides the kindness she has shown us during our stay, she has become my friend. I hope to repay her in some measure by helping her secure a proposal of marriage from Louvel. But if he is too blind or stubborn to marry her, then she will have the means to be free of him should she choose."

"You just cannot stop matchmaking, can you?" Deverill asked with cynical amusement.

Kate ignored his teasing. "That is not my sole reason. It is more because Gabrielle has no fortune and no family to rely on. I have never had to face being penniless and all alone in the world, dependent on the charity of others, but I fully comprehend the indignities women suffer as the legal property of men, subservient to their slightest whims. I am wealthy enough that I won't miss the funds, and it will enable her to determine her own fate."

"Very well," Deverill finally consented. "I will instruct Halsey to convey the sum to the bank and establish an account for her. But I'll wager Louvel will not be pleased when he finds out."

"No doubt," Kate muttered. "But this step may prod him to treat her with the respect she deserves."

On the following day, they held a small service and

symbolic burial for the late Marquess and Marchioness of Beaufort, the Earl and Countess of Traherne, and the other shipwreck victims.

Kate was glad to have the presence of both Cornelius and Rachel, and of course, Deverill. She had vowed she would not cry, but as she stood beside the newly dug grave and traced the new headstone for her mother and father, she felt the sharp loss all over again and couldn't hold back her tears.

Yet this moment marked the end of her mission to honor her parents and relatives. The company was subdued afterward when they discussed the plan to return to England and decided to set sail late the following afternoon with the tide.

Meanwhile, Kate and Deverill would return to St. Georges this evening, and in the morning, settle their business with Louvel and Gabrielle and gather their belongings from the cottage.

That plan also afforded them another visit to the Roman bath—which, Kate suspected, Deverill would use to ease her sadness.

Claiming a saddle horse from the livery rather than using the hired carriage, he mounted first, then took her up in front of him. He held her closely the entire way, speaking little while she leaned back against him, willing to let him take the lead.

When they reached the cove and brought the horse to a halt, Kate bestirred herself to observe their surroundings. The three pools rippled with silver light, possessing the same luminous beauty as the sea that shimmered beyond the bath.

The spellbinding scene held an aura of enchantment, as sensual as anything she had known before with Deverill. Yet the moment also held a special poignancy since it would be their last time alone together.

He helped her dismount, then led her to the edge of the center pool. When she started to remove her gown, he stopped her.

"No, allow me."

He undressed her slowly, as if she were a helpless rag doll. His eyes were so soft. His touch so tender. His lips brushed the corner of her mouth with tantalizing gentleness before he lowered her into the heated water.

She was right, she realized; he intended to provide her comfort. He wanted to distract her from her melancholy thoughts of loss and grief, just as she had yearned to do for him upon learning of his hidden war wounds.

A sigh that mingled sorrow and need escaped Kate as she sank deeper.

Deverill shed his own clothes quickly and joined her. Guiding her to one side of the pool, he positioned her back against the sloping wall. She could feel his gaze like a tangible caress drifting over her as he scooped up water and let it run over her naked shoulders. His hands moved in a light murmur over her skin . . . yet offering more solace than arousal.

The moon, casting slivers of light through the tree

limbs overhead, sculpted his features in shadows, but his gaze held the same disarming gentleness as his hands; that dark, intense, beautiful gaze that had haunted so many of her dreams. She felt as though she were falling into his eyes.

Then he took her in his arms and bent his head. His lips moved over hers, his kiss slow and soft and designed to burrow into her heart, she feared.

After a time his embrace grew more intimate. He began stroking between her thighs, and in only a short while, he glided into her.

The passion Kate felt rising from deep inside her had less to do with physical sensation than the emotions pulling at her heart. She was suddenly seized with longing. She was frantic to be with Deverill, to ease the fiery ache in her chest and limbs. She kissed him back with an edge of desperation, and he responded in kind, increasing his rhythm, taking her with hard, possessive thrusts, his lovemaking the primal expression of life to chase away the darkness of death.

When it was over, he gathered her close again. Kate buried her face in his chest, the water swirling around them in heated currents.

The ripples faded eventually, the pool growing still once more. Yet inside, Kate felt her heart swelling with frightening tenderness. She kept her eyes closed, trying to quell the longing still clamoring inside her, but it was no use.

She loved Deverill. There was no other explanation.

She'd mistakenly thought she could manage him. That she could keep her heart safe. She should have known better.

I love him.

Strangely, the realization was not in the least shocking, although she acknowledged an element of surprise. Since her girlhood, she had imagined ideal love, had fantasized about how it would feel. In truth, however, real love was vastly superior to her romantic ideal, and far more painful.

Painful because it wasn't reciprocated. At least not yet.

So what should I do now?

Most immediately, what point was there in confessing her love? She couldn't force Deverill to develop deeper feelings for her. They had to grow naturally, without coercion. Indeed, divulging her love might actually do more to drive him away.

Therefore, she had to pretend that nothing had changed.

"Thank you," she murmured against his sleek wet skin.

"For what?"

"For all you have done for me and my late family. Now you and I can return to England and resume our normal lives."

He drew back, giving her a quizzical look. "Normal?"

Looking up, Kate manufactured a smile. "You can have what you have wanted all along—an uncomplicated marriage of convenience, without my silly notions of love and romance plaguing you."

Deverill's frown was immediate, and he searched her face for a long moment.

When he remained silent, she explained further. "You can find a bride who will better fit your requirements. You won't be compelled to deal with my unreasonable demands, or suffer my hounding you to share your feelings. When we arrive home," she added for good measure, "we can announce that we don't suit after all. We don't love each other, so there is no reason to continue our betrothal."

He started to reply, then apparently thought better of it. "Perhaps that is the best course."

It astonished Kate, how much his simple agreement hurt.

His willingness—even eagerness—to end their betrothal was an admission itself. Deverill didn't love her—and probably never would.

With effort, she forced another amiable smile. "We should return to the cottage and begin packing, don't you think?"

Not giving him time to reply, she pulled out of his arms and struck out for the pool steps, doing her level best to hide the hurt that was lashing at her inside.

Brandon woke early the next morning with Kate still sleeping beside him. The unease he felt was not full-blown panic, but he'd sensed her distance for the remainder of the evening.

Kate was pulling away, and he needed to decide how best to deal with her withdrawal.

For that reason alone, he was glad to be leaving France. In England he would have allies. He could solicit Lady Isabella's help, for one thing. Kate loved and revered her aunt, who was something of a matchmaker herself.

He could also enlist Kate's brother, Ash, and even her cousin Skye, Lady Hawkhurst. With her family aligned with him, he would wage a full-fledged campaign to win her hand in marriage. And no matter the obstacles, Brandon vowed, he was not giving up.

That pledge was prime in his mind when he gently roused Kate awake, and later as they breakfasted, and still later as they walked the short distance to Louvel's mansion.

Upon admission, they found the pirate and his mistress finishing their breakfast. Louvel seemed satisfied with the final payment for the excavation, but frowned when Kate asked to speak to Gabrielle alone.

His suspicious gaze followed the two women from the dining room and lingered on the doorway they had passed through. Hearing their lowered voices out in the corridor, Brandon could infer the scene taking place: Kate offering her unexpected financial gift, and the Frenchwoman responding with shock and delight.

As if wondering at the cause, Louvel rose from the table and strode to the door. Brandon followed in time to see Gabrielle flushed and beaming.

"What is the matter?" Louvel demanded of her in French.

She turned excitedly, waving the bank draft for three hundred guineas, which Brandon knew had been converted to francs. "You will not credit Mademoiselle Wilde's generosity! She has given me a fortune."

Snatching the draft from her, Louvel first examined the amount, then narrowed his eyes on Kate. "I will excuse your mistake, mademoiselle, but any recompense belongs to me."

Brandon saw Kate stiffen, but she kept her tone amiable when she replied. "There is no mistake, monsieur. I wish to thank Gabrielle for her kindness in allowing us to stay in her friend's cottage all this time. She is due remuneration for our room and board at the very least."

"I will keep it all the same."

Gabrielle spoke up then. "Jean, you have no right to claim—" She gasped when he suddenly grasped her elbow, whether in surprise or pain wasn't clear.

"You are not to question me, do you comprehend?" he declared. "I expect you to obey me."

Immediately Kate stepped forward in protest. "I'll thank you to unhand her, monsieur."

He turned back to her, his jaw hardening. "You will keep your opinions to yourself if you are wise."

"Then I am not wise," Kate retorted in a tightly controlled voice. "Abusing a lady like this is hardly the behavior of a gentleman."

"Fortunately I make no claim to being a gentleman." Even though he released Gabrielle, who rubbed her arm, his smile was almost a sneer. "I will brook no interference from you, Mademoiselle Wilde."

With a cold smile of her own, Kate stepped even closer, obviously willing to challenge him.

A bystander thus far, Brandon felt tension knot his muscles. The situation was fast spiraling out of control, with Louvel's temper on a short leash and Kate's eyes flashing.

"It does you no credit to rely on brute force to gain your way," she added in a caustic tone.

Brandon shifted his stance, preparing to intervene, as Kate spoke again. "That draft belongs to Gabrielle. You will return it at once."

"Or what?" Louvel's smile turned dangerous.

Kate visibly suppressed a shiver as the pirate towered over her, but she did not back down. "Or I will make you."

Brandon understood her motivation: She deplored injustice and refused to impotently stand by while Louvel committed violence against the weaker sex, particularly a woman who was her friend. But while the threat brought out her natural passionate nature, her intervention was foolhardy, given Louvel's savage nature . . . as was her boldness in seizing the bank draft from the pirate.

As fast as a snake striking, he grabbed her wrist with one hand and reached for her throat with the other, as if intent on strangling her.

Brandon lunged foward, but Kate acted first by twisting away, then yanking her arm from Louvel's grasp, and in one smooth motion, raising her knee to his groin in a punishing blow.

The pirate doubled over in pain, groaning. With clenched fingers, Kate stood over him, braced for retaliation. But Louvel sank to his knees, struggling to breathe, no longer an immediate threat.

Her male relatives had taught her how to defend herself even against a lout of superior strength, Brandon remembered.

By then, however, several servants had heard the commotion and come running. Now they were gathered at one end of the corridor, gawking in shock at the spectacle of their master being publicly humbled.

In another moment Louvel recovered enough to lift his head, giving a view of his enraged features. He was livid—a woman contesting him in his own home, making him lose face.

Stepping in then, Gabrielle quietly dismissed the servants, who wisely scurried away.

Fire still flashed in Kate's eyes, but evidently realizing she had gone too far in confronting Louvel, she inhaled a breath and made an effort to soften her approach. "If you must know, monsieur, I had your own welfare in mind as well as Gabrielle's. I wished to provide her with a dowry. It is customary for a bride to bring a financial stake to a marriage."

His furious gaze narrowed on her, although he still

panted for breath. "What the devil . . . are you talking . . . about?"

"Gabrielle wishes to marry you."

"Marry?" He turned his head to stare at the Frenchwoman.

"Yes, marry," Kate insisted. "She happens to love you. I am almost certain you hold her in affection. If not, that is your choice. But you have no right to mistreat her."

Louvel continued to eye Gabrielle while he fought to recover his voice. "Is this true?" he finally asked.

The beauty ducked her head rather shyly. "I confess it is so."

"Why did you . . . say nothing before?"

"Because I feared how you would respond."

Kate waited another moment to let Louvel absorb this new intelligence, then said more kindly, "Allow me to point out that with these funds, she will have a choice whether or not to remain with you. If *you* are wise, you will propose to her without delay. Although why she would have you as her husband after this is beyond my understanding."

Louvel shot Kate a deadly glare, which again set Brandon on edge, ready to leap to her defense. He disliked how she was provoking the pirate; she well knew that Louvel was a dangerous man to have as an enemy. Once he made sure Kate was safe, he was going to give her a good tongue-lashing.

At the moment, however, Louvel seemed more fixated on his mistress. "Forgive me, *chérie.* I acted out of anger."

Gabrielle returned a soft smile. When she helped him to his feet, Kate spoke yet again.

"Well then, we will take our leave and allow you to sort out your feelings for each other. Thank you again, Gabrielle, for all you have done to make our stay as pleasant as possible. And to you, Monsieur Louvel, for allowing me to properly lay my family to rest." She hesitated, then added, "I will deliver this draft to the bank in Royan where it will be waiting for you when you choose to claim it."

The pirate gave Kate another dark glance, but his attention was chiefly for Gabrielle. Judging by his intent gaze, perhaps he was considering a marriage proposal after all.

When Kate joined him, Brandon ushered her down the corridor to the front entrance. For the first time in several minutes, the protective fear that had gripped him eased and his rapid pulse began to slow. But his own ire increased in direct proportion to their distance from Louvel.

Brandon felt his jaw lock with the effort of holding back the chiding he wanted to give her. However, he forced himself to wait until they were out of earshot, when they were descending the front steps of the house.

"That was foolish in the extreme, defeating Louvel in front of witnesses," he said through ground teeth.

Hearing his tone, Kate glanced up at him in surprise. "Why are you angry with *me*? You would have acted similarly, had I not stepped in first to protect Gabrielle."

"My anger is because you made yourself a target for Louvel's vengeance. He will view it as the ultimate humiliation, being vanquished by a woman."

"What can he do to me?" Kate asked dismissively. "We will be gone shortly and will never have to deal with him again."

Brandon bit back a sharp reply. Having witnessed some of the pirate's previous altercations in America—which had ended in assault, and worse, death—he knew the lengths Louvel might go to now. For that reason among others, he was eager to leave St. Georges as soon as they loaded their valises into their rented carriage.

He escorted Kate to the cottage and left her there to collect their belongings, then made his way to the nearby livery and ordered his team hitched. While he waited in the stable yard, Brandon recalled her naïve question, *What can he do to me?*

His unease increased as memories of Louvel's gravest offenses came flooding back, and he couldn't suppress the dark images flashing through his mind. A scoundrel unconstrained by civilized boundaries, Louvel could easily act out of revenge, doing Kate physical harm, up to and including killing her.

The possibility made his gut clench. Perhaps he'd been unwise to leave her alone in the cottage after all. He should have brought her with him to the livery.

Unable to shake his ominous thoughts, Brandon had decided to return to the cottage when he heard footsteps behind him. Turning at the sound, he went very still.

Barely ten feet away stood two of Louvel's underlings, with four more at their backs, all of them armed with pistols or knives or cudgels.

He recognized three of the brutes by name: Ancel, Raoul, and Gaston. The ringleader, Ancel, waved his pistol while speaking in French.

"You are to come with us, monsieur. Louvel wishes a word with you at once."

Chapter Nineteen

Assessing his odds took Brandon only a heartbeat. Fighting his way out of this situation would not be easy—one against six hulking corsairs brandishing weapons at close range. A quick glance at the rear of the stable yard told him that the head ostler and livery hands had all slipped away, no doubt unwilling to cross a man as powerful as Louvel.

Brandon voiced a silent oath. He should have been on his guard, especially after the emasculation Louvel had recently suffered. But self-recriminations were useless at this point.

Just then Louvel himself rode into the yard and drew to a halt, followed by a lumbering wooden wagon pulled by a pair of sturdy horses.

"What is this?" Brandon asked the pirate. "Retribution?"

Smiling, Louvel rubbed the scar on his cheek. "*Mais oui*. I have a long memory. You never paid for the humiliation you dealt me years ago. Did you think I would permit you to leave here with impunity?"

"I suppose I should be honored. You sent an entire army of your cohorts to apprehend me."

A gloating grin spread across the pirate's swarthy features. "I could not risk your overpowering them."

"I suspect the reason is more because you are too spineless to fight me man to man."

Louvel's grin disappeared. "Why should I risk myself when there are more certain methods to ensure your demise?"

Brandon ignored the sudden tightness in his chest. "You mean to shoot me, then?"

"I have in mind something more original."

"Do tell," Brandon drawled, knowing that provoking Louvel to boast was the swiftest way to discover his plan.

"I have merely to leave you to drown. There is an underground cell in the caves where our contraband is stored that will flood at high tide." Louvel glanced around the yard. "Where is Mademoiselle Wilde? I expected to find her with you."

The constriction around Brandon's chest drew tighter, and he spoke before he could stop himself. "If you dare lay a hand on her . . ."

"What will you do?" Louvel's expression turned to a sneer. "You cannot escape with your life."

Once again Brandon contemplated taking on the entire band of pirates. He could possibly commandeer a pistol and shoot Louvel before being overwhelmed. But if he fought and failed, Kate would be alone, undefended, at Louvel's mercy. No, his only leverage was to bluff.

"Would you care to test me?" When the pirate hesitated, he added a warning. "Clearly you suffer from an unnatural belief in your own immortality. Even should you eliminate me, Miss Wilde has powerful friends who will hunt you down like a rabid dog."

Louvel continued to pause, although judging from his scornful expression, the threat was ineffective, Brandon realized.

Perhaps there was a better alternative: Keeping Louvel occupied so Kate would have time to escape. With luck, she could even ride to Royan to fetch help from Halsey and his crew. Yesterday he'd instructed the captain to bring reinforcements if he and Kate hadn't returned to Royan by noon today. But by then his fate might be sealed.

He decided it wise to change tack.

"Shall we negotiate, Louvel? I will offer no resistance on one condition."

"What condition is that?"

"Give me your word you will leave her unharmed."

"You would trust my word?"

"No, but I know your *chère femme* will not be happy if you harm mine."

"That is true. Gabrielle would be none too pleased. I suppose I will settle for harming you."

Brandon considered it a fair bargain. Louvel would likely make good the threat to kill him, but at the moment he only cared about keeping Kate safe. He was willing to die if necessary.

His best and only choice was to buy her time to avoid capture. And he had to pray that she wouldn't attempt to come after him. Kate was clever and brave, sometimes too brave for her own good.

Nodding his agreement, Brandon allowed his hands to be tied behind him and a cloth hood to be dragged over his head.

As they prepared to load him into the wagon, though, he heard footsteps to his left. Then a sharp pain in his head led to total blackness.

As he struggled to consciousness, his first awareness was of the sway and jostle of a vehicle. He was lying in the bed of the wagon, he realized. In all likelihood, he'd suffered a blow from a cudgel, since Louvel wouldn't want to risk his defiance.

He couldn't tell how long he had been unconscious, nor could he hear voices, so he had no idea how many men were accompanying him, or if Louvel himself was riding beside the wagon, or if the pirate had ordered his minions to dispose of his prisoner while he went to apprehend Kate.

The thought struck fear in Brandon's heart, along with a savage anger. There was a chance she had already been seized.

If any harm came to her, he would kill Louvel with his bare hands. *If* he could get free. At the moment he was at a supreme disadvantage, unable to protect her or help her in any way. Louvel could be carrying out his revenge at this very moment. Kate could be lying wounded somewhere, or, God forbid, dead.

Brandon felt his heart give another violent lurch. If she were to die, he couldn't live with the guilt. He wouldn't be able to live without her. He wouldn't *want* to live without her. Not when he loved her—

The realization caught him like an unexpected blow to his ribs.

He was in love with Kate.

No doubt his affliction had been developing for some time, despite his frequent self-denials. How blind to have only just now recognized his feelings when it might be too late to act on them. He'd waited far too long to come to his senses.

In truth, he had actually believed he could resist her. He'd sought to avoid any pain or remorse or guilt in his life, fearing being sucked into a spiraling whirlpool of emotion and, yes, love. But with Kate he'd had no choice. There were countless reasons he had fallen—

The thought splintered with the jagged pain in his head as the wagon rolled over one deep rut and then another.

Brandon gritted his teeth to hold back a groan. This was certainly not the time or place to be pondering his ardor for Kate.

Even if they managed to escape this predicament alive, there would still be obstacles. He could still lose her. She didn't love him yet, and she refused to marry without it. Furthermore, after all the times he'd denigrated her romantic dreams, she might not even believe his sudden profession of love. He would have to prove his sincerity and convince her to give him another chance.

First, however, he would have to figure a way to escape. It was galling to be this helpless, trussed up like a sheep at shearing time, being carted to his likely death.

Worse, the woman he loved could be in grave danger from his nemesis, and just now there wasn't a damned thing he could do about it.

After futilely waiting nearly half an hour for Deverill to return with the carriage, Kate went in search of him at the livery. Initially, the head ostler was disinclined to answer her queries, but she could tell from his odd apprehension that he had news he didn't wish to share.

"What troubles you, monsieur?"

"I dare not tell you, mademoiselle."

When Kate pressed and pleaded, though, he finally mumbled a curse under his breath and revealed that Monsieur Deverill had been taken captive by that dog Louvel. As it turned out, the ostler despised Louvel for hurting his brother some years past but feared incurring the pirate's wrath.

Dismay filled Kate as she stared at him. "Where was Deverill taken?" she managed to ask in a hoarse voice.

Again the ostler hesitated, before confessing that he had overheard talk about a certain cave that filled with the tide. "It is how Louvel keeps his cutthroats in line—by threatening to toss them in the drowning cell."

Kate tried to remain calm, but inside she was reeling. "How do I find this cave? Please, if you know, you must tell me."

"I know not, mademoiselle. I have never visited there before. I swear it. Although I have heard it is in one of the coves to the south of here."

Kate clenched her hands into fists in an effort to stem her fear. By now Louvel could have injured Deverill, or worse. Much worse. Or alternatively, Deverill could have been confined in the cave to drown. If her inexpert calculations were correct, the tide should be coming in about now. . . . Dear heaven, she had to act—but how?

The wise choice would be to seek help from Captain Halsey, but by then it could be too late to aid Deverill. No, she had to send a message to the captain at Royan and then try to confront Louvel herself. Perhaps she could delay him long enough for help to arrive.

"I must find Louvel," she murmured almost to herself.

"But he did not accompany his fellow tars, mademoiselle."

She stared at the ostler. "Where did he go?"

"I regret, I do not know. Is it possible that he returned to his home and sent his underlings to do the deed without him?"

The ostler had no more information to share, but at least her promise of an ample reward made him agree to send a message to the harbor at Royan. With an unsteady hand, Kate wrote her note to Halsey and watched as a stable boy was dispatched.

Then turning, she picked up her skirts and ran.

She headed directly for Louvel's house, hoping he was there, praying Gabrielle would help her if not. By the time she arrived at his doorstep, she was panting for breath and frantic with worry, for she couldn't help imagining what had befallen Deverill.

Not bothering to knock, Kate burst into the foyer and startled one of the serving maids who was dusting the staircase banister with a feather duster. When the girl stammered that her master was away from home but revealed her mistress's location, Kate raced to the kitchens, where Gabrielle appeared to be occupied with arranging flowers in a vase.

"What is the matter?" she exclaimed in alarm.

Kate put her palms against her midriff as she struggled for air. "It is Louvel! He has taken Deverill . . . and means to kill him!"

Gabrielle's face drained of color. "Surely you are mistaken."

"There is no mistake. There were witnesses. He plans to exact retribution and so ordered Deverill apprehended by his men. Please, do you know where I can find Louvel? I must speak to him."

Gabrielle shook her head in dismay. "He is not here. He intended to visit the bishop in Royan about a license to wed. You see, shortly after you left, he professed his love for me and offered his hand in marriage—" She frowned deeply as she set down her flowers. "What will you do if you find him?"

"I am not certain. I can offer to pay a ransom . . . or I can beg him for mercy—"

Gently, Gabrielle put her hands on Kate's upper arms, saying in a calming voice, "You are not thinking clearly, my friend. I know Jean. Once he is slighted, he does not forget. Pray, believe me. It would be best if I entreat him instead. I suspect I am the only one who can persuade him to abandon his quest for vengeance."

Her sincere concern had the intended effect on Kate. Inhaling to compose herself, she nodded in agreement. "Yes, you are right. But I cannot stand idly by and do nothing while Deverill dies. At the very least I must try to stop Louvel's men. What of the place where they took Deverill? A cave that floods with the incoming tide. Can you direct me there?"

If anything, Gabrielle looked even more alarmed. "*Mon Dieu* . . . I will draw you a map."

"Yes, please. . . ."

Carrying pen and paper to the kitchen table, the Frenchwoman quickly began to sketch while speaking out loud. "You will need a horse, Kate. You may borrow one from our stables."

"The livery will have horses already saddled. It will be faster if I hire one from there."

"But you cannot go alone—"

"I must. There is no time to waste."

"Some of our footmen could accompany you."

"You can send them after me if you wish."

With the discussion of such specific details, Kate finally began thinking more clearly. Her pistol and dagger were in her valise at the cottage. She should stop there first.

"The map, Gabrielle," she urged her friend. "Please hurry."

She detoured to the cottage to fetch her weapons, then retraced her steps to the livery, where she claimed a horse and showed the map to the head ostler. Fortuitously, he recognized the inlet where the cave was located and, although still reluctant to risk greater involvement, promised to direct Captain Halsey there if he arrived.

As soon as possible, Kate set out on the coastal road, which was flanked by a pine forest. Yet once away from Gabrielle's steadying influence, she could feel panic welling in her stomach again. And even though she managed to find the first junctions and other identifying markings indicated on the map without much difficulty, the journey gave her too much time to think.

Her darkest imaginings returned to assault her, and

in addition to fear, she was filled with regrets and re-criminations. Deverill could die without ever knowing how she felt. She had waited too long to tell him of her love. Just now she would have married him in an instant, even if he never returned her regard, but she might never get the chance.

After some quarter hour, Kate turned off the road, onto a sandy lane that wound down to the estuary and a pretty cove the color of aquamarine.

Upon reaching the shore, she turned left to ride along a narrow beach toward a rock cliff where the cave was supposedly located. The sun sat at its zenith, making the sand hazy with heat. Soon Kate was perspiring, and yet chilled with nerves at the same time.

She slowed when, ahead, she glimpsed a waiting wagon and team, along with several saddled horses. But with no sign of their owners in sight, she felt a measure of relief.

The strip of beach was fast disappearing when she dismounted and made her way on foot. Thankfully, she soon spied an entrance in the rock face of the cliff, worn smooth by centuries of tidal waters. Upon reaching it, Kate paused to hide her dagger under her skirts, tucked inside her garter. Then, taking a deep breath, she gripped her pistol and ducked inside.

The tunnel was far darker than the beach, but high enough that she could stand upright. Kate knew another temporary moment of relief, for the waves rolling in from the cove had not quite reached the passageway.

It was unlikely that Deverill would have drowned just yet.

However, moisture from sea spray clung to the walls and made the rock surface slippery beneath her feet. Treading warily, she carefully felt her way along the wall. When her eyes grew more accustomed to the dimness, she could see a faint glow at the end of the tunnel, perhaps from a burning torch.

She had only moved another few steps, though, when a harsh male voice called out in challenge, setting her heart thrashing in her chest.

Gritting her teeth, Kate disregarded the command to halt and continued moving forward. The tunnel opened into a cave roughly half the size of a country barn. When she stepped inside, she saw three of Louvel's brigands standing guard at the rear of the cave. However, she failed to notice the fourth who suddenly appeared on her right. She was no match for the brute, so although she put up a struggle, he disarmed her with humiliating ease.

He grinned, flashing a gold tooth, then taunted her in French. "Now who have we here? You seem to have lost your way, mademoiselle."

Ignoring him, Kate glanced around the cave, which was indeed lit by torchlight. No goods were stashed there, but the contraption at the rear of the sloping cave floor resembled a low cage with rusted metal bars. Worse, the sharp downward slant ensured that any seawater entering the tunnel would collect there at the end, submerging the cage, until eventually draining through fissures in the rock with the receding tide.

The drowning cell, she realized with horror.

Deverill sat inside, leaning back against the bars, his knees upraised casually but his arms tied behind him. He watched without expression as Kate's captor herded her toward the cell.

With a key retrieved from a shelf cut in the rock, the pirate unlocked the padlock that secured the cell door, then shoved her inside. Kate had to crouch to avoid hitting her head, but at the moment she only had eyes for Deverill.

He looked half angry, half exasperated, and when he spoke, his drawl was biting. "What the devil are you doing here?"

Taken aback by his ungrateful tone, Kate sank to her knees before him. "I had some notion of trying to prevent your drowning."

"All you accomplished was to get yourself captured."

Her alarm rose as she searched his face. He must have suffered a head wound for the cravat around his neck was darkly stained where his scalp had bled.

"You are injured," she murmured in dismay.

"It is nothing," Deverill replied tersely.

Behind her, one of the pirates called out to the others. "The tide is rising, so we must depart."

Looking back in time to see the key being returned to the shelf, Kate heard booted footsteps for a moment, then silence, which suggested that their jailers had snuck out of the cave, leaving her trapped inside the cell with Deverill.

His ire didn't diminish just because they were alone, however. "I had hoped you were safely in Royan by now."

"Did you honestly expect me to act the coward? Of course I would never leave without you."

"I came here without a fight so you would have a chance to escape."

Kate's vexation rose to match his. "So you thought to sacrifice yourself to protect me? I am not amused!"

A muscle ticked in his cheek, and he looked as if he was trying to bite back a smile. "No?"

"No. I was mad with worry for you."

"As I was for you. However, it was foolish of you to search for me. What did you expect to achieve all by yourself?"

"I am not entirely witless. I sent a lad to Royan to fetch Captain Halsey."

Deverill shook his head. "I had already instructed Halsey to come in search of us if we didn't appear by noon."

"Well, you might have informed me!" Kate began, before realizing they were spending precious moments arguing. "Would you like me to cut you free of your bonds?"

His expression arrested. "Can you?"

"Yes. I brought my dagger."

Raising the skirt of her gown, she pulled out the

sheathed knife. "I didn't think they would search my person."

He stared at her for another instant, then started to laugh. "I should know better than to underestimate you, darling Kate."

Crawling around behind him, she applied the sharp blade to the rope that tightly bound his hands, and with effort, managed to slice through the knots.

Turning then, Deverill leaned closer and hauled her into his arms, his grip so strong and tight she could scarcely draw breath.

His embrace was infinitely reassuring, even if they might be destined to die together.

Yet this was not a romantic moment in the least—which made his next action all the more puzzling: Deverill reached behind her and began to take down her hair from its sleek chignon.

Kate was startled into asking, "What on earth are you doing?"

"Not seducing you, if that is what you imagine. I need a hairpin if I am to pick the lock."

When he found a pin, he held it up to the light and gave a smile of relish. Then startling her yet again, he cupped her face and kissed her, swift and hard, before crawling across the cell and turning his attention to the padlock.

"Take heart, princess. We are not defeated just yet. I have no intention of dying here today, much less letting you die."

As it happened, however, the bars were too closely

spaced for Deverill's muscular arms to fit between, so he turned the task over to Kate, giving her detailed instruction on what to feel for and how to tease the tumblers.

It was painstaking work that took precious minutes. Despite the coolness of the cave, Kate was beginning to perspire again when the first trickle of water seeped into the cell, followed shortly by a greater one.

Fresh fear twisted in her stomach. The cave would fill presently and the entire cell would be underwater, rendering them unable to breathe. *Heaven help us.*

"Steady," Deverill urged. "Take your time."

Biting her lip, Kate reapplied herself to her task. He doled out more encouraging words while the passing seconds ticked by in her head.

Her skirts were soaked with seawater by now, and Kate was about to utter an oath of despair at her lack of progress when Deverill's head jerked up. "Someone is coming."

Kate followed his gaze to the tunnel entrance. It was then that she heard a sound that was sweet music to her ears: Gabrielle's voice whispering in French, "Kate, *mon amie,* are you here?"

Chapter Twenty

"*Yes, Gabrielle!*" *Kate* called out. "We are here, locked inside the cell!"

Entering the cave, the Frenchwoman rushed toward them. "*Mon dieu,* I did not believe Jean would truly attempt murder. . . ."

"You were mistaken, as you can see," Deverill said dryly. "Are you alone?" he added in an oddly suspicious voice.

"But, yes," Gabrielle answered. "When Jean did not return from Royan, I feared it would be too late to save you, so I came in search of you." She held up a fist-sized rock. "With this I shall attempt to break the lock."

"There is no need. The key is on the shelf, there to your left."

When she fetched the key, an enormous relief filled Kate—evidently a premature reaction, for Gabrielle paused. "Please, I must have your promise. I will gladly release you if you swear you will not seek revenge and harm my Jean."

"I will only promise not to kill him," Deverill replied grimly.

Kate used a softer tone. "Please, Gabrielle. You cannot leave us here to die."

Apparently she agreed, for she nodded her head as if coming to her senses. "No, certainly not. I will aid you because you aided me, Kate. You defended me to Jean when more easily you could have abandoned me. You had nothing to gain by interceding on my behalf, and much to lose by incurring his wrath. But I beg you both, do not harm him."

Without waiting for a reply, she used the key to remove the padlock. Deverill pushed open the cell door and guided Kate through, then followed.

Their rescue was just in time, Kate thought. By now the cell was two inches deep in seawater. Gratefully, she hugged Gabrielle. "Thank you, my dear friend," she said before Deverill put an end to their reunion.

"Come, we must hurry."

Taking first her hand, then Gabrielle's, he carefully retraced a path through the tunnel. For the next two minutes they slogged through the rushing waves that flooded the rock floor until they reached the end.

After the dimness of the cave, the bright sunlight was almost blinding. By squinting, though, Kate could see that the beach at the tunnel entrance was fully submerged.

Sitting on the ledge, Deverill eased himself into the surf, then lifted each woman down in turn. With his support, first Gabrielle, then Kate waded through the swirling water to dry land.

Kate's first urge was to throw herself down on the sandy beach in gratitude, but she settled for turning her face up to the warm sun. They were wet and bedraggled but alive.

Transportation was the first order of business. Surprisingly, her horse was where she had left it, grazing on seagrass, as was Gabrielle's. Deverill helped both of them mount, then swung up behind Kate.

They had reached the coastal road and were halfway to St. Georges when they heard the thunder of hooves up ahead. A score of men were galloping toward them, all brandishing weapons.

Thinking the pirates had returned, Kate felt her heart leap to her throat. But at her back Deverill relaxed and offered reassurance. "They are friends, not foes."

When the riders drew closer and reined to a halt, she recognized half of the men as Captain Halsey and his crew. Among the others, she was startled to see, were Deverill's cousin Trey and Beau Macklin.

Frowning in puzzlement, Kate glanced back at Deverill, who explained, "I didn't trust Louvel to accept our final payment and so sent to England for reinforcements over a week ago."

"It appears your misgivings were warranted," Macky said.

"What took you so long?" Deverill asked.

"We only arrived in port this morning," his cousin answered. "You look a trifle worse for wear, old man."

Deverill returned a humorless laugh. "You are a master of understatement."

"Do you even require our services?"

He nodded. "Yes. I prefer to make a show of overwhelming force."

A hint of amusement curved Trey's mouth. "No doubt you could have handled your difficulties without us. I am all admiration. Clearly you rescued yourselves."

"We have Mademoiselle Dupree to thank for our rescue," Kate interjected.

Trey tipped his hat to Kate. "Well met, Lady Katharine."

From the corner of her eye, she saw Gabrielle give a start at the use of her noble title, but there was no time to defend hiding her station because Deverill gave his orders. "Let us ride."

Unsure what action Deverill would take, Kate spoke not at all during the journey. She could feel anger coming off him in waves, vibrating with the rhythm of the pounding hoofbeats. And when they reached the pirate's house and slowed their pace, she could see Gabrielle's expression of dread.

Raising his hand to bring the other riders to a halt, Deverill drew rein himself and shouted out, "Show yourself, Louvel!"

Without waiting, he swung off their horse, leaving Kate mounted, and strode toward the front steps. Gabrielle remained frozen, as if afraid to move.

Kate held her breath as they waited. Perhaps the servants had been watching from inside the house, for eventually the front door opened and the pirate stepped out.

Seeing the army at Deverill's back, Louvel turned pale.

Deverill modulated his voice to be clearly heard. "I will give you the chance you never afforded me, Louvel. To fight me like a man rather than a coward."

"As you will."

By now a crowd of spectators was beginning to gather in the street. They all stood gawking as the pirate slowly descended the front steps.

Except for the snorting and huffing of labored horses, silence reigned.

Kate found herself murmuring a prayer, but when she saw the flashing gleam of a knife clutched in Louvel's hand, she gasped.

Deverill's expression of contempt showed what he thought of such treachery, and his tone turned livid. "Ever the coward."

For an interminable moment, Louvel stood staring belligerently, knife raised, feet spread in an offensive stance. But then evidently he thought better of attacking an unarmed man in front of witnesses and threw the blade aside.

Then, shockingly, he bowed his head, as if waiting

for his punishment. "Do your worst. I am prepared to go to my death like a man."

Kate was surprised to feel a flicker of admiration for the pirate.

"I comprehend why you must have your revenge," Louvel said.

"I doubt you comprehend anything," Deverill ground out. "I care little for my own skin, but you nearly killed the lady under my protection." He took two strides forward, prepared to engage the battle. "Defend yourself, you mangy cur."

Kate watched, not daring to breathe. The two men circled each other warily at first, fists at the ready. After a few moments, they came together, intent on knocking the other off balance, but with neither immediately succeeding. In the next encounter, Deverill ducked the pirate's jab and landed a blow to his rock-hard belly, eliciting a grunt.

Although of similar height, Louvel's physique was more massive. But Deverill's athletic litheness served him well during the next onslaught as he sidestepped nimbly and leveled a well-aimed hit to his opponent's chin.

With a curse, Louvel redoubled his efforts. Bending low, he suddenly charged, using his head like a battering ram and wrapping his powerful arms around Deverill's waist, causing him to stagger backward.

Deverill swiftly recovered, however, first delivering a hard knee to Louvel's groin, then sinking down on his haunches while stiffening his arms against the pirate's chest. Louvel went somersaulting overhead and catapulted face-first onto the pavement.

Giving a groan, Louvel jumped to his feet with the desperation of a cornered animal. When he lunged a second time, Deverill delivered a blow to the man's gut that doubled him over. Louvel's grunt of pain was cut off abruptly when Deverill's fist struck the pirate's jaw with a force that sent him reeling.

Slow to regain his footing, Louvel stood swaying and gasping for breath. He didn't relent, however.

When rushed a third time, Deverill ducked the swinging fist and drove his own fist into Louvel's face. This time the pirate fell with a thud and remained down, dazed, although still conscious, judging by his groans.

Crossing to his vanquished foe, Deverill stood over him, breathing heavily and flexing his bruised knuckles as if contemplating continuing the fight.

Kate thought it time to intervene. "Deverill, please . . ." she said urgently. "You cannot kill him. You gave your word."

"Never fear. I will only beat him to a pulp."

"It is more honorable to show mercy. If you maim him, what kind of life could he give his wife?"

She could see Deverill struggle to control his rage, but slowly his fierce expression began to fade.

"I believe you should stay your hand," Kate added for good measure.

"It is more than he did for you."

"I know, but you are the better man."

Another moment passed, but when Deverill lowered his fists, Louvel recognized his reprieve.

"I . . . thank you . . . monsieur."

Deverill gave a snort of disgust. "Lady Katharine is the one who deserves your gratitude. She is more merciful than I could ever be."

Nodding weakly, Louvel climbed unsteadily to his feet. When he took a step backward, as if to retreat into the house, Kate spoke up. "Not so quickly, Monsieur Louvel. There is one condition for our leniency."

"And what is that?"

"You must wed Gabrielle or set her free."

Shifting his gaze, Louvel shared a long, intent look with Gabrielle. "I will wed her if she will still have me. *Chérie,* I will love you and treat you as you deserve, I swear on my life."

Seeing his unexpectedly humbled expression, Kate somehow believed him. He had earned much greater punishment, he clearly knew, and stood to lose the woman he professed to love.

Deverill addressed the pirate again. "We shall call it a draw, Louvel. I trust I have seen the last of you, but if not, be warned: You cross me again at your peril."

"I fully comprehend."

When Gabrielle slid off her horse, Kate did the same, then moved to embrace her. "Again I thank you, my friend."

"But, no, it is I who is indebted to you," Gabrielle said.

"I truly hope this is the right course and that you will be happy with him."

"I shall, my lady."

They clasped hands in farewell, then stepped back from each other.

Going to Louvel's side, Gabrielle put her shoulder under his arm and helped him limp up the front steps and into the house.

As she watched, Kate at last felt her fear begin to ease. Turning, she met Deverill's intent gaze and offered a faint smile.

For the first time in hours, she could breathe.

Chapter Twenty-one

Kate was highly eager to return to Royan, but before departing, Deverill conferred with his cousin and Macky while she was near enough to overhear some of the conversation.

"My thanks to you both for voyaging all this way."

"Think nothing of it," Trey answered. "You would have done the same for any of us."

"Hawk did not accompany you from England?"

"No. He offered, but I felt he has done enough for our league."

Deverill nodded as if understanding the cryptic comment. "I mean to ride to Royan with Lady Katharine. You may follow us, but I'll thank you to keep your distance."

The odd arrangement surprised Kate, but she had no chance to question his plan.

Deverill borrowed a sturdy mount from one of Halsey's men, then left the captain in charge of returning Kate's hired horse and retrieving their carriage from the livery, fetching their luggage from the cottage, and most especially, thanking the head ostler for his aid. If not for him, Kate knew, Deverill might not be alive, and perhaps herself as well.

In short order, Deverill had mounted and set her up in front of him.

"I suppose you have a good reason for riding double?" she said when they were out of earshot.

"Two reasons: One, I am not letting you out of my sight until we are safely on board the *Galene*. And two, I require privacy for what I have to say to you."

Kate bit back a reply. After all of this morning's turmoil, she was very grateful to have Deverill's strong arms around her, but she suspected she was in for a scold. In fact, she had a few choice words of reproach to deliver to him as well.

She decided to begin with something less confrontational, though. "Thank you for sparing Louvel. He did not deserve such compassion, but for Gabrielle's sake, I am grateful."

"You needn't thank me. I want no more killing in my life."

Kate was glad for that sentiment also, but now that her anxiety and tension had largely drained away and their sheer survival was no longer in question, her lesser emotions came to the fore—vexation being the chief among them.

"You might have told me that you had sent to England for your cousin and friends."

"I didn't want to distress you unnecessarily."

"I would not have been so terrified had I known reinforcements were coming."

"Is that so?" he asked skeptically.

Kate stiffened at his tone. "Well, perhaps I would have been. Nothing could have lessened my horror at seeing you in that cell."

"I believe your words were, 'mad with worry.'"

His teasing made her bristle. "You needn't make light of my fear, Deverill!"

To her distress, he bent to kiss the nape of her neck. "Why are you so incensed, princess?"

The casual gesture did nothing to soothe her ire. "Because I am just now recalling how inappropriate your response was to my panic. I was ready to drown you myself for allowing yourself to be captured just to spare me—and then calling me a fool because I searched for you. And to add to your transgressions, you kept a significant confidence from me, summoning your friends from England without telling me. After all we have been through together, there should be no more secrets between us, Deverill. We need honesty—"

"I agree entirely." His perfectly amiable reply took the wind out of her sails.

"You do?"

"Yes, sweetheart. How is this for honesty? I love you."

Even though Kate thought she must have misheard, his pronouncement set her heart banging against her rib cage. She twisted awkwardly in the saddle to stare back at him.

Her shock must have registered on her face, for he lifted an eyebrow. "Did I fail to mention my feelings? How grossly remiss of me. I happen to love you quite madly, darling Kate."

His dark eyes held amusement as well as unmistakable tenderness. "What, have I rendered you speechless? Fancy that."

Kate swallowed past the sudden dryness in her throat, but her voice still sounded a trifle hoarse when she finally found her tongue. "When did this happen?"

"When did I fall in love, or when did I realize it?"

"Both."

He pursed his lips. "I expect the realization has gradually been coming over me for weeks now, but culminated in the past few hours. I felt something akin to panic last evening when you said you wanted to end our betrothal because you didn't love me, and abject fear this morning when Louvel threatened you over the bank draft. But I knew for certain when I thought you might die at Louvel's hand."

When she remained silent, Deverill prodded her. "What have you to say to my declaration?"

Kate narrowed her eyes at him. "I say that I cannot quite credit your change of heart. You might merely be claiming to love me so I will wed you and save you the bother of hunting further for a wife."

"I promise, that isn't the case. I would never deceive you on so serious a matter. And I want much more than a marriage of convenience or a wife to bear my children to carry on the title. I want *you*, Kate. I want a future with you, complete with all the joy and possible pain that entails."

Kate felt her heart turn over. "So do I, Deverill. Will you please marry me and make an honest woman of me?"

"Is this a proposal?"

"Yes, indeed."

His beautiful mouth curved. "I felt sure it was the gentleman's responsibility to offer matrimony."

"Normally it is. But everything about this day has been upside-down."

His hesitation was calculated to keep her on edge, she knew. Although the warm light in his eyes was endearing, Kate decided to give back some of his provoking teasing. "Forgive me for wounding your manly sensibilities. I would not expect you, of all men, to be intimidated if the lady offers."

He gave an exaggerated sigh. "You have not wounded me. I am resigned to going through life with you occasionally wearing the breeches in the family."

Kate laughed and wrinkled her nose at him. "Occasionally, I will."

"I wouldn't have it any other way. Very well, I accept your kind offer." An instant later, he chuckled. "I suppose I will have to marry you. You've completely spoiled me for anyone else."

Suddenly he drew the horse to a halt, then took her

chin in his warm fingers. "Be warned, Kate. I could never be satisfied with the cold marriage of convenience my parents had. I won't settle for less than your entire heart."

His declaration made her melt. "You have my heart, Deverill. I love you, and I always will."

He studied her intently for a long moment. Then his gaze grew even more serious, if that was possible. "Until you, I never realized what I was missing in my life. I love you, Kate. Quite dearly."

Briefly she closed her eyes. "I think I should pinch myself to see if I am dreaming. I hoped you could learn to love me someday, but I had begun to doubt you ever would."

"With you advising me, I never stood a chance at resistance."

Realizing she was developing a crick in her spine, Kate swung one leg over the horse so that she could sit sideways. Smiling up at Deverill, she looped her arms around his neck. "No doubt your arrogance will be intolerable, now that you have gained my surrender."

His expression softened. "My surrender is just as profound, Kate. From the first moment we met, I felt an affinity for you that no other woman ever came close to inspiring. But these past few hours have shown me how badly I need you. I can't imagine living my life without you. I wouldn't want to try. I want you in my life, in my bed, in my heart."

And with that he bent to capture her mouth.

It was a kiss of pure possession . . . deep, consuming. Not hard and desperate as in the cave, but savagely tender and passionate and full of promise.

Yet all too soon Deverill pulled away. Kate felt the loss keenly, until he explained, "As much as I desire to continue, we should wait until we are on board my ship. Not only is embracing on horseback exceedingly uncomfortable, we cannot count on privacy with our friends following close behind."

Kate cast a glance at the road behind him as he urged the horse into a walk. "I confess I am glad to have their escort back to Royan. I was also impressed that they heeded your call and traveled all the way to France without hesitation."

"Fighting tyrants and extricating innocent citizens from perilous situations is their forte."

"You said they were an elite branch of the Foreign Office, but they seem very accustomed to charging into danger."

"You don't know the half of it," he said enigmatically.

"Oh? More secrets?" she responded, disapproval in her tone.

"I swore a sacred oath to protect their confidences. But I can tell you considerably more once we are wed. Meanwhile, let us hasten back to Royan. I intend to sail with the ebb tide."

Although her curiosity had been piqued, she let Deverill change the subject. "Will we manage it?"

"I will make certain of it. I want to return to England so we can begin our life together. We need to make up for lost time."

Kate flashed him an arch smile. "How well I know it. Six years is an excruciatingly long time."

Deverill's laughter sounded low and rueful. "The blame is wholly mine. I should have come to my senses much sooner. But now that I have . . . Kate, I promise to love and cherish you always."

The words were softly spoken, but she felt their power. Looking into his eyes, she could fully believe that he meant his vow. This was what she had yearned for—for Deverill to love her truly, deeply, forever.

"I shall hold you to your promise," she replied just as softly.

Turning to face forward again, Kate leaned back against his solid chest. As he spurred the horse into a canter, his arms wrapped around her tightly in support and affection, causing hope and joy to fill her.

Perhaps her most treasured dream would come true at last.

When they returned to the inn in Royan, her aunt and uncle were delighted to learn they had made their provisional engagement permanent. With the focus on departing quickly, however, there was no time to celebrate.

Rachel was not eager to brave the high seas again, even with Deverill's assurance that the voyage would be far smoother without a violent storm lashing at the ship. When the *Galene* finally set sail some three hours later, they all stood at the starboard quarter railing, watching the coast fade from sight. Even with Deverill's arms around her, Kate felt the solemnity of the occasion. She was exceedingly glad to see the last of France for the moment; in truth, they couldn't leave quickly enough for her. And her uncle and aunt felt similarly.

Cornelius's disappointment was palpable when he conveyed the priest's final report: They had never discovered what became of the crested gold locket Lady Beaufort was wearing when she washed ashore. Lord Beaufort's signet ring had never been found, either, nor the last of the missing jewels that had gone down with the *Zephyr.* And yet Kate knew a sense of peace, having properly laid her lost loved ones to rest after so many years.

Another hour had passed when the *Galene* reached the more turbulent waters of the Atlantic, where the gusting breezes blew cooler, despite the summer evening sunlight.

When Rachel claimed to be feeling queasy, Kate gave her a wry glance. "There is no need for you to pretend illness any longer, Aunt."

Rachel had the grace to blush. "During our last voyage, I might have exaggerated my seasickness a little, but only a little. I truly was ailing."

"But once we arrived in Royan, you made certain Deverill and I had every opportunity to be alone."

"That was the chief purpose for our chaperonage, I

believe. To provide Lord Valmere the opportunity for a courtship."

"Indeed?" Kate cast an amused glance at Cornelius. "And you, Uncle? You sanctioned her deception?"

His flush showed his discomfiture. "I fear I am not adept at subterfuge."

"I convinced Cornelius to play along," Rachel declared loyally.

Which explained why he had frequently disappeared whenever Kate had come near.

"I take full responsibility," Deverill interjected.

Rachel gave him a faint smile. "We will leave you to explain, then."

Kate watched her aunt and uncle cross the deck to the companionway hatch, then focused her attention on Deverill. His windblown, ruffled locks and stubble shadowing his jaw made him appear the ruffian, but he had never looked more dear to her.

"I am waiting for your explanation," she prodded.

"There is not much to explain. I intended to use this voyage to woo you."

"But you enlisted my family's aid and united them against me."

"Not against you. For your benefit. I needed every advantage I could muster. As it was, I nearly had to die for you to admit your feelings. I plan for us to share a cabin tonight, by the way."

When Deverill held eye contact with her, heat sizzled between them, but Kate recognized his tactic.

"You are attempting to change the subject," she accused.

He ignored her complaint. "If you are worried about a scandal, there is an obvious solution. We can be married tonight. Captain Halsey can perform the ceremony."

"We had best wait until we return to England to hold the wedding. My family will want to witness my downfall." Kate flashed a wry smile. "I have badgered them for so many years about their romantic affairs, I owe them the satisfaction of seeing my nuptials. And Aunt Isabella would never forgive me if she weren't present. She takes matchmaking almost as seriously as I do."

"I will forever be grateful. Bella was my biggest champion these past few months. I asked for her aid before ever leaving America."

"I suspected that was why she remained in Cornwall. So I would fill her role as matchmaker and conduct your search for a bride."

"She had a hand in convincing the other members of your family also. They all made various excuses to avoid the voyage to France."

Kate shook her head in mock indignation. "My own family in league against me."

"Perhaps because they could see what even I could not: I long ago joined the ranks of the countless men who are smitten with you."

She couldn't help but laugh. "Now that I cannot credit."

"Ask your brother. I told him as much before we left England, when I sought his permission to marry you. He gave his blessing, if you care to know."

She arched an eyebrow at Deverill. "More secrets you have been keeping from me?"

His mouth twisted with regret. "Guilty as charged—but in future, I promise to eschew all secrecy."

"I trust you will."

"What of the secret *you* have been harboring? Cornelius mentioned your matchmaking theory based on legendary lovers. You sought to retell the Greek myth of Pygmalion and transform me from American scoundrel to English lord."

Kate felt her face warm a little at his ragging. "My theory has been highly effective at predicting ideal matches for my family and friends, I'll have you know."

Deverill planted a kiss on her temple. "Whatever basis you chose for our union would not have mattered. I've wanted you for years, and I was determined to claim you. In fact, you were the prime reason I came to England."

"You came to England to claim the title," Kate retorted.

"That was only my rationalization. You are the bride I wanted all along. I would never have wed anyone else."

"What of Daphne Farnwell? You showed great interest in her at that last ball."

"I only pretended an interest to make you jealous."

Kate felt a tightness ease inside her. "You succeeded

quite well. My jealousy is what led me to propose our engagement."

"Thank God. You made it very difficult for me to win you, particularly forcing me to confront my own demons. But you could never have gotten rid of me, princess. I was not about to give you up."

He punctuated his declaration by bending his head and kissing her, which sent her pulse soaring. Breaking away, she cast a glance around the ship. None of the crew was paying them any attention.

"Let us go below and cement our pledge," Deverill said in a husky tone. "I am not waiting any longer to claim you as mine. We have wasted too much time as it is."

When he took her hand, Kate went willingly, her heart pounding in anticipation.

Upon reaching his cabin, he shut the door behind them and took her in his arms again. But there he paused. His warm palm cupped her nape and he stood staring down at her.

There were countless emotions in his eyes: affection, need, want, hunger. His dark eyes burned into her, rousing heat and fire and desperate longing inside her. When he began to undress her, Kate aided him urgently. She craved to feel the heat of his hands on her bare skin.

In short order she was naked with her hair down, so they turned to undressing him. Every perfect inch of him was devastating, she thought as he shed the last of his clothing and they came together again. Flaring excitement ignited inside her at the familiar, erotic feel of him.

Just as she expected, his hands were strong and possessive and hot against her skin, his touch sending desire vibrating through her body—the driving desire to be part of him.

Unwilling to wait any longer, she led him to the bunk. Then, staring into dark eyes that were heavy with his own desire, Kate lay back and drew him down to her.

Brandon felt the same urgency as Kate but forced himself to go slowly. Instead of kissing her fiercely as he knew she wished, he savored the moment, savored *her* . . . the silk of her skin, the taste of her, her luscious breasts . . . He cherished her with his hands and mouth, and by the time he began caressing the curls concealing her sex, she was whimpering in need.

When he made to part her thighs, though, Kate opened her eyes. "The sponges . . ." she reminded him.

"We no longer have need for sponges. If a child comes from this night, then we will welcome it."

She smiled, really smiled, and his breath stopped.

"Be with me," she whispered.

"Gladly."

He complied readily with her plea, sliding into her with ease. He was rock hard and aching for her, his cock so swollen he thought he might burst, and she was all luscious wet heat.

A wave of intense pleasure shimmered through him as he settled more deeply in the cradle of her thighs. His fingers tangled in her glorious mass of hair, and he closed his eyes and breathed her in. Her scent settled inside him, filling the last empty spaces. . . .

His stillness made Kate shift restlessly beneath him. When finally he began to move his hips, hers rose eagerly to meet him, but Brandon remained set on drawing out the moment.

Apparently his pace was not intense or swift enough for her, for suddenly she pressed her hands against his chest, staying him. Taking command then, she urged him to roll over so that she lay on top, still joined to him.

"You are taking much too long. . . ." she complained against his ear.

"And you think you can do better?" Brandon taunted.

With a sultry smile curving her lips, she raised her head. "I know so."

Gazing up into bright eyes that challenged him, that desired him, he felt charmed and utterly seduced. The fire that infused his veins surged in his loins, and his rigid erection thickened still more.

Perhaps Kate felt his response, for she gave a breathy little moan. Then she retaliated by tantalizing him with a fleeting kiss before offering him the taut peak of her breast. He accommodated her, suckling her nipple, making her whimper. At the erotic sound, he felt a fiery ache shoot throughout his groin.

The same fire was tormenting her, he knew. Stirring restlessly, Kate pushed herself up to straddle his hips.

Once again Brandon felt his breath catch. The sight of her like this, so wanton and eager, ravished his senses: Her bare breasts proud and perfectly shaped, her narrow waist tapering to sweetly curving hips. The rose-gold sunlight streaming into the cabin brought out the sunset in her unbound hair, which flowed like ribbons around her body and wound around the globes of her breasts.

She was a natural temptress, and the magic of her green gaze was working its spell on him. She was a man's private fantasy, beautiful and passionate, his own personal siren, calling him to the rocks.

Passion throbbed between them as, holding his gaze, she lifted her weight slightly, only to lower herself slowly onto his swollen shaft. Brandon sucked in a ragged breath as her sleek, hot passage enveloped his cock. Impaled on his erection, she fit around him to perfection.

Craving to touch her, he reached up and filled his hands with her breasts. Kate gave a throaty moan and closed her eyes. Then covering his hands with her own, she let her head fall back and rode him.

Soon her breath became more rapid, as did his, while a look of ecstasy claimed her expression. As if she could no longer control her longing, she began to move, setting an urgent rhythm. Brandon grasped her hips, urging her on, intensifying his own pleasure as well as hers. She was more passionate than ever before, panting for him, clutching fiercely at his shoulders, throwing her head back in wild abandon.

Moments later she cried out, a high, keening pleasure sound. Desire surged through him, as intense as any he'd ever felt.

Desperate to satisfy this feverish need she'd set burning deep inside him, Brandon finally sought his own explosive release.

Afterward, she collapsed upon him, her skin smooth and warm and damp with sweat against his own. His arms closing around her, he remained unmoving, sheathed in her slick heat, exactly where he wanted to be.

Eventually their harsh breathing slowed while his thoughts drifted to the amazing change Kate had wrought in him. It was incredibly tender, this sweet ache he felt for her. It was unquestionably love. She had taught him that.

He needed her, he wanted her, he loved her.

It was remarkable how far she had reached inside his heart. And yet some part of him had always recognized her as his mate. He'd wanted someone who mattered. Someone special and irreplaceable. A woman strong enough to challenge him, who made him a better man.

He wanted Kate, now and forever.

Shifting his position, he rolled to face her, so that they lay on their sides, gazing at each other.

Love ran through him as he contemplated the pleasure of being ensnared for life, and he knew Kate felt similarly. She remained there watching him, her eyes indescribably tender and pleasure-hazed.

"I do love you dearly, you know," he murmured.

"I am beginning to believe you" was her satisfying reply.

For the second time today, he was struck by the dreamy, dizzy joy in her smile. That smile had been his undoing from the very first, Brandon realized.

There were countless other reasons he'd fallen for her, though. She fired his blood; she made him burn from the inside out. Yet it was her spirit, her zest, her fearlessness, her persistence, that had ultimately captured him.

She'd refused to let him languish in his own cold, emotionless world. She'd made him confront his own demons, spurring the rebirth of feeling inside him, dredging it up from where he had long ago buried it.

He felt as though he was coming back to life. For Kate, he had let down his guard. For her, he'd opened his heart and let the wave of unwanted emotions flood him.

Slowly Brandon raised his fingers to her lips to trace her soft smile.

Loving her felt *right*, like filling a hollow space inside him that had been empty for too long. And he would vanquish any lingering doubts she might have by proving his love to her for the rest of their days.

Epilogue

Kent, England, July 1817

Remarkably, his feelings for Kate grew stronger by the day, so that when they married five weeks later, Brandon wondered how he had ever managed to live so long without her.

Yesterday, with all the Wildes present, poignant memorial services had been held at both the Beaufort and Traherne estates in Kent in remembrance of their late family members. But Kate's grand wedding had been deliberately set for the morning afterward, the timing designed to counterbalance sadness with happiness.

Which was why just now as they spoke their vows in the chapel at Beauvoir, it concerned Brandon when he saw a tear roll down her cheek.

"Good God, are you crying, princess?" he murmured under the droning tone of the vicar.

Kate wiped at her eyes and whispered back, "You

know I tend to cry at weddings. But they are tears of happiness."

"Ah yes, you are a hopeless romantic."

"On the contrary. I am not hopeless any longer, thanks to you."

She gazed up at him lovingly, making his heart swell. When it came time to kiss the bride, Brandon couldn't help but marvel at the depth of his own happiness.

After the ceremony Kate stood by his side, accepting the good wishes of the wedding guests, her smile warm and joyful. He wanted to give her reason to smile like that always.

She made a stunning bride, he thought watching her. Kate was only one of the fiery, sensual Wilde clan, but the glow of life that surrounded her evinced a special quality all her own. She was vibrant, almost incandescent. Clearly a woman in love.

Lady Isabella Wilde was the first to crow about their obvious love match. Bella, the vivacious, half-Spanish, half-English widow whose third husband was Cornelius Wilde's late brother, Henry, sounded smug in her exultation. "I knew all along you were right for each other. You were destined to marry."

"Perhaps so," Brandon agreed before remarking to his new wife, "I'm fated to love you for the rest of my life, and there's nothing you can do to change it."

Amusement danced in Kate's green eyes before she turned to greet her former companion, Nell, with an affectionate embrace.

Amusement also laced his cousin's voice moments later when Trey slapped him heartily on the back. "We are elated to have you join our ranks of happily married men, old fellow."

"I am exceedingly fortunate."

In more ways than one, Brandon added to himself. Several of his former colleagues in the Guardians had attended his wedding, and he was gratified to be welcomed back into their ranks, knowing this was his second chance for the life he wanted.

Kate would be the center of his life, however.

During a brief lull in the congratulations, Brandon took her hand and brought her fingers to his lips for a tender kiss—and then found himself captured by her enchanting gaze.

He could see everything she felt, every nuance of raw emotion in her eyes. But most satisfying was how she looked at him as if he were the most fascinating, wonderful man alive. There was no defense against that.

He wanted no defense, either. She made his world a better place. She made him feel again; she made him complete. He wanted to share every part of himself with her. And he was counting the minutes until he could get her alone and express his desire in more reassuring ways.

Kate felt a similar urgency to be alone with Deverill. Yet when the company moved to the elegant manor where a lavish wedding breakfast was to be served, she paused to drink in the moment, surrounded as she was by family and friends. Once again a lump clogged her throat and tears blurred her eyes as she gazed around the room at so many happy married couples: Ash and Maura, Jack and Sophie, Skye and Hawk, Quinn and Venetia, Rachel and Cornelius. She was thrilled that her dearest relatives and friends had found wedded bliss, most recently Nell with her husband of barely two months.

And then there was her own handsome husband. Deverill looked more relaxed and content than she had ever seen him. He no longer had the uncivilized appearance of a pirate, either, although his elegant coat of blue superfine cloth only partly disguised the width and power of his shoulders.

A short while later when libations were poured, Ash raised his glass to the newlyweds and followed with a toast to Kate specifically.

"I wish to thank my sister for her dogged persistence. As much as it pains me to acknowledge it, Kate, my love, we are all deeply indebted to you for your hounding. And we are doubly grateful that you have finally met your match."

"As am I," Deverill said, his mouth curving. "Even if she wanted to mold me like a Greek statue."

Kate felt warmed by the fire in his eyes. She no longer wanted to change him. On the contrary, she wanted Deverill exactly as he was: exasperating, provoking, stimulating, loving. He was her ideal match and his bold brand of love was perfect for her, even if it had taken time for her to see it. They were good for each other, they completed each other.

She endured her family's ribbing with good grace. Evidently they expected her to abandon her attempt to inspire more legendary lovers, but she could have told them that she hadn't given up her matchmaking in the least.

Daphne Farnwell was among the guests also, and Kate had someone particular in mind for Daphne, although she would wait to share her plans when they were better formed.

As for her immediate family, the first children of the new generation of Wildes had been born, which meant in fifteen years or so, she could begin searching for a new crop of legendary lovers.

Meanwhile, she had her own romance to nurture. At the thought of her future with Deverill, Kate was swamped again by a surge of pure happiness. She had dreamed of a once-in-a-lifetime, passionate love, and he had fulfilled her dream in spades.

A half hour later, Deverill took her hand and pulled her out of the drawing room, down the corridor to the library. He was reaching for her before the door shut completely, capturing her in his arms.

"I couldn't wait. I want you all to myself."

His warm fingers gripped her chin, and he lowered his head. He could work magic with his mouth, so his kiss silenced her for several enthralling, pulse-pounding moments. And when at last he let her up for air, he made clear his purpose.

"I intend to have you now, Kate."

His promise made her feel faint, but she felt obliged to make a token protest. "Deverill, we have a house full of wedding guests."

The gleam was back in his eyes, a distinct challenge in his gaze. "What does that matter? I am not waiting until tonight to consummate our union."

Kate hesitated. They planned to spend their wedding night at the nearby Valmere country estate. Shortly after returning to England, she'd visited there with Deverill and seen the enormous amount of work to be done. The grounds and land and tenant farms appeared in good order, but several years of his late uncle's invalid status had left the manor in disrepair. They had started hiring more staff, but refurbishing the main rooms would happen while they travelled certain regions of England for their wedding trip, beginning with the Cotswolds and the Lake District—remaining on dry land for now.

A fortnight ago she had asked Deverill if he minded the vast change in his circumstances. "Will you be truly content to give up the sea?"

"For a life with you? Without question. It is only fitting for a man to settle down with the woman he loves. Besides, I expect to share any number of adventures with you."

The prospect appealed greatly to Kate. She was even willing to sail again with him, in no small part because Deverill kept her fears at bay. She hadn't suffered a single nightmare about sinking ships since that stormy night on board the *Galene*.

They would be leaving in the morning on the first stage of their journey, so he would have her all to himself then. However, she shared his impatience for the consummation.

Looping her arms around his neck, Kate contemplated Deverill with a provocative smile. They were learning to trust, learning to love with open hearts, with only occasionally a clash of wills. This, however, was one of those moments when they were in complete accord.

"I don't wish to wait, either," she said huskily as her gaze settled on his mouth.

Reaching up, Kate slid a hand into his dark hair and dragged him down for another kiss. His taste was hot and heady and infinitely satisfying. When his embrace tightened and his kiss intensified, desire washed over her like warm honey, while joy whispered through her.

This was what it meant to truly love, this sweet, soul-deep ache.

Deverill was her husband now, and she had absolutely no doubt that their love would be legendary, a lifelong adventure of the heart, with every moment to be savored.